MARY ROBINETTE KOWAL

Ghost Talkers

★ ★ ★

TOR

A TOM DOHERTY ASSOCIATES BOOK • NEW YORK

GHOST TALKERS

Copyright © 2016 by Mary Robinette Kowal

A Tor Book
Published by Tom Doherty Associates, LLC
175 Fifth Avenue
New York, NY 10010

www.tor-forge.com

Tor® is a registered trademark of Tom Doherty Associates, LLC.

The Library of Congress Cataloging-in-Publication Data
is available upon request.

ISBN 978-0-7653-7825-5 (hardcover)
ISBN 978-1-4668-6073-5 (e-book)

Our books may be purchased in bulk for promotional, educational, or business use. Please contact your local bookseller or the Macmillan Corporate and Premium Sales Department at 1-800-221-7945, extension 5442, or by e-mail at MacmillanSpecialMarkets@macmillan.com.

First Edition: August 2016

Printed in the United States of America

0 9 8 7 6 5 4 3 2 1

For my niece, Katherine Harrison

The War Sonnets: The Soldier

If I should die, think only this of me:
That there's some corner of a foreign field
That is for ever England. There shall be
In that rich earth a richer dust concealed;
A dust whom England bore, shaped, made aware,
Gave, once, her flowers to love, her ways to roam,
A body of England's, breathing English air,
Washed by the rivers, blest by suns of home.

And think, this heart, all evil shed away,
A pulse in the eternal mind, no less
Gives somewhere back the thoughts by England given;
Her sights and sounds; dreams happy as her day;
And laughter, learnt of friends; and gentleness,
In hearts at peace, under an English heaven.

—Rupert Brooke

Ghost Talkers

★ ★ ★

Chapter One

★ ★ ★

16 July 1916

"The Germans were flanking us at Delville Wood when I died."

Ginger Stuyvesant had a dim awareness of her body repeating the soldier's words to the team's stenographer. She tried to hold that awareness at bay, along with the dozens of other spirit circles working for the British Army. Even with a full circle supporting her, she ached with fatigue, and if she weren't careful that would pull her back into her body. It wouldn't be fair to force Helen to assume control of the circle early. The other medium was just as exhausted. Around them, the currents of the spirit world swirled in slow spirals. Past events brushed her in eddies of remembrance. Caught in those memories, scent and colour floated with thick emotion. The fighting at the Somme had kept the entire Spirit Corps working extra shifts trying to take reports from the dead, and the air was frigid with souls.

The young soldier in front of her had been with the 9th Scottish Division, 26th Brigade, the Black Watch. Technically, Pvt. Graham Quigley was still a member of the Black Watch, until his unfinished business was completed and he could cross beyond the veil.

Belatedly, Ginger realized what he'd said. "So you could see the Germans? You know their positions?"

His aura rippled black with remembered pain, but a flash of amber satisfaction shot through it. "Oh, ma'am. Don't I just. The shell that got me made it clear as all that I'd not live through the day, so I had the boys prop me up." Quigley grinned. "I saw the Huns set their guns up not fifteen feet from where I lay bleeding."

"When did you die? The time. Did you see the time?"

"Eleven forty-seven." His spirit winked at her. "I had one of the blokes hang up my watch so I could see the time. Remembered my training, I did."

Most soldiers came in within a few minutes of their death, but sometimes their confusion, or the sheer number of them, meant that their report didn't come until hours later. Knowing when they died was vital. Ginger's shift would end at noon, so Quigley had only been dead for a few minutes. "Can you show me their positions?"

"Aye. That I can." The amber of his pleasure suffused and buried the dark pain of dying. If the Spirit Corps did nothing else, it gave these young men some meaning for their deaths.

"Give me a moment." Her circle, well trained as they were, made the necessary changes to their configuration. Taking care not to break contact with her, Mrs. Richardson, on her right, slid her grip up Ginger's arm so that her hand was free. An aide, seated in the centre of the circle, positioned the drawing board in front of her. Edna had already clipped a map of the village

Longueval and Delville Wood to the board. Neither woman had the Sight, so to them the soldier was only a dim shadow, and only that much when they were in full contact with the circle. Without it, they'd feel nothing more than a spot of uncanny cold where he stood. But while the circle was in effect, with a strong medium to lead, all six of the sitters could hear him, and the countless drills they had done stood them in good stead.

If Quigley had seen where the Germans were, the command centre could hopefully find a way to stop those guns. A cluster of other ghosts waited, crowding the warehouse until another circle was free to take their report. Dimmer flashes of living people walked through the room carrying stenographers' reports or updated orders as the casualties poured in.

Ginger reminded her body to take a breath before she turned her attention back to the soldier. She pushed her soul farther out of her body. The relief sighed through Ginger as her mortal weight lessened. Her soul blended with the radiance around her, but there was not time to permit herself to drift in the spirit plane and delight in the tangible flow of ghosts. "Show me, please."

She reached out for Quigley and let his soul wrap around hers so she could drop into his memories.

He is leaning against a wall trying not to look at where his legs used to be. The pain is not as bad as he'd thought it would be, but he'd give anything for a drink of water. He is so thirsty. The blasted Huns have overrun their position and are setting up their guns behind the wall of what used to be a church. No proper respect, shelling a church like that. He blinks, trying to focus, but the world is starting to go grey around the edges. The lance corporal had told them how important it was to the war effort to remember what they saw as they were dying. There are five Huns: three to handle the gun, plus another two to manage the horses that pulled it into place. The sound of the gun going off is deafening, but he's too tired to flinch. It's cold. It's a relief after the oppressive July heat. But why is it cold? The gun fires again, and he stares at it, willing himself to remember. It's a heavy field Howitzer—a Five-Nine—and the Huns look to be settling in to stay.

Ginger pulled herself back, sinking toward her body. It had gotten even colder in the vast warehouse—no. No, that was just a residual from Quigley's memory. Her body shuddered with it anyway, and she wanted to push back away from her heavy mortal flesh. The circle pulled her soul down, anchoring her. Ginger checked to make sure her body was still breathing and nodded to the soldier. "Thank you. That is very good information. I will make a commendation to your superior officer."

Back in the mortal sphere, Edna was slipping the map from the board. Upon it, Quigley had used Ginger's body to draw the location of the gun and the Germans at the time of his death. A runner would take the map to the intelligence officers, and they would relay the information back to the front line. Ginger sent up a prayer that they could stop the gun, even while knowing that there would be more deaths. There were always more deaths facing her.

At the edge of her awareness, a familiar spark entered the room among the living. Captain Benjamin Harford. Even from here, his aura crackled with anger and worry. The worry wasn't unusual. It seemed that Ben was always worried about something these days. The anger though, and the way it twined into the heavy grey worry like a scarlet serpent, was not like her fiancé.

"Am I finished, ma'am?" Quigley's presence pulled her attention back to where it belonged. "They said in the training that we could send a message after we reported in."

"Yes. Of course." Ben and his worry would have to wait

another ten minutes until her shift ended. "What message would you like to pass on?" She would just repeat his words, and let the stenographer take a note instead of spirit writing. It seemed unjust to complain of being tired when speaking to the dead, but her entire body ached with other people's memories.

"Tell Alastair Olsen that he owes me five bob. He'd bet that I was too daft to remember to report in, and I guess he was wrong." The soldier twisted the memory of his cap in his hands. The amber faded, and for a moment his aura went deep purple with grief. "And tell my mum that I love her and that I'm sorry about the table leg. I meant to fix it before I went to war. Tell her I'm sorry I didn't. Hell—tell Alastair Olsen to give the five bob to Mum and she can use that to get the leg fixed. Only don't say I said *hell*." He looked behind him, and the edges of his spirit blurred. "Oh . . . that's the light the lance corporal was telling us about, I guess. Huh. It's yellow."

With a sigh, Quigley let go and diffused away from them. The eddies of his passing tugged on Ginger's soul, nudging her to go along with him on his journey. Her circle stood fast, holding her to this mortal coil. With her spirit, she held a salute as Pvt. Quigley's soul passed fully through the veil to the next plane of existence.

And then another soldier took his place. "Private John Simmons of the 27th Brigade, reporting."

Ginger brought her soul into alignment and passed control of the circle to Helen. Together they waited to find out how Pvt. Simmons had died.

★ ★ ★

At noon, a soft chime echoed through the great warehouse. Ginger could feel the relief from her team that their shift had ended. She held them steady while Helen finished with the soldier she was taking a report from.

He had lied about his age and was only fifteen. Ginger bit the inside of her cheek as he gave his final message for Helen to pass on. He was hardly the only boy shot down so young, but his death seemed harder because his commander had held him back, knowing he was too young to be there, and a chance grenade made it over the lines to kill him in the trench. Likely the two other boys he was with, as well. He hadn't even seen anything useful to report. Not that Helen had let on. She let him believe that he'd died with purpose, for a higher cause.

Still, it was a relief when he felt released and slid past them to go through the veil. Ginger clamped down on Helen, using the weight of the others in the circle to keep her soul from billowing out in the wake of his. She waited as the other medium settled back into her body. Across the circle, Helen lifted her head and took a deep, unsteady breath.

"Well . . . that's done, then." Her Caribbean accent came through more clearly in her fatigue. Her dark skin did not show the circles under her eyes as clearly as Ginger's, but it had gone ashy at the effort expended today. Even alternating control, their three-hour shifts were soul-numbing. The sheer number of deaths over the past two weeks had forced all the mediums to go to double shifts, and Ginger was not at all sure how long they could continue that pace. Already one girl had lost her grip on her body. They were keeping her physical form comfortable, in hopes that her soul would find its way back, but it seemed unlikely.

As a group, they dropped the circle and let go of each other's hands. Ginger's palm chilled as the film of sweat, which always formed during their long sessions, met the cool air. At least they would not have to be back on rotation until seventeen hundred today.

Letting her soul slip a little out of her body, Ginger paused to do the required check on their team. They had seven members in their team, as per regulations. A circle consisting of two mediums and four unsighted, with an aide for corporeal needs. Mrs. Richardson and Mr. Haden were clearly well and had matching rosy glows to their auras.

She flexed her fingers and turned to Mrs. Richardson on her right. "Thank you for the support during the drawing."

The elderly woman smiled and patted Ginger on the knee. "Of course, dear. It is the least I can do for the war."

"Aye. That and knitting." Mr. Haden gave her a sly wink. He wore a pair of fingerless gloves that Mrs. Richardson had made for him out of a thick grey wool. His arthritis bothered him in the perpetually cool warehouse, but he hadn't complained. It was simply hard to hide aches and pains from a circle. Even those without the Sight could sense at least a little of what the others felt when the mediums linked them. Which is how she also knew that Mr. Haden was sweet on Mrs. Richardson. Neither of them admitted it aloud though, pretending to be oblivious and flirting the old-fashioned way.

Lt. Plumber picked up his crutches and gave her a brief nod as he levered himself to his remaining leg. He could have sat the war out on disability, but he opted to be an anchor in the Spirit Corps instead. He wore the blue uniform of the disabled with pride. The dark tinge of pain in his aura seemed no more pronounced than usual.

Joanne was already leaning in to whisper to Edna. They were no doubt planning to head straight to the WAC's hospitality room to dance with as many officers as they could, if the cheery mixture of light red and yellow were any indication.

Ginger stood and stretched with a groan. She glanced to the side of the room where Ben waited for her. He was leaning against the wall of the warehouse, scribbling something in the tiny black notebook he kept perpetually tucked in his uniform pocket. His long, lean figure had always been dashing in evening dress, and seemed to exhibit the British Army uniform to equal advantage. His hat was tucked under his arm, and a lock of his dark curls had worked its way free of its pomade to hang over his forehead. The line of his mustache was turned down in a scowl as he concentrated on his notes.

He looked up, as if he felt Ginger's gaze, and a smile briefly lifted the worry from his face, though it did nothing for his aura.

Helen caught Ginger's eye and gave a nod toward Ben. "Looks like you have other duties awaiting you."

"Yes, well." Blushing a little, Ginger tried to appear nonchalant. "We do have to prepare for a staff meeting."

"Mm-hmm." Helen winked. "I'm sure he's looking forward to your report."

Laughing, Ginger crossed the floor past the other circles that were still in session. Most of the mediums were women, but some were men who were unfit for duty on the front. Their anchoring circles were also largely women, mixed with injured veterans and men too old to fight. Braziers stood every few feet, trying to knock back the perpetual chill of the vast warehouse—Potter's Field, they called it. Ginger kept her head down as she walked and her soul tucked tightly in her body, trying to keep her awareness of the dead soldiers to a minimum. Without being linked in a circle, she wouldn't see a full vision of any of them, but their auras still tugged at her, begging for a chance to tell how they died. She pulled further into herself, trying to confine her sight to the mortal sphere.

Ginger stepped past the line of salt that marked the edge of the working area. The temperature was a trifle warmer here, but that might have been simply due to Ben. Just his smile of greeting heated her skin.

"Good morning, Miss Stuyvesant." He tucked his little notebook into his pocket.

"Captain Harford." Their engagement was not a secret, and the wedding had only been delayed because of the war, but the brass still preferred them to be discreet. It was "distracting," apparently. "To what do I owe the pleasure? Come to help me collate my reports?"

"I thought I'd take advantage of the cool." His smile did not reach his eyes, and his aura stayed dark. "Walk with me?"

"Into the heat? You are a contradiction."

"I like to keep you guessing." He gave her a little bow and gestured to the door. "It is the role of an intelligence officer to avoid predictability at all costs."

"Mm . . . and here I thought you just enjoyed being difficult."

"It is an occupational hazard, I fear." With a passable imitation of a heartfelt sigh, he opened the door and ushered her into the corridor that ran along the length of one wall. Doors to a warren of offices opened off the side of the hall opposite Potter's Field, but Ben walked her down to the exterior door. The hall was warmer and mercifully clear of ghosts. A swirl of men and women filled it as they hurried outside, away from the cold of duty. "Speaking of occupational hazards, Axtell ruined my copy of Chaucer."

"The one I gave you? Humph. I never did like him."

He laughed and shook his head. "Darling, I would not trust him with one of your gifts. Besides, he doesn't read Middle English. This was my Pitt-Taylor translation."

"Even so. I am surprised he had any interest." Ginger's sensible boots clicked against the sharp green and white tiles as she walked with Ben to the end of the hall. She was simply fatigued at the end of a shift. Nothing more. "Or was this an illustrated edition?"

"He was using it for a book code."

"Well . . . if it was for the war, I suppose you had no choice." She paused by the door. "How did he ruin it?"

"He was shot. It stopped the bullet, apparently." He pushed open the door to the outside, and a wall of warmth met them.

Ginger wore a heavy linen skirt as part of her uniform, and a shawl on top of that to ward off the chill of Potter's Field. It was easy to forget, while locked in the dim and cool warehouse, that France was in the midst of July.

"Perhaps we should put a copy of Chaucer into the standard kit." She took the shawl off, folding it over her arm. In sticky, humid New York City, this would have been accounted a pleasant day, but it was still overly warm in her uniform.

"I would not object, but the troops already carry nearly fifty pounds in their kit." He gestured toward the trees that lined the walled yard surrounding the warehouse. "Shall we seek the shade?"

The members of the Spirit Corps broke into knots of twos and threes as they left the confines of the warehouse. Likely, most of the mediums would go back to their billets at the old asylum, to rest before their next shift. If her own fatigue level was any guide, they simply must figure out a better staffing arrangement. With luck, her aunt would have found some new recruits on her most recent trip back to England.

In an odd way, Ginger envied the mundanes who would go on to their volunteer hospitality duty at the Women's Auxiliary Committee's hospitality room. The WAC provided a convincing excuse for the vast number of women who were in Le Havre and would, hopefully, help keep the precise nature of the Spirit Corps secret as long as possible. Serving tea to living soldiers sounded very appealing. Perhaps she could convince Ben to go out. After she had a nap.

Ben settled his hat back on his head and steered them to the long row of plane trees that lined the wall surrounding the warehouse's large cobbled yard. Their papery bark peeled in a thousand shades of brown beneath vast spreading crowns of bright green. Ginger let him carry on in peace for a moment until they had reached some undefined appropriate distance from the warehouse.

He glanced back at the building and sighed. People still thronged around it on the way to and from their shifts. Stopping, he leaned against the trunk of a tree so his back was to the building. "Ginger . . . pretend I'm trying to wheedle a kiss?"

"Am I to take it that I won't get one, then?" She smiled and turned her back on the building as well, shaking her head as if denying him. They had acted out this ruse before when he needed to listen in on something at a party. She would rather have had a kiss.

He took her hand, running his thumb over the backs of her knuckles. "Assume I've given my standard disclaimer about this being completely confidential, please."

"Always."

"We've received reports that the Spirit Corps is being targeted by the Central Powers."

"Ah . . ." She resisted the urge to look back at the building. "Do they know where we are?"

"We aren't certain, but they most certainly know about the program." He let go of her and tugged at the cuff on his uniform jacket. "They've started blinding our wounded."

"What—"

"We thought that they knew . . . reports that I can't go into. But one of the reports that I *can* talk about came in today through the Spirit Corps—one you'll hear about at the staff meeting. A soldier was left behind enemy lines, dying—all standard thus far—but when the Germans found him, they put his eyes out."

She swallowed against nausea. Bad enough that these young men died, but to have their body desecrated in such a manner was an unlooked-for horror. "Surely that's just brutality. They may not have even known he was alive. I mean, that's part of what we count on, isn't it? That our boys can stay behind after their positions are overrun, and report what they've seen."

He gave a bitter laugh. "The last thing he heard was, *Noch ein gespenstiger Spion* . . . Another ghost spy."

Chapter Two

★ ★ ★

During the year it had been in operation, the Spirit Corps had begun to turn the tide against the Central Powers, but it had been too much to hope that they could keep the mediums a secret for the entire war.

If the Germans now knew about the program . . . Ginger sighed and shook her head. "I'm not certain that there is anything we can do to stop them, but that doesn't mean the Spirit Corps should be discontinued."

"I don't care about the program—I mean, I do, and we'll talk about this at the staff meeting. The reason I'm telling you now is that I think the Germans' next step will be to target the mediums. I want you to go away for a while."

"Absolutely not."

"Just until we can sort this out. Put some security precautions in place, that sort of thing."

"The rest of the Spirit Corps. What are you doing for them?"

He took his hat off and ran his fingers through his hair. "Well, they're British, aren't they? This isn't even your fight, since America hasn't entered the war."

"I beg to differ. My mother was British, and since I am also engaged to a British officer, I most certainly have a stake in England's future."

"And as your fiancé, I have a stake in yours. How many mediums have died from exhaustion or from losing their connection to their bodies? Hmm? And that's before we add a threat to your physical self."

Ginger gestured back towards the entrance to Potter's Field. "I see the toll of war every day. Every day. And every day I wonder when I will see you report in. Not if, but *when*. Whereas the danger to the Spirit Corps is very much an *if*. Even were that not the case, I am bound by duty as much as you."

"Not so. As a man, I would be branded a coward were I to respond rationally to the danger of war. As a woman, no one expects you—"

"As a woman—!"

"Ginger—you are raising your voice." Ben straightened and took her hand, raising it to kiss as a pantomime for any onlookers. At the touch, his eyes widened a little. Though not a medium, Ben was a sensitive and, as such, could see her aura clearly when touching her.

She wanted to yank away from him, but managed to tilt her head and smile. In another setting, the heat in her cheeks might look like a maiden's blush instead of the anger it was, but Ben certainly could not miss that her aura had gone as red as her hair. With as sweet a voice as she could produce, Ginger simpered. "Oh, Captain Harford. You are so brave. I am only a simple girl."

"That is not—" He stopped himself and bent his head, sighing. "Let me try again? If I were allowed to leave this pointless war, I would. But I would be shot as a coward. The expectations for women are different—I am not saying that they *should* be, only that they are. You have the choice to stay or to—"

An explosion cracked through the air.

Ginger was on the ground, face down in the bottom of the trench. Mud squelched between her fingers and filled her nostrils. Her side burned despite the cold of the mud. She couldn't see for all the mud. Tubby was screaming again. Good God, couldn't someone get the big baby to shut up? She tried to push up, but only clawed at the mud with one hand. The other—her other hand was gone. No—no! She wasn't supposed to die in the bottom of the trench. She hadn't even gone over the top yet. She had to get up, she had to get out of all of this mud. She had to—

"Ginger!" A hand rested against her back. "Ginger, darling . . . it was just a truck backfiring. Ginger?"

She coughed, her face pressed against the dry earth of the yard. It had only been someone else's memory. Shuddering, she pushed herself up, with Ben guiding her. His hat was upside down in the dirt. Hands shaking, Ginger picked it up and brushed the dust away. "I am so sorry."

"Darling, sh . . . don't worry about that." Ben took the hat from her and set it aside. He fished in his pocket and pulled out a handkerchief. With tender care, he dabbed the tears from her cheeks. "It was just a truck. The Huns won't be able to get close enough to Le Havre to bomb it."

"I didn't—" Ginger took the cloth from him so she could wipe her own cheeks. "I thought I was . . . one of the reports today was a boy who died in the trenches."

"Ah . . ." He pulled her into an embrace, and she leaned into the warm circle of his arms. For the moment, Ginger let Ben rock her in his arms and closed her eyes, concentrating on the solid physical sensation of his firm chest and the tickle of his mustache against her forehead. Surrounding her like a shield, his aura spread in the amber and rose of his love.

★ ★ ★

Before the war, if anyone had told Ginger that she would find paperwork and filing reports the most pleasant part of her day, she would have laughed, directed them to her social secretary, and then gone off to a soiree. Now, though, the monotony of going through reports and merely *reading* about deaths seemed a welcome respite. During the shifts, aides ran reports immediately to central intelligence, who then telephoned the chiefs of staff so they could adjust their strategy. All Ginger had to do was present a weekly report on the efficacy of the Spirit Corps program, with lists of the mediums in active service and those lost to burnout or a circle failing to hold.

By the time she had left Ben to get her papers in order, Ginger was tolerably calm. Her legs, at least, were no longer shaking. Ben met her outside the meeting room and held the door for her. His aura had swirls of steel blue concern and a faint tinge of brick red guilt.

She laid a hand on his arm and leaned in to whisper. "Why are you guilty?"

"I have my reasons." He opened the door. "And no fair peeking."

"Thank you, Captain." She narrowed her gaze at Ben, but he only gave her one of his winning grins, dimples and all.

As she entered, the men in the room rose to their feet, nodding in greeting. Captains Keatley and Lethbridge-Stewart each had a sheaf of papers as usual. Captain Axtell had dried mud on his uniform as though he had come straight from the field. Even his blond hair was dimmed by the layer of mud.

From behind his desk, Brigadier-General Davies peered over his glasses at her. His aura was tinged brown with annoyance. "No Lady Penfold today?"

"She sent me in her stead, sir." As her aunt had done with almost every general staff meeting. Lady Penfold was the titular head of the Spirit Corps, only because of the dratted British insistence upon a title. Not, of course, that they would give a woman a rank in the army proper. Not even if they were doctors, or ambulance drivers, or mediums. In any event, if they wanted the person who understood the spiritual mechanics of the corps best, they should have had Helen here.

"Mm." He turned to the papers on his desk. "Well then, might I prevail upon you to make us some tea? My man is terrible at it, and I would kill for a decent cup."

Ben cleared his throat before Ginger could respond. "I can have Merrow do that, sir."

His soldier-servant, Pvt. Merrow, had not yet left the room with the other aides. He jumped as Ben spoke. The wiry young man's aura was quite shot through with pinks of embarrassment. The poor thing's shoulders were perpetually hunched, as if he were constantly afraid of coming to notice. But he immediately went to the door with a murmured, "Very good, sir."

Trying and failing to catch his eye, Ginger said, "Thank you, Private Merrow. That would be very kind."

"Damned if I don't envy you, Harford." Captain Axtell slapped his hand against his leg, raising a cloud of dust. "My fellow can't make a decent cup to save his life. Or mine."

"It seems my books are what save your life."

"Right! Ho! You have that true enough." Axtell boomed with laughter at odds with the dark reds of his constant anger.

Ginger stepped a little away from him. While he'd been away at the front, she'd forgotten how easily Axtell laughed and how viciously bleak his aura was. The combination of laughter and rage made him seem more dangerous than Keatley, whose dour expression was at least matched by mossy browns of disappointment.

Brigadier-General Davies rapped his papers against the desk, straightening them with a series of sharp taps. "Shall we get down to business, gentlemen? And Miss Stuyvesant."

Ben pulled out a chair for Ginger and nodded to it to ask her to sit. The other men settled into their usual spots around the table, putting reports down in front of them.

"Let's get right to it." Davies peered at one of the papers. "The Spirit Corps passed us a report today that confirms what we've been suspecting for some time now. The Germans definitely know about the program. Blinded one of ours and said, 'Another ghost spy.' Now, my first question is: Why did they blind him? Will that have any effect on the men's reports?"

Ginger shook her head. "No, sir. If soldiers carried their wounds with them into the spirit realm, most of them would be unable to report at all."

He grunted. "So why blind them?"

"I would expect because they don't know any better. Perhaps a sign of their desperation?" She shifted in her chair so that she faced the brigadier-general more directly. "I mean, the Germans have less experience with spiritualism, so they may misunderstand the capabilities of ghosts."

"I thought a German invented it."

Ginger clasped her hands together in her lap to hide her

annoyance, grateful that Davies could not read her aura. "A German? No. Or do you mean Emanuel Swedenborg?"

"That's the fellow." Davies pointed his pen at her.

"Ah. He was Swedish. And—and, though mediums have occurred naturally throughout history, there were enough charlatans that it wasn't considered scientifically provable. So, really, we count the beginning of the formal study of spiritualism as 1847, which is when the American Andrew Jackson Davis wrote his seminal book. The movement spread to England, but it's been slow to take hold on the Continent." Ginger tapped her nose, thinking. "In fact, Germany likely has a dearth of trained mediums, given their history of burning witches."

Lethbridge-Stewart grimaced. "The mustard gas they introduced last September . . . I wonder if they actually created it specifically to blind our Tommies, and the lung damage was a side effect."

Ben said, "I had the same thought. It would explain why they're increasing the frequency of gas attacks."

"Right. Our boys can't report on things they can't see." Davies turned to Ginger. "Or can they?"

"No, sir. Or . . . more properly, while it is *possible* for a ghost to linger in an area and observe things after death, the dead have no sense of time passing. That's why our soldiers are conditioned to report in *directly* upon their death, else they might linger for days or weeks with no awareness that time had passed."

"Any way to mitigate that?" Lethbridge-Stewart leaned forward in his chair.

"Even if there were, the longer a spirit remains on this side of the veil, the more likely it is to lose coherence." At his look of incomprehension, Ginger simplified her explanation. "Ghosts shed their memories without a body to anchor them. The haunt-ings you've seen have diminished to a single point of trauma."

"Still—"

"Please. Consider what you are asking." Ginger looked around the room at the men. All of them, save the brigadier-general, were in their prime, with the lean, fit physique of sol-diers. "Would any intelligence be worth trapping our boys in the memory of their death?"

Axtell swore and shuddered visibly. The dried mud on his clothes was a grim reminder that he'd seen the horrors of the war more recently than any of them, save Ginger.

In that silence, Merrow opened the door with the rattle of a tray full of cups and saucers. The company turned as one at the welcome aroma of strong tea. Flinching, Merrow blanched vis-ibly at the scrutiny.

Young men like him, full of fear, were braver to Ginger than brash fools like Axtell. Surely Merrow had lied about his age to join up; he couldn't have been more than seventeen, but neither his age nor his fear kept him from doing his duty. Nor would Ginger allow the simple fact of her sex to give her reason to shirk. If Merrow could fight, then by God, so could she.

Brigadier-General Davies took his tea from Merrow and waited until the young man had left the room again before re-turning to business. "Axtell, is there any indication that the Huns know where the mediums are located?"

"Nothing from my usual sources. Calling the mediums 'the London Branch' seems to be effective misdirection. The decoy hospitality huts here are working, so people continue to believe that the Spirit Corps are just a part of the WAC."

"By contrast to Axtell . . ." Ben took a cup from the tray Merrow had left. "I'm hearing murmurs in my network, sir. I'd say it's only a matter of time before they guess where Potter's Field is located."

Sighing, Davies nodded. "I am afraid you have the right of it. And have they figured out how the conditioning ritual itself works?"

"Hell if I know." Axtell wadded up a piece of paper and tossed it at Ben. "It'd be easier if I knew what the ritual entailed."

"Not my department." Ben held up his hands with a grimace, but his aura went yellow-green with caution.

There were a handful of people who knew how the soldiers were primed to report in. Ben was not one of them. However, he had been instrumental in getting the program up and running, and the other men were aware of that much. It wasn't surprising that, as intelligence officers, they might try to prompt him for more information, even while knowing that he was unlikely to give it.

"Still . . ." Axtell shifted in his seat. "It's deuced hard looking for signs that people know how something is done when I don't even know what I'm looking for."

The brigadier-general snorted. "The classification level is high enough that I don't know either."

"How the hell they can keep it a secret when they condition the entire bleeding army is beyond me." Axtell shuddered and then chuckled. "It gives me the creeps, knowing that the Spirit Corps mucked about with our minds like that and not a one of us remembers it."

"Let us count our blessings that the conditioning is holding, rather than being frustrated that we don't know the process." Davies made a mark on his paper, and his aura filled with orange frustration. "Meanwhile, we shall have to make plans for the evacuation of the corps. Perhaps relocate them preemptively."

Ginger managed not to roll her eyes at that suggestion. "That is not a possibility, I am afraid. The soldiers are primed to report to the nexus at this location, rather than to a specific medium."

"That seems stupidly shortsighted." Keatley, who to this point had not spoken, looked up from his ever-present papers.

"We had no way of knowing who would be on duty. And given the rate of attrition among the corps, if we *had* primed men to return to mediums, a goodly number would find their way across the channel to haunt some poor woman who could do nothing with the information."

He snorted. "Ah yes . . . the attrition. How unfortunate that the poor women are overcome by sitting quietly all day."

Lifting her chin, Ginger opened her mouth to retort—

"Here now—" Ben sat forward, back stiff as he glared at Keatley. "None of that. The mediums suffer more from this war than you can possibly know."

"Please, spare me."

"They live through the deaths of every soldier who reports in." He rose to his feet and leaned over the table. "Every soldier. So I will thank you not to mock them."

Ginger compressed her lips. Ben was overstating the case a little. The only deaths she experienced were ones for which it was necessary to enter the soldier's memories. A simple report could be taken verbally and, sad to say, most soldiers saw nothing of use.

"Sit down, Captain Harford." Brigadier-General Davies shifted in his chair. He rubbed the back of his neck, scowling at his cup of tea. "Though his point was not made politically, Keatley is correct in that we *were* shortsighted. When we implemented the Spirit Corps, we thought the war would be over by now. Keeping it a secret for a few months: difficult, but possible. For a year . . . well. We were pushing our luck, and, as Harford notes, it's only a matter of time before the Huns find the corps. So—what can we do?"

Ginger offered, "We could prime new recruits to report to a different location and gradually relocate."

"What of the Tommies currently in the field?" Davies asked.

"They will continue to report here."

"It might be wise to decentralize the department." Ben's aura turned a self-satisfied amber. "If we set up several branches of the Spirit Corps in different locations, it would slow the Huns' ability to find any of them since they'd get conflicting reports. Since Miss Stuyvesant established this location, she would be admirably suited to setting up additional ones."

Ginger narrowed her eyes at him, knowing full well what he was attempting. "Lady Penfold depends upon having me here as her liaison. I am afraid it would be too disruptive to send me away."

"Perhaps we can appeal to Lady Penfold." Ben turned from Ginger to the brigadier-general. "I really think Miss Stuyvesant would be best suited for the task."

"I can draw up a list of mediums who would be appropriate." Besides, being at the Le Havre offices was her only opportunity to see Ben. "The challenge is that we're short staffed as it is. Everyone is already pulling double shifts just to keep up with the deaths. Some mediums will be required to stay here, regardless, and since this is where HQ is, I think one can hardly argue that it makes sense to send your Spirit Corps liaison away."

Davies nodded and resettled his glasses. "You make an excellent point. It would be different, of course, if her ladyship ever deigned to come to a meeting. Make up that list for me, will you?"

"Yes, sir."

"Good. Meanwhile, I want efforts made towards the security

here. Keatley, Lethbridge-Stewart: I want you on that. Harford—you said you were getting murmurs in your network?"

"I am, sir. Nothing definite, but rumors of rumors of the Germans looking for witches. Now, if that's them trying to establish a Spirit Corps of their own, or trying to find ours, I cannot tell you. Yet."

"Mm . . ." He made another note on his papers. "Well . . . I want you to go back out and see if you can find anything definite."

"Of course, sir." Ben darted a glance at Ginger.

Axtell brushed at his trousers and laughed. "What about me?"

"Good God, man." Davies waved at him. "You couldn't sneak up on a blind nun as badly as you reek. Go bathe. The rest of you lot, just clear out. I have work that needs doing."

Which was just as well, because Ginger had words for Ben. Very serious words.

Chapter Three

★ ★ ★

Their walk out of Brigadier-General Davies's office had more strain than Ginger would have liked. If they had not both been sensitives, then their attempts at light banter might have fooled them into complacency. As it was, by the time they reached the exterior, Ginger was more than ready to let her temper fly.

"Well done with the tea, Merrow," Ben called over his shoulder. "I shan't need you till supper, so you are at leave."

"Very good, sir." Merrow saluted and headed toward the main gates.

Ginger counted to ten, walking at Ben's side, and waited until she was confident that Merrow was out of earshot. "Do not ever do that sort of thing again."

"Ask him to fetch tea instead of you?"

"I was speaking of your effort to send me away. Against my express wishes."

"Your wish is that you be able to continue to do your duty. My wish is for you to be out of harm's way. This would have given us both what we wanted."

Ginger threw her hands in the air. "There will be danger wherever I am. A zeppelin might get past our aeroplanes and bomb us. Or my circle might break and my soul could detach from my body. Or I could fall down our billet's stupidly steep stairs and break my neck."

"Ginger—" He reached for her hand.

"I am not finished." She pulled her hand away. He could see well enough how angry she was without the addition of her aura. "The problem is not whether there is danger or not, but that you are making the decision for me. That is what makes me angry."

Ben held up his hands in placation. "You cannot fault me for making the attempt, and I did not press the issue. I mean . . . as your fiancé, it would have been within my rights to have taken Davies aside or appealed to Lady Penfold. But I didn't."

"Do not even think of such a thing."

"Of course I am going to *think* of it, darling. Acting on it would be a step too far, and I promise not to do that." He glanced up and gave her a lopsided smile. "Probably."

Ginger raised one eyebrow, knowing full well the effect it had upon Ben. As she hoped, he looked abashed.

Pulling off his cap, he swept a hand through his hair. With a sigh, he settled the hat back upon his head. "Please, Ginger . . ." Ben took a step closer and held out both his hands, palms up. "Look. You can see I am contrite, can you not? Please forgive me."

"I can." Even without touching him, the steel blue of contrition weighed down the whole of his aura. The brick red that had been there before had faded so it only tinged the edges. "And you are also guilty. What are you planning?"

Ben gave a wry smile, kicking the dust. "Ah . . . the guilt is because I knew you would be angry with me."

"And you did it anyway?"

"Truly? Yes." He took a step closer, holding his hands out until she took them. His palms were warm and lined with unfamiliar calluses, a gift of the war. When they made contact, his aura sprang into clearer focus. Beneath the steel blue contrition and the embarrassment lay a layer of fine black mist. Fear nestled against him like a second skin. "I would rather have you furious with me and know you are safe."

She could not doubt his sincerity. Nor, truly, could she pretend that she did not understand his impulse. She tried to look sternly at him, lips drawn together in a line, but when they held hands, he could see her aura and already know he was forgiven.

She said it anyway, because the willingness to act was more important than mere intentions. "I forgive you. This time."

"Oh, thank God." He squeezed her hands. "Otherwise, I do not know who I would take dancing tonight."

"Dancing, is it?"

"There's a touring company at the hospitality room. I hear they have a fine cornetist. Join me, Miss Stuyvesant?"

"Thank you, Captain Harford. I would be delighted." Ginger checked the watch she wore on a chain around her neck. "My next shift ends at eight p.m."

"Twenty—"

"Twenty hundred. Yes, I know. But this is a social call, so . . . pick me up at my billet at half past?"

"I shall await your pleasure." He gave her a bow. "At half past eight o'clock."

★ ★ ★

Ginger paused at Helen's open door, caught by a flash of an elegant yellow gown. Inside, Helen sat in a chair with her head tipped back against the plaster wall of the asylum. She stirred the air lazily with a wooden fan. The elegance of her gown was broken by the skirt hiked up over her knees.

Ginger leaned in the door. "That's a lovely gown. Are you going out?"

"I was." Her aura fluttered for a moment with a shade of orange frustration. "Too hot."

"Should I have left a ghost in here?"

Helen snapped her fan shut and shook it at Ginger. "Maybe I make you the ghost. Keep me cool."

She snorted in response. "I have a long list of people who might serve the army better as cooling units."

"Ooo . . . the meeting went that bad?" Helen patted the bed with the fan before opening it again. "Was it Davies or Axtell this time?"

Rolling her eyes, Ginger crossed the room and sat on the rough linen of Helen's bed. "Both, and Keatley. And Ben. Do you know that the brigadier-general actually asked me to make tea? At the staff meeting!"

"He wouldn't have asked your aunt that. That's for sure."

"Exactly. As much as I try to tell myself that it has to do with age—"

"You don't have a title. She does." Helen shrugged one shoulder. "It's why we asked her to be in charge."

"Yes . . . I know. I just thought that once I got in and proved myself, they would stop overlooking me."

Helen's mouth pursed as though she had tasted a lemon. "Trust me. Doesn't matter how good you are. It won't ever be enough for them to take you out of the box they put you in. What did Ben do?"

"Tried to be his usual heroic, gallant self." Ginger hesitated, then stood and closed the door to the room. She pressed her hands against the worn wood to reassure herself that it was shut all the way. "He wants me to go away—tried to engineer it, in fact, with the brigadier-general—because he thinks the Germans are targeting us. The Spirit Corps."

Helen sucked in a breath and closed the fan. She leaned forward and rested her elbows on her knees. "Why do they think that?"

Ginger quickly relayed the details of the "ghost spy" report. If there were any sense in the world, Helen would be the person in charge of the Spirit Corps. She had more experience and a better theoretical grasp of spiritualism than Ginger, and definitely more so than Aunt Edie. But the army brushed all that expertise aside and saw only her colour.

When Ginger finished, Helen studied the opposite wall, with her eyes narrowed. "So . . . so we need to move the mediums from here."

"Do you think it would be possible to set up a relay from the nexus to a different location?"

"The problem . . . so, let's think. Right now, we're using the soldier's ID discs to bind them to the nexus here. It's set so that they have to report here before they can rest."

"Right. Making replacement ID discs with soil from a new location would be simple enough. It's getting all the soldiers back in for another blood draw that's the tricky part."

"It doesn't have to be blood. Spit would work, or any other bodily fluid."

"It's the pretext I'm worried about." The soldiers had to know something about the Spirit Corps program, or they wouldn't take note of their surroundings as they died. But the ritual that they went through . . . it was all a mum show. They actually primed the soldiers during their medical examination. They simply did a blood draw, and added the blood to resin ID discs made from the soil at the nexus in the warehouse.

Helen raised one finger. "Maybe for a vaccination?"

"As a long-term solution, that might be what we have to do."

"So the question is . . . can we relocate the nexus in the meantime?"

"Right." Ginger had gotten the original idea from a spiritualism concept that souls will imprint upon specific places. But Helen had been the one who'd figured out that they could embed that location in each soldier's ID disc and then bind it to them with their name and blood. "I've been thinking of a sort of relay, but I think we'd still need a group here to manage it."

"Hm. A relay . . . the problem is, we've made it so that the soldiers don't get released until they report at Potter's Field. I think that after reporting, they'd still have to be sent back here for release to the next plane. We'd have to change the way the binding is structured so that they give their report and then come here—only the nexus won't pull them if they . . . let me think on it."

"It sounds like you are hitting the same stumbling blocks I was."

"It's all a jumble." Helen opened her fan again. "See if you can get me a list of the places where they are thinking about setting up other branches."

"Have you an idea?"

"Nope." She shrugged. "But more information is always good."

Ginger stood, brushing the soft gauze of her skirt smooth. "Why don't you come dancing with us? A break might do you some good."

"No. Thank you though."

"Oh. Do come. You're already dressed."

Helen cocked her head and raised an eyebrow. "I don't know whether to be pleased that you've forgotten or annoyed."

"Forgo—oh." Of course. Helen could not join them at the hospitality tent. She was black. Ginger's cheeks heated with embarrassment, and her aura must have been just as ruddy. "I'm—I am so sorry. We can go elsewhere. Or—"

"Ginger. Go dancing with your fellow." Helen brushed her skirt off her knees and stood. "I'll step out with my friends. The music will be better anyway."

★ ★ ★

Laughing, Ben swung Ginger around in a tight pivot to avoid another couple on the crowded dance floor. The hospitality room was little more than a tent, but panels had been laid out to create a space for dancing. It seemed half the Western Front had found their way into that tent. At the far end, the small brass ensemble drowned out the distant sound of guns.

The cornetist was as brilliant as promised. And black, but no one seemed to have any objection to *him*, so long as he was playing. It was absurd that Helen could not join them here. And yet . . . Ginger recalled with unease how she would have reacted before she worked with Helen.

She rather hoped that Helen was also enjoying a night out. It was such a delight to be out of the shapeless uniform and pretending to be part of a normal couple in love.

Across the floor, Joanne and Edna had found partners and danced away, while Ben's hand at Ginger's back guided her through the slow-slow-quick-quick of the new dance craze.

The blue gauze of her skirt billowed as they spun about the floor. It would be nicer if Ben were in evening dress instead of Army drab. Still, under her left hand, his shoulder was delightfully firm. Ginger gave it a squeeze. "How did you have time to learn the foxtrot?"

"When I was in Paris." He tilted his head and deployed his dimples. "It was an assignment. You don't mind that I danced with other women, do you?"

"Hardly. I dance with other men."

He rocked her in a three-part turn. "Part of your hospitality duty. I know. I try not to be jealous."

"Do you succeed?"

"Not really. No." But he winked, and his aura was amber with pleasure. "Oh, bother. Speaking of duty . . ."

Ginger glanced around as Ben steered her off the dance floor towards a beefy man with an aquiline nose. His blond hair had been darkened by a coat of brilliantine and lay flat against his head as if it were painted there. Over the wool and sweat of the assembly floated a scent of musk and honey. "Ben! Old man. I see you have found the prettiest lady available."

"Reg." Ben released his hold on Ginger and shook the big man's hand. "May I present you to my fiancée, Miss Virginia Stuyvesant. Ginger, my cousin Captain Reginald Harford."

"Ah . . ." Ginger offered her hand. "So you are the infamous heir presumptive?"

Laughing, Reginald revealed that dimples were a family trait. "He delights in teasing me with unlikely scenarios. Though I won't deny that I'd hoped Ben wouldn't marry." He bowed over Ginger's hand as if he were in evening dress. "But, meeting you,

I would guess that my chance of inheriting just shrunk significantly. Have you a sister?"

Ginger laughed. "An only child, I'm afraid."

"Pity." Reginald eyed Ben, and then the dance floor. "Would you mind terribly if I borrowed your fiancée for a dance?"

Ben shrugged and shook his head. He was all affable on the outside, but his aura suddenly flared green. "Bad timing, I'm afraid. We were just going to call it a night."

"Ah well. Another time, Miss Stuyvesant."

"I hope so, Captain Harford." Ginger looked around the crowded tent, spying the girls from her circle. "Over there . . . do you see the brunette in the blue dress? That's Edna Newbold. Ask her to dance. Joanne, the girl next to her, will want to, but she'll step on your feet."

Reginald winked at her. "I appreciate the warning."

"Reg—" Ben took him by the arm. "Edna is a nice young woman. Don't do anything I wouldn't."

"But that so limits my opportunities." He gave a little bow and, with a wink, made his way into the crowd.

The dancers quickly swallowed him, but Ginger still waited a moment before leaning in to whisper in Ben's ear. "What was that about?"

"I told you I was not good at suppressing my jealousy." Ben offered her his arm and led her through the tent to the outside. "Besides, he had a . . . certain reputation at university that I cannot be altogether easy with."

Alarmed, Ginger looked back toward the tent. "But I just sent him to Edna."

"For one dance, in a crowded tent full of servicemen. She will be fine." Ben frowned. "Unless she has a habit of going home with any man she meets."

Ginger smacked his arm. "Don't be vulgar."

"Ow!"

"Edna is a respectable young lady, and so are the other girls in my circle."

"Good." He rubbed his arm. "Truly though, she's only in danger if she's an heiress. He's perpetually short of funds."

"Her father is a shepherd."

"Then she is definitely safe from him."

"Well . . . next time, say something anyway."

"I did! I told him to behave."

"I mean to me."

"What am I supposed to say? 'Ginger—this is my cousin. He's a cad. Don't trust him with your friends, horses, or money.'"

"I wouldn't object." She regarded him with some concern. "You have never said a bad word about him before."

He sighed. "I have to be pleasant to him, or my father will have my head."

"And what of me?"

"You . . . you make me be a better man than I am naturally inclined to be."

"You do say the sweetest things."

He offered her his arm. "Walk you home, Miss Stuyvesant?"

"I would be delighted." She settled her hand in the crook of his arm, and leaned close to feel the warmth of his body.

The streets of Le Havre were dark, save for the moonlight and, in the distance, the flash of guns. Outside the hospitality tent, the constant crackle and bang reasserted itself. It was strange what one could get used to hearing. It sounded so different in the memories of the dead.

"Are you all right?" Ben put his free hand over hers.

"Only tired, but that is true for everyone, I think." She leaned her head upon his shoulder as they walked. It was a delicious intimacy to be out together, unchaperoned, for a stroll at night. Before the war, it would have been unthinkable. "Must you really go away tomorrow?"

"Alas, yes. It won't be a long trip, though." He steered her to the side to avoid a refugee sleeping in the doorway of a building. "Ginger . . . have you—I was thinking about lucid dreaming."

"It isn't reliable for spy work, dear. The dreamer is too likely to shape the dream into what they want to see."

"No—no, I know that. I was thinking more . . . for us." Ben cleared his throat, looking at the moon. "If we both tried at the same time. While I was away, I mean."

In theory, they could share a dream, though Ginger had never tried it outside of her training as a medium. "I suppose, though I already dream about you every night."

"Do you? Really?"

"Well . . ."

Ben cupped her cheek with one hand. His thumb left a trail of warmth as he caressed her cheek. "May I steal a kiss, Miss Stuyvesant?"

In answer, Ginger smiled and tilted her head up, lips parting. Who cared for proprieties? Ben grinned back at her and bent—

A sharp whistle cut through the night. "Nicely done, Captain. Is her hair red all over?"

Ben turned from Ginger, his hands bunching into fists. A man with the pips and crown of a captain sat in a doorway, collar undone and hair hanging into his eyes. Ben took a single step toward him. "Apologize to the lady."

"For what? Asking you a question? I didn't ask her, now did I?" He leaned to the side to look around Ben. "Hey, lady. Are you red all the way down?"

Ginger's mouth hung open a little in astonishment. She had

heard cruder language in some of the memories, but none addressed directly to her. Her heart speeding a little, she put her hand on Ben's arm. "Let's go."

"How much is she? Maybe after you finish, I can have a turn."

A flare of red exploded through Ben's aura, wiping out every other colour. With a guttural cry, Ben rushed at the man, who rose to meet him. Their breath huffed out so she couldn't tell which of them had cried out at the impact. With scuffling sounds, they staggered across the sidewalk. In the moonlight, it was almost possible to think they were dancing the foxtrot.

"Ben! Stop." Ginger darted closer. "Stop! It doesn't matter."

Without a doubt, neither man heard her. A dull series of thumps accompanied an exhalation and a groan. The other man staggered back, one hand clutching his nose. "Jesus. We're supposed to be on the same side."

Ben growled. "Apologize to her."

"Fine. Fine! Lady, I'm sorry your fellow is a prick."

Ben lurched forward, but Ginger caught him by the arm. "Stop it, Ben. Do you want to get called up on charges?"

He stood, tense and panting, then spat at the man. Without saying anything else, he turned and put his hand at the small of Ginger's back. The pressure guided her away from the encounter, but Ben stayed stiff and silent as they walked several streets away. He walked with one hand pressed against his ribs, while his aura roiled around him in angry reds and blacks. Flashes of deep brick red sparked through the maelstrom of emotion.

"Ben?"

They walked past a few more buildings. Ginger's heart was still racing. That flash of temper was so unlike him. Before the war, Ben had been the most even-tempered man she'd ever met.

Now . . . and what had been the point? If they had just continued on their way, the fight would not have occurred.

"Ben? What was that?"

He slowed and then came to a stop, staring at the paving stones. After a moment, he shook himself. "Sorry." He raised a hand to run it through his hair and stopped with a wince. "That was . . . I wish you hadn't heard that."

"I've heard worse."

His eyes widened, and then he gave a crooked grin of recognition. "Right. I forgot who reports to you."

She shook her head. "I meant, why did you attack him?"

"He was—well, I couldn't let that stand."

"Actually, you could have. If we had continued walking, the man would have been behind us in no time at all. And . . ." She laid her hand over his where it pressed against his ribs. "You would not be injured."

"This? I'm not—" He glanced at her and grimaced. "You're looking at my aura, aren't you."

She nodded.

"That's not fair." He shrugged with one shoulder. "He landed a good punch, but nothing is broken."

"Still. The point remains that you don't even need to be bruised."

"I couldn't very well let that sort of comment—I mean, what if you had been alone?"

"Ben." She sighed, exasperated with him for bringing up unlikely scenarios. "The fact that I am out with you, without a chaperone, is not a sign of my usual behaviour."

"But if I hadn't said anything, that fellow would have thought that his comment was acceptable and might have escalated with another woman." He rubbed his face. "It's conduct unbecoming an officer."

That might be the case, but neither was brawling. What worried her more than either was Ben's aura. The anger had evaporated and left behind the grey of despair and the deep purple of grief.

"What is the matter? Ben—I mean . . . what, truly, is the matter?"

He looked at her, and for a moment the grief was visible on his face as well. He gave her a lopsided grin, making his dimples flash. "Let a man have some mystery, what?"

"Not too much." She took his arm again. "Or I shall feel I don't know you."

"Some days, my dear, I don't feel that I know myself. So we're on even footing."

Chapter Four

★ ★ ★

17 JULY 1916

Ginger walked onto the floor of Potter's Field, shivering as she stepped over the line of salt. Most of the team had assembled already. They were only missing Mrs. Richardson and Mr. Haden. Ginger's shoulders relaxed a trifle when she spotted Edna, none the worse for wear and with a satisfied amber haze to her aura.

Helen looked up and smiled at her. "How was dancing last night?"

"Mostly lovely." Ginger took her seat in one of the armchairs, grateful that the mediums rated padding.

"Mostly?"

Ginger thought of the fight Ben had had and shook her head. "He left on a mission this morning."

Helen *tsk*ed. "That means I'm going to have to listen to you mooning over his letters, aren't I?"

"He's suggesting lucid dreaming as being more reliable than the post."

"Ha!" Helen shook her head and then sobered. "You serious?"

Ginger shrugged. "Well, I don't think it will actually—"

"No, no." Helen shook her finger at Ginger. "No. You are that tired. Already your soul is loose in your skin, same as mine. Don't do nothing that will loosen it more. You hear me?"

"I . . . yes. Of course. You're right." After half the sessions, she had to remind herself why returning to her body was important.

The simultaneous arrival of Mrs. Richardson and Mr. Haden made Ginger's brows rise. They both had auras that were even deeper in amber than Edna's, and . . . was that a pink haze of embarrassment? Ginger glanced across the circle at Helen, whose eyes were round with surprise. Covering a smile, she met Ginger's gaze and raised her brows. Ginger had to bite her lip to keep from laughing. It did, indeed, look as if the flirtation between the two elder members of their team might have been taken to a new level.

Joanne cleared her throat. "That's a very nice jumper, Mr. Haden."

She giggled, nudging Edna, as Mr. Haden brushed the soft brown wool of the sweater he wore under his jacket. He beamed at Mrs. Richardson. "Aye. I needed sommat for the cold, and look here." He pulled the fabric a little away from his body so they could see the green twined through it. "See how fine a stitch it's got? Master craftsmanship, that is."

"It's just Fair Isle knitting, only a simple knit stitch." The silver glow of pride in Mrs. Richardson's aura said the stitch was anything but simple. She patted the tight grey bun at the back of her head.

With a wink at Mrs. Richardson, Joanne leaned over to

Mr. Haden. "Well. It brings out the colour of your eyes. I had not noticed what fine hazel eyes you have until this very moment."

"Is that a fact?" He blushed, rather charmingly.

Across the circle, Lt. Plumber said, "I may need a jumper like that."

"But you'd need one in blue or grey, because your eyes are like the sky." Edna suddenly coloured.

The gong sounded, its low single tone rolling across the warehouse. Time for their shift to begin in earnest. Ginger held out her hands to either side. Mrs. Richardson took her right hand and Lt. Plumber took her left. Closing her eyes, Ginger felt the links in the circle form, leading from her to Mrs. Richardson to Mr. Haden to Helen on the other side. And then back from that medium through Joanne to Lt. Plumber and then Ginger herself.

In the spirit realm, hosts of soldiers billowed, waiting to report. It was Helen's turn to lead, so Ginger acted solely as one of the anchors in the group. The other medium stretched her soul out of her body in a coruscating wave. It bore her form and figure, but with a delicate translucence.

The dead soldier in front of her seemed perversely more solid, being fully in the spirit world. He could not be more than twenty, and held his cap in his hand. "Oh—a lady medium? I thought—"

Likely he'd thought he'd meet Houdini. Helen gave no sign of noticing his confusion, which was fairly common. "May I have your name, rank, and how you died?"

"Private William McIndoe, 12th Battalion, Gloucester Regiment. I was carrying orders to the listening post off of Whitehall and a sniper got me." He held out his hands helplessly. "I didn't even see him. I got nothing useful to report. I'm so sorry."

Helen soothed him. "Of course you do. We'll let your commanding officer know to send the orders again. Do you know what time you died?"

In the centre of the circle, Edna wrote the message for their runner and passed the note to the lad. He would drop it in the communications room and they would relay it to Pvt. McIndoe's commanding officer.

"I left at quarter till six, just as it was getting light."

"Good. And do you remember the direction you were facing or where you were hit?"

He shook his head, grey with misery. "I was crawling, and then I was dead."

"That means a head wound. See? You do have useful information. Have you a message for home?"

"Yes, please. Tell my da that I died doing my duty and that I didn't mind it. I just didn't mean to die so young. That'll do." He hesitated and then turned back to her. "Wait—tell my brother that I hid his knife in the leg of my bed. I only meant to tease, and thought I'd be home to fish it out for him at Christmas."

"I will."

"Thank you. Oh? Is that the . . ." He faded before the sentence finished.

Helen rippled in his wake and Ginger bore down to keep her anchored. When Helen was settled, the circle balanced for a moment, with each of them supporting the others. And then Ginger took the lead as their attention shifted to her. She lifted out of her body, reveling in the loosening of her bonds. The colours of the auras mixed with a crackle of scents as spirits swirled around them. The bright cinnamon red of attraction lay between Lt. Plumber and Edna, which was a new thing. Perhaps the young woman should ask Mrs. Richardson how to knit.

Ginger steadied herself and had her body take a deep, filling breath. She turned to the soldier in front of her.

It was the officer from last night. His eyes widened in surprise. "You're a—aw, geez. I'm real sorry, ma'am. I thought you were a—"

"That was obvious." Ginger smoothed her soul. She felt Helen's query through the circle, but it wouldn't be fair to ask her to process two souls in a row. "And it doesn't matter now."

"So . . . wait. We're in Le Havre? I thought the Army Corps of Mediums was in London. With Conan Doyle and Houdini and the lot."

"You were meant to, so I'm glad to hear that you did."

He hit his head. "Spirit Corps . . . all you hospitality ladies in the WAC's Spirit Corps. You're mediums—God. I feel like a prize idiot."

That was not the epithet Ginger would have chosen to call him, but at the moment she had a job to do. "May I have your name, rank, and how you died?"

"Right. Right . . . Captain Harold Norris, D Company, Heavy Branch, Machine Gun Corps. Pretty sure I was murdered."

He had been in Le Havre last night. There wasn't time for him to have gone to the front. Lt. Plumber squeezed her left hand, tugging on her awareness. Why was he bothering her? Lt. Plumber shook her hand again and—

Ginger realized that she had stopped breathing. She inhaled, and even in the spirit realm she could feel the burn of air rushing into her lungs. She focused on Capt. Norris. "Did you anger another boyfriend?"

"No. Look—I was drunk. All right? As if it weren't clear. So after your fellow roughed me up, I went to the baths. Which, yes, were closed, but I'm good with locks. So I'm in there soaking and I hear these guys talking, and then one of them drowned me. So. Spies. In Le Havre."

Given that Capt. Norris had been drunk and that he did not appear to have the steadiest of characters, there was no telling how reliable his testimony was. She should pass control of the circle to Helen and ask her to relive the man's memories, but—but after all Ginger's complaints to Ben about being allowed to do her duty, it would make her the worst sort of hypocrite not to do this herself.

Ginger reached out a tendril of thought and brushed the soldier's soul.

He is soaking in the giant vats they use for bathing the soldiers who are fresh out of the trenches. Big steaming things, kept hot all day round because it would take too long to warm up that much water. Used to be for making wine in, before the war. He can slide all the way down to his neck, and the weightlessness is enough to almost make him forget the past three days. Shell, after shell, after shell, till he was the only one left of his company. He ducks his head under the water, scrubbing at his hair. Keeps thinking he feels bits of stuff stuck to his scalp, but he's bathed enough that it can't still be pieces of brain.

The water stings his split lip. Couldn't really blame the guy who'd slugged him. Not when he was trying to pick a fight.

He lifts his head above the water and just lies there. It'd be so easy to slip under the water and not come back up.

He must've dozed off some, which was a mercy, because someone is talking. A man. Sounds posh.

"The key is the skirts. You understand? The skirts."

"I have the list right here."

"Good. Start with an—"

He lifts his head from the water. "Speaking of skirts . . . you know a place where I can get a quick tumble?"

There are two men, one of them in a British Army uniform,

but the only light is from the window behind them, and he doesn't see much more than that before the officer is on him. Has him by the shoulders and pushes him down under the water. He thrashes, trying to get free, but in the big tub there is no leverage, and he is still too drunk to be coordinated. Dammit. He didn't survive the shelling to die like this. His lungs burn and he coughs, sucking in water.

Ginger yanked herself out of his memory, shaking and cold. Skirts . . . that had to be related to the mediums.

Capt. Norris eyed her, wariness circling him in leaf green and silver grey. "So?"

"You were murdered. Forgive me for doubting you."

He shrugged. "Under the circumstances, I'd doubt me too. You find those guys, you hear? That one in the uniform . . . he's a traitor."

"I will. I'll report this at once." Her circle steadied her, and Ginger took another breath. "Have you a last message?"

"Yeah. Ask Paddy McIntyre to take a cricket bat to my kid brother's knee. I'd rather him crippled than in this damn war." He hesitated and then grinned. "And *are* you red all over?"

"Really? *That's* your unfinished business?"

He shrugged. "I was always the nosy type. Would've made me a good spy."

"And an unsubtle one."

He held out his hands. "No . . . no. I'm sorry. My mum raised me better than that. It's just the war . . . not a real good excuse, is it? We're all in it. So. I'm sorry I asked. It was rude."

"In that case, you're forgiven."

He winked. "Thank you. Hey . . . that's the light. Thought they were foo . . ." And he was gone.

Without opening her eyes, Ginger said, "Edna. Will you see that this report goes directly to Brigadier-General Davies?

He'll want someone to examine the scene in case there are further clues to the men's identities."

"Yes, madam."

Helen asked, "Do you need to take a break?"

"No." Ginger forced a laugh, even though everyone in the circle would be able to feel how shaken she was. Sometimes, external appearances could help shape her internal response. "We've only just begun. But I am happy that it is your turn to lead."

"Hmm. We'll talk after," Helen said, and she took the lead on the circle.

Ginger subsumed herself in her physical form and helped the rest of the circle anchor Helen as another soldier stepped forward.

★ ★ ★

As Ginger crossed the line of salt, she sighed with relief at leaving the cool pressure of death behind. God, but she was tired. Given her druthers, she'd have gone straight back to the dormitory to sleep until her next shift. Duty, however, meant talking to the brigadier-general. Given Capt. Norris's report, it was all too likely that Davies would want to question her as the closest thing he had to an eyewitness to the crime.

"Oh, no you don't." Helen linked her arm through Ginger's and steered her away from the offices toward the front door. "We both need some sunlight and life before more work. Have lunch with me?"

Ginger cast a glance back over her shoulder toward the offices. "I should really go talk to the brigadier-general."

"Mm-hmm. About that soldier who was—no, wait. What is

it in the manual? The irregular death." She shook her head. "As if any of them are regular, after what we doing to them."

"Speaking of which . . ." Ginger glanced around to see if anyone was listening, but the other people in the hall were either chatting with forced animation to cast off the memories of work, or so turned inward with exhaustion that they likely did not even hear the distant sound of the armaments. Still . . . it was better to be safe than sorry. Ginger tightened her hand on Helen's. "I think that stepping out sounds very nice."

Helen pursed her lips and snorted, clearly reading Ginger's aura.

Arm in arm, they walked outside. The sun brushed the chill from Ginger's fingers and wrapped itself around her like an aura. "The temptation to go find a grassy field and wantonly lie down in it is very strong."

Helen chuckled. "Now you sound like me. Except that I want a proper beach."

"Rocky cliffs are not satisfying?"

"Cold water is more the problem." Helen tugged her arm and steered her to an unoccupied bench near the wall. "Come. Sit in the sun for a bit. Then I let you talk business."

It did feel good. Ginger sank onto the wood slats and leaned against the back. "Oh, my."

Helen nodded. "I told you. Now—what happened with that Capt. Norris?"

"I thought you said we weren't going to talk business!"

"This is about your soul." Helen nudged Ginger with her elbow. "You knew him?"

"Not really. He said some unpleasant things last night while I was walking, and then got into a fight with Ben."

"You don't think—" Helen cut herself off. "Sorry. I shouldn't have even thought that."

"Thought that . . . thought that *Ben* killed him? Because of me?"

She shrugged. "Men change during the war."

"Not that much." He had changed, that was true. But not so much as to murder a man over a few words. "Besides, neither voice was Ben's. And anyway—the important thing is that I think it was related to the Germans looking for us."

"'The skirts'? I wondered that too. Do you think he was going to say the name Anne, or something like 'an apple'?"

"Could be either. There are half a dozen Annes in our ranks, to say nothing of the regulars."

Helen shrugged. "I wouldn't know."

Wincing, Ginger bit her lip. Of course, Helen and the other West Indian mediums were not assigned to work the hospitality tents. "I'll get the list from my aunt."

"And ask that fellow of yours if he's got any ideas."

"Next time I write to him." Ginger looked sideways at Helen. "Speaking of gentlemen. How was your evening out?"

"Better than it had any right to be."

"The heat?"

Helen hesitated and then shook her head. "My cousin—he was supposed to have come back from the front yesterday, but he didn't."

"Oh. Oh, my dear, I am so very sorry."

"It's okay. He's in hospital. And I know this because I met one of his squad mates when you *forced* me to go dancing."

"I suggested."

"Forced."

"Be that as it may, I am glad to hear that he is alive." Ginger watched Helen with some interest. It had not occurred to her that Helen would have family in the war. "Have you other family here?"

"Two cousins. A brother in Egypt." Helen drummed her fingers on her knee and leaned back against the bench. Closing her eyes, she turned her face up to the sky. "I think I am going to sit here and ponder the question of how to move our mediums."

"You look more as if you are going to nap."

"It is all the same thing." Helen waved her hand to shoo Ginger away. "You go talk to the brigadier-general."

★ ★ ★

Helen had probably been correct that Ginger should have gone for lunch first. But given what had happened to Capt. Norris, she could not put off talking to the brigadier-general any longer. She was the closest they had to an eyewitness to the crime. Marshalling her strength, Ginger leaned against the wall outside Davies's office. The wood scraped against the cloth of her uniform, and she concentrated on the sensation of the fibres sliding across the grain to ground herself in the here and now.

Straightening her shoulders, Ginger put a professional smile on. Thank God Davies couldn't read auras, or it would not have fooled him for a moment. She rapped on the door.

"Enter!"

Turning the cool brass knob, Ginger followed orders and entered the brigadier-general's office. "Sir. I am here to follow up on my report about the death of Captain Harold Norris."

"What? Who?"

She faltered. Edna was supposed to have the runner take the report straight here. "The officer who was murdered in the baths last night . . . did you not get the report?"

"Oh . . ." He pawed through the pile of papers on the desk. "Oh, that. I sent someone round to fish him out of the baths. Devil of a mess, but not murder."

"He was held under."

He snorted. "He was drunk, which has been confirmed by multiple witnesses. He fell asleep in the baths. Have to have the bloody thing drained."

"Sir—I think you must not have received my report. He heard two men talking and then one of them, in a British uniform, held him under. He was quite certain that they were spies."

"Because that would make him seem less foolish, right?" The general pinched his nose. "I see men who shoot themselves in the foot, quite literally, in order to be sent home from the front."

"Yes, but—"

"I am not a medium, but I know men. This man had a history, and was going to come to a bad end with or without the war, and he did."

"Sir. I relived his last moments. I *saw* the men who—"

He waved his hand to cut her off. "You saw what he wanted to think his last moments were. But really . . . if we had spies in our midst, why would they bother with the murder of a drunk gunnery captain? Now go, sit down and be quiet, and leave the war to the men."

That was not how it worked. When she relived a memory, it was as if it had actually happened. Shaking with fury, Ginger gave a brief nod and thanked the stars that the British and their goddamned regulations wouldn't allow women in their ranks, so she did not have to salute or listen to this arrogant ass. She would write to Ben, and he would take her seriously.

Capt. Norris was murdered. He might have been a drunk, but his death would not be in vain.

Chapter Five

★ ★ ★

When Ginger's aunt Lady Penfold was in town, she stayed in the Hôtel de Ville, the only hotel of any note in Le Havre. As the maid escorted Ginger into the sitting room of her suite, a flurry of lace erupted from the chair. "Ginger, darling! You are too thin, poor dear. Come. Sit. Have some chocolates. No—cheese. Have you eaten today? Hush—I can see by your aura that you were about to lie to me. Sit, my dear. Sit."

Ginger's aunt patted an overstuffed chair the way she would to call her pug.

Laughing, Ginger sank into the chair. "Truly Aunt Edie, I had lunch before I came."

"Piffle. I have seen what they serve you." She set a cheese board in front of Ginger and cut a slice herself. Placing it atop a piece of bread, she handed the whole to Ginger. "I do so wish you would stay here. I hardly use the place, and even when I am here, there is more than enough space."

"The dormitory is small, but convenient. You are all the way across town."

"First of all, your 'dormitory' is an unused asylum. Second, you say 'across town' as if you were talking about London distances. Across town? I can walk 'across town' in half an hour! Even were that not the case, there is a streetcar that stops just across the Jardin Publique, and runs nearly to your door."

"And some days, I am so tired . . ." Too late, Ginger saw the trap her aunt had laid. Edith, Lady Penfold was the younger sister of Ginger's mother and had taken a vested interest in her niece, even when the Atlantic Ocean had separated them.

"Ha! I knew you were exhausted."

Ginger held up her hands and shrugged. "We've had to schedule double shifts. Please, please tell me that you have some new recruits for us."

Aunt Edie cut herself a slice of cheese and nibbled on the corner of it. "Well . . . I do. But not so many as either of us would like. My efforts to discredit the spiritualist movement have been a trifle too successful, I think."

Ginger winced. "The fake séances?"

"Not as well attended as they have been, although—I've been working with Houdini, and we have found ways to fake most of the effects of an actual ghost. So the spectacle still draws some people. Mm! I brought six women who all have actual talent—completely undiscovered. Charming things."

"And their discretion?" Charming, unfortunately, did not always mean discrete.

"From excellent families! And all so, so eager to do their bit for king and country."

"That is a relief."

She sighed and shook the piece of cheese at Ginger. "What you are actually thinking is perhaps closer to *only six*, isn't it?"

"Would it help if you no longer had to pretend spiritualism was a fraud?"

Narrowing her eyes, Aunt Edie tilted her head. "Yes . . . but I thought the whole point was to keep the Germans from realizing what we were doing for as long as possible."

"They might have figured it out."

Aunt Edie clapped her hands over her ears. "Good heavens, girl! Do not tell me that. You *know* I cannot be trusted. It is a miracle I have managed not to tell people that I am faking the fakery. If that even makes sense. Oh . . . Ginger, dear. I am a gossip. Please, please, do not tell me anything more."

And that was why her aunt avoided the staff meetings. The same thing that made her such a success in society and so able to recruit mediums was also her greatest liability. Ginger sat forward and set the cheese and bread aside. "I'm afraid I need to tell you one more thing, because there is a matter I need your help with."

Her eyes brightened. "Ooh! Do tell."

"I took a report from an officer who was murdered while in Le Havre by someone who appeared to be a British officer. I stepped into the man's soul and experienced his death, so I'm absolutely certain it was murder."

"My God."

Ginger took a breath. "My problem is that I told Brigadier-General Davies about it and he believes I'm making it up. Could you speak with him? I think he might take your title more seriously. He's always annoyed when I come to meetings instead of you."

Snorting, Lady Penfold sat back in her chair. "I will do one better than that. I will speak to his wife. We will get this sorted out, posthaste."

★　★　★

The chime sounded, ending their second shift. Ginger settled back into her body, and the entire circle groaned in unison. Joanne giggled. "Lord. Don't we sound like the worst choir in the world?"

Lt. Plumber shook his head and gave a weary grin. "Not near as bad as some of the singing in the trenches."

These were good people, and she was fortunate to have them. Aches ran through her limbs with half a dozen phantom memories. Maybe she would take Helen's advice and have a stroll by the shore, just to get some air untainted by death. Then, too . . . she finally had a letter back from Ben. With the uncertainty of the post coming to the front, it could sometimes take only a day for a letter to reach her, and sometimes two weeks. This looked to have been a week in transit. She'd had to fight the urge to open it immediately when she received it, but she was so tired she hadn't been sure she would be able to make sense of it.

Ginger scrubbed her face, trying to chafe some feeling back into her form. When she lowered her hands, the entire circle was staring at her. "What?"

Across the circle, Helen stood, stretching. "What are your plans this evening?"

"I was thinking about a walk to the shore."

"Bother." Joanne clapped her hands over her mouth and looked around at the group.

Ginger's soul was still unsettled enough that the sudden flashes of brown annoyance from the group were as plain as text on a page. "Again, I ask, what?"

Joanne lowered her hands and gave a sheepish shrug. "We had a pool about how long it would take you to read Capt. Harford's letter."

Ginger glanced around the group in disbelief. "A pool . . ."

Mr. Haden nodded. "Aye. 'Twas my idea, and I was out of the running first thing."

Helen said, "Well, we all knew you got it. It was written all over you during the first shift."

"Figured you'd open it straightaway, I did." Mr. Haden shrugged. "It's what I would have done with a letter from my sweetheart."

Helen smirked. "And I said you would wait until right before bed tonight, so you had no other distractions."

"I see . . . and Joanne thought I would go straight back to my room, I take it. If I open it right now? Who wins?"

Mrs. Richardson raised her hand and waggled her fingers. "I said that you'd think about waiting, but you wouldn't be able to stand it."

Mr. Haden frowned at Joanne. "Although now that *someone* let you know there was a pool, it won't count."

"In that case, I shan't worry about playing favourites." Ginger pulled the letter out of her pocket and waved it at them. "I am going back to my room straightaway and will read it there."

The cheer they let out did more to restore her than any other measure, short of Ben arriving in person.

★　★　★

Ginger settled at the small table in her room. Its past as an asylum meant that, though she had a window, it was close to the ceiling and barred. At least the building no longer held restless souls. When the Spirit Corps had first moved in . . . it had required some effort to make it habitable by the sensitive.

On the table, she had a pad of paper and her copy of *The Story of an African Farm,* both of which were absolutely necessary to read a letter from Ben. She started with the salutation.

> *My dearest, darling, beloved Ginger—*

With that, she breathed a sigh of relief. In their private cipher, it meant that he was not going to see combat or venture into enemy territory. She only worried when he wrote a simple *Beloved.*

The paragraphs of the letter, by agreement, would contain nothing coded, though sometimes there were veiled references.

> *I received your letter of 17 July and so wish that I could be there with you. Or you with me, if that didn't mean bringing you closer to the front lines. I'm indulging myself by imagining that you are sitting just behind me. You laugh. I can hear that sweet mocking tone. We are currently in a meadow under an apple tree, drinking mint tea sweetened with honey. The hive is not one field over. If it were not for the constant thunder and rattle of the guns, it would be a lovely holiday.*
>
> *Ah . . . my dear. I miss you so very much.*
>
> *Damn this war that keeps us apart. In fact, it has inspired me to commit some verses. Pray, bear with my attempts at doggerel. I never claimed to take any prizes for my poems in school, but it is supposed to be the mark of an educated Englishman, so I continue to try. There is so much more that I want to say, and I do not think these verses will be able to touch upon my feelings about this war with any degree of justice.*

Ginger slid the pad closer to her. Here was the meat of the letter.

Death vanquishes brave and daring men.
Consider a captain, pacing near a quagmire found within.
Even valour escapes consideration now.

The heroes accept pain. Even frightened. Even vets.
Any restless, angry fighters are facing threats
Powerless over their sacrifice and death.

Death follows, as death is part of corporeal war.
Such anyone can reasonably abhor.
Certainly others find victory inside death,
Justice and freedom inhabit flesh.
Reach, find another path constantly.
And seek any path that the inner dream offers passionately.

The verse, as Ben said, was not very good, although better than it had any right to be. What mattered was that the poem converted to the numbers in a book cipher. Only the first letter of each word mattered in the cipher. The consonants represented numbers zero through nine, while vowels or the end of a line indicated the end of number. So "Death vanquishes brave and" became 260. That was the page number. The next number would be the line, and then the third would be the word, and so on through each set of three numbers.

The line break at the end of a verse represented the end of a phrase. Going through, Ginger converted the poem to a string of numbers, and was left with:

(260, 29, 1) (110, 2, 6) (237, 6, 7) (168, 6, 10)
(55, 1, 3) (9, 3, 3) (351, 1, 1) (54, 2, 1)
(23, 2, 1) (174, 13, 1) (36, 26, 3) (333, 11, 4) (155, 2, 1)

She rubbed the bridge of her nose, trying to massage away the ache behind her eyes. Next came the book. Each number was part of a book code that linked to *The Story of an African Farm*. She flipped through the pages and found page 260, line 29, first word . . . *Gas.*

It took the better part of an hour to find all the references and check her work. When she was finished, she sat back and stretched. Her neck popped audibly, sending a jolt up behind her right ear.

She bent forward and read Ben's words, in her writing:

GAS NEEDED DEVELOPMENT TIME.

GERMAN IN LEADER SHIP.

CURIOUS EXACT WORDS CAP HEARD

Ginger sat back and shivered. If the Germans had needed development time to create the gas, then that potentially meant a long-standing leak. German in leadership . . . a spy in the command structure? God.

And then the last—if Ben wanted to know the exact words Captain Norris had heard, which she hadn't been able to relay in verse, then it likely meant he was worried it related to the mediums.

She almost would rather not have been right.

Chapter Six

★ ★ ★

22 JULY 1916

Ginger ducked into the relative shade of the hospitality hut. Edna followed, with her notebook clutched over her chest. Her rosy complexion had reddened into blotches at her cheeks. The sides of the tent had been drawn up to allow for a breeze, but the July heat still stuck Ginger's chemise to her back and left an itchy layer of sweat on her scalp.

The six recruits her aunt had brought from England looked just as wilted as Ginger felt. Why, oh why couldn't their uniforms have been cotton?

She let her soul expand a little so she could see their auras. Mostly the grey-brown of boredom, although the older woman with grey hair had a layer of grief over her. Ginger pasted on her society smile and approached the small café tables they sat around. "Good morning, ladies."

Most of them turned to face her, but one young woman, with her dark hair pinned up in a complicated twist, kept chattering to the girl across from her. Her conversational partner shifted in her seat and glanced meaningfully at Ginger, with a flurry of ruddy embarrassment clouding her aura. She cleared her throat, but the dark-haired woman kept chattering on.

". . . so I sailed over the fence on my beloved Golden Galleon and landed smartly on the other side, just in front of Lord Tipley. Such a fine-looking gentleman, and he said—"

Ginger cleared her throat. "Pardon me. I do so hate to interrupt, but I'm afraid I haven't much time with you today."

"Oh." The woman sniffed and brought her distinctive silhouette around. The pert nose, the low forehead . . . Ginger would recognise her anywhere, and by the flush of poison green disdain that coloured her aura, it seemed that Abigail Giddeon recognized her as well. "Miss Stuyvesant! What a pleasant surprise."

"Miss Giddeon, did my aunt not tell you I was here?" She looked down at her list of six names and did not see an Abigail Giddeon anywhere on the list. All respectable girls from good families . . . ha. Miss Giddeon would only qualify as "respectable" under a very narrow set of definitions.

"Ah—it's Lady Winchester now."

"I congratulate you. I had not heard. Unfortunately . . . married ladies are not allowed to serve."

With a sigh, Lady Winchester lowered her lashes. Her remorse would have been convincing had she not been in a group of mediums. As it was, her aura remained a placid blue. "Alas. My husband died in the first year of the war. I'm only just out of mourning, but I shall miss him always."

"You have my condolences for your loss." Ginger looked at her papers briefly, and then faced the group with a smile. "Now.

Ladies, I must thank you all for volunteering to help with the war effort. You've had a week to acclimate yourself to Le Havre and become familiar with your duties here at the hospitality hut. There is another duty, far more important, that your country needs your aid with, but—and I must stress this—it requires the strictest of secrecy."

"May we tell—" one of the older women began.

"No." Ginger shook her head. "I am very sorry, but you may not even tell your own mothers."

Lady Winchester sniffed. "I'm sure I won't tell anyone."

"Thank you for that reassurance." And the devil of it was that she probably wouldn't. As much as Ginger disliked Abigail Winchester, née Giddeon, it had more to do with her habitual flirtation with men for the pleasure of the hunt than anything else. Even then, Ginger might have liked Lady Winchester better if she hadn't been able to see the mustard-green spite of her aura while she flirted.

And, of course, all of these women were capable of seeing Ginger's own aura, if they took the time to look. The only thing saving her, likely, was that none of them yet had the wartime habit of keeping their souls a little out of their body. But . . . just in case, it was time to think of kittens and other pleasant things, and attend to business. "We will require you to sign a declaration of secrecy before proceeding. At that point, if you violate it, you not only compromise national security, but will face charges for treason. If you feel that you are incapable of this, your work in the hospitality hut will continue without change and with the sincere thanks of your country."

She gave a nod to Edna, who passed the papers to the women. The tent quieted till it held nothing but the sound of paper rustling. Outside, the distant boom of guns rolled over the canvas. All six women signed their declarations, and then Edna collected them, placing them into a folder. When she was finished, the room was more solemn than it had been.

With a breath, Ginger faced the group again. "How many of you have attended a séance?"

All six hands rose, which was not surprising, since that was how Aunt Edie had been finding people. Before the war, séances had been fashionable ways to pass the time. Now, they were both discredited *and* a desperate way to say good-bye to lost soldiers.

"Good. Now, have any of you led a séance on your own?"

Five of the six hands rose. Only a widow with a white streak shooting through her hair, who must be Mrs. McCarty, kept her hand down. She peered around at the other women, and her aura took on the green-brown of uncertainty. Ginger smiled at them, making sure to catch the older woman's gaze. "Don't worry. We'll still be putting you all through training to make certain that you are all using your skills in accordance with regulations. Even if you don't have much experience, by the time you leave here, you will be one of the most experienced mediums in the world."

Silver questions wrote themselves across everyone's soul. The little blond woman in the back actually made an "Oh!" of surprise.

Ginger smiled at her. "Yes. We've asked you here to be mediums."

Lady Winchester scoffed. "But mediums are just charlatans."

Ginger cocked her head. "I'm sorry. I saw you raise your hand when I asked if any of you had lead séances on your own."

"Well, yes. But I faked it." Lady Winchester gave a self-satisfied smile and drawled, "I mean, really. Sitting in the dark with eligible gentlemen? Anything might happen."

Mrs. McCarty raised her hand. "I faked it too, which is why I did not feel I could, in honesty, raise my hand previously. Of course, at the time, I did not realize I was faking, but once I read Mr. Houdini's article about the ideomotor effect, I understood that I was moving the Ouija board pointer myself without realizing it."

Ginger swallowed and wet her lips, feeling a little ill. "Well . . . this is to be expected, I suppose. Ladies, the British government has employed the services of Mr. Houdini and Sir Arthur Conan Doyle to discredit spiritualism to the public, hoping to keep the Germans from knowing what we are doing. They have invented terms to explain away genuine phenomena, and created stage illusions that duplicate a genuine séance but which can be unmasked as the work of charlatans. I assure you, spiritualism is a very real thing."

"But I know I faked it," Lady Winchester said.

"Always?" Ginger concentrated on her aura, watching browns and greens play across it in muddy confusion. "Or did you used to perform them and believe in what you were doing?"

"I—I was very young. So naturally, I thought it was working, but believing in ghosts? It's too silly."

"And yet, that is precisely why you are here." Under normal circumstances, Ginger would lead them through some simple training first, but with this group, restoring their faith in their own abilities seemed paramount. "If you'll follow me, please."

★　★　★

Passing through the tall walls surrounding the yard at Potter's Field always made Ginger feel a bit like she was entering the grounds of a castle. Though that might be because she was from America, where they did not have such things. She'd visited actual castles since coming to England, and the only comparison to the brick warehouse was in the thickness of the walls.

Ginger led the small group up the stairs and into the building. The cool leaking from Potter's Field was a welcome relief after being outside.

They followed in a tight group down the hall, and she paused outside the door to the main floor of Potter's Field. "Ladies, I must ask you to keep your voices low, as our sisters are working diligently at the moment."

And then she opened the door on the vast warehouse, leading them through to the area cordoned off from the rest by a line of salt.

Even a person without a sensitive bone in their body would feel an undefined sense of discomfort about Potter's Field. To the mundane eye, it consisted of nothing but circles of women— and the occasional man, sitting with hands held and heads bowed as if at a prayer meeting. Quiet murmurs blended with the hush of pencils on paper as young women took notes of what the mediums said.

There was nothing on the surface to inspire unease, save for the unnatural chill. Ginger's charges had a far different reaction.

The little blond woman in the pink dress—Miss Ainsley— gave a little shiver. "Oh! Oh, my."

Ginger made a note to herself that Miss Ainsley might have more sensitivity than the rest of the group. "Yes. I think you are beginning to understand what your work here will really be."

"Are they . . . are they all mediums?" Mrs. McCarty had a hand pressed to her bosom as she watched the circles.

"Only two per circle. The rest are unsighted people, who act as anchors. You'll be partnered with an experienced medium after we finish basic training." Ginger gave them a smile. "You, my dear ladies, are a rare and valuable commodity for the war effort. And spiritualism is very, very real."

★ ★ ★

Ginger rolled over in bed, blinking. The moon was just visible through the high window of her room, accompanied by the ever-present rolling thunder of distant guns. What had woken her?

Someone pounded on her door. "Miss Stuyvesant!"

That was Edna. Ginger sat up, throwing off the covers. Merciful God. Not another surprise push from the Germans. In the hall, she could hear other doors being knocked upon, other mediums being called from their sleep.

"Miss Stuyvesant!"

"Just a moment, Edna." Ginger staggered out of bed, dizzy for a moment, and had to brace herself against the wall. "What is it?"

"It's an all-hands call, ma'am," the young woman said through the door. "Massive influx of dead."

Closing her eyes for a moment, Ginger grimaced. She had already worked two shifts that day. Even with the new recruits in the roster, there just weren't enough mediums. Steeling herself, she crossed the room and opened the door. "Rouse the—"

"The circles are already there, ma'am. We waited till the last minute for the mediums."

Ginger squeezed Edna's shoulder. "Bless you. Give me five minutes to get dressed, and I'll be there."

Down the hall, Mrs. McCarty followed an aide with a steely cloak of resolve wrapped around her aura. One of the other young recruits hurried after, still pulling on the jacket of her uniform. She seemed almost eager for her first all-hands. They would do well. She hoped.

★ ★ ★

"I was in bed when I died."

Ginger had a dim awareness of her body repeating the soldier's words to Edna. This was the . . . she had lost count of how many nearly identical reports she had taken. And the air was still thick and frigid with souls.

The soldier in front of her, Pvt. Winfield Sullins, had been asleep at camp 463, miles away from the front, as had all the other young men who were reporting in tonight.

"Please, ma'am. How did I die?"

And that was the unfinished business all of them had tonight. Was it even still night? "There was an explosion at your camp. It appears to have been the work of a saboteur. Did you see or hear anything suspicious before you went to bed?"

Sullins's brows went up. "Everything? I'd just come in. This was my first night." He looked around. "Am I really dead? This isn't just a dream."

"No. I'm so very, very sorry. Do you have a last message?"

He blinked. "I hadn't—I mean, the lance corporal said we were supposed to think of our last message, but . . . but I thought I'd see some fighting first."

"Take a moment. Perhaps a word for your mother?"

"She's dead. Will I get to see her?"

"I don't know what lies behind the veil, but I very much hope so."

"That'd be nice." He tugged at the memory of his earlobe, frowning in thought.

After a moment of silence in which he pondered, Ginger prodded him. "Is there anyone else you might wish to send word to?"

"Um . . ."

The desire for compassion warred with the urge to rush the man so that Ginger could get to the next one and then be done with this blighted night. With the battles, at least the soldiers had died doing something. Even knowing the angle of entry from the bullet that killed them could help narrow down a sniper's location. These men . . . And why? Camp 463 was of no strategic importance. To be sure, the loss of life would be felt, but even there, the numbers were minuscule compared to the thousands who died during each military push.

God. But they had to clear these young men from the queue. Without a sense of resolution, their conditioning would keep them from crossing beyond, which would be an immoral act. And even if *that* weren't enough to motivate her, they were clogging the report queue. If there was a German offensive today, all the critical reports would be delayed.

A queasy certainty rippled through Ginger. At her side, Lt. Plumber gripped her hand, and she took a shaky breath.

If one wanted to cripple the Spirit Corps, and couldn't find the location, then an excellent strategy would be to clog the lines and burn the mediums out. She had a sudden surge of fear for the new recruits. Please, God, let their partners keep an eye on their fatigue levels.

She focused on Pvt. Sullins again. "Who raised you?"

"My da."

"Shall I tell him that you died honourably and that your last thought was of him?"

"Yeah! That sounds real fine, only . . . I died in bed."

"It was still in service to your country, and you are to be commended for it." Ginger tried to project reassurance. "At ease, soldier. You are relieved of duty."

He gave a beatific smile and his soul brightened. "That's the light! It's all gold and—" His soul billowed upward and away through the veil. Ginger held a salute as he passed out of the middle realm.

Sinking back into her body, she relinquished control of the circle to Helen. The other medium's fatigue radiated back through the circle to her as another soldier stepped into place.

Exhausted, Ginger rested as much as she could while still serving as an anchor for Helen. The soldier who was reporting had also died in his sleep. So many pointless deaths. Across the room, a familiar spark entered Potter's Field. Ben. Thank heavens he was back from the front. As soon as she could break the circle, she would tell him immediately of her suspicions about *why* the attack had occurred as it had.

But maybe he already knew. His aura was full of distress. He was—

Ben was dead.

Chapter Seven

★ ★ ★

Ben stood among the dead, his soul dark with pain and grief.

He was dead.

How could he be dead? She had a letter from him only days ago. No—no! Ginger hurled herself outward, reaching for him. In the distance, her body stood, ripping away from the circle. Her physical form swayed for a moment and then crumpled to the ground.

Someone corporeal was shouting, and a weight dragged Ginger back down toward her body. She tried to shrug it off, wriggling away to reach Ben. He could not be dead.

Ben backed away, shaking his head. "Stop—Ginger. Stop! You have to stay with your body."

"No." She tore at whatever was holding her, and sank into Helen's bared soul—

She is teaching in a dusty schoolroom. Her students are passing pebbles back and forth, pretending it's money for an exercise. They want to stop for story time, but in Antigua, knowing how to make correct change at the market is a necessary skill. Later, as a reward, she'll let the one who wins the game pick what she reads to them. Last week it was H. G. Wells. This week, it might be—

Ginger yanked free of the memory. "Don't try to soothe me!"

She writhed and slapped at Helen to make her release her hold. Helen held firm. She didn't understand. She had to let Ginger go. Grabbing a memory of her own, she shoved Helen into it.

She is sitting on the back of her cousin's gelding. It stretches her legs wider than her own pony and is not at all comfortable. A goose startles in front of her, and then the horse is rising. The ground smacks against her, and she looks up. The sky is grey and dappled and falling on her.

Helen jerked free, and Ginger became untethered. Freed of the encumbrance of her physical form, she turned to Ben again. His face was white with horror, and grey sprouted from his back in wings of despair. Shoving aside the souls between him and Ginger, Ben grimaced. He staggered as each soul brushed against him, leaving traces of memory in its wake, but he kept coming.

Ginger flowed out to meet him partway.

"You have to go back."

"Why?"

"I need you to live." He put his hands on the memory of her shoulders to push her down.

And he is shaking again. Goddamn it. It's one thing to kill a man in the heat of battle. A terrible thing, but understandable.

Behind him, Merrow is cleaning the dust off Ben's uniform, as if it matters what he looks like. The fabric rustles as the boy hangs it on the peg in his borrowed room at the camp. "Shall I fetch your dinner, sir?"

"I'm not hungry." *That was too harsh.* "Thank you, Merrow."

The boy hesitates. Please, God, do not let Merrow say anything sympathetic, because it will break him. God—and Ginger will know. She'll know that he killed one of their own.

For a moment, Ben released Ginger, and the anguish around him stunned her into stillness. The memory of Helen's voice tickled Ginger: *You don't think he . . .* Ben couldn't have killed Capt. Norris. That wasn't—it wasn't possible. She had heard the murderer's voice, and it hadn't been Ben's.

Gritting his teeth and wrapping resolve around himself, Ben grabbed her again.

He can't sleep. The man had been a traitor. There had been a trial and a firing squad. It was all correct.

But Ben had liked the fellow.

That is the devil of it. He had been charming and brave. And Ben had enjoyed his company. But he was a traitor, and now he is dead. Had he reported in? Maybe Ginger already knows that Ben—

The cabin is too confining, so he creeps out, trying not to wake Merrow. The guns boom, sporadically, in the night. He fishes in his pocket for the cigarettes the Red Cross shipped over. A damn sight easier than rolling his own, but he'd give a lot for a pipe. The match flares in the dark, almost like an aura. He cups his hand around the cigarette, guarding the flame as he inhales. Mint and shit fill his lungs. He shakes the match out and tosses it on the ground. Crushing it underfoot, he takes another drag.

Someone scuffs the dirt behind him. Ben starts to turn, and then he's hauled backward. His throat burns. He can't breathe. Why can't he breathe? The burning darkens into pain, and he claws at his throat. A garrote.

He tugs at the hands holding the piece of wire around his neck and staggers, trying to throw the man off. They stumble together, and, for a moment, there's a distorted reflection in the window of Ben's cabin.

A man with light hair and a British uniform.

He can't breathe. He can't breathe. He is on his knees. Breathe. He can't. He—

He was dead.

Ginger slammed back into her body. The weight of it lay upon her like a blanket of rotting meat. Her breath wheezed as she inhaled. She opened her eyes, and the cracked plane of the floor stretched away from her, ending in a horizon of fabric and flesh. She could not make sense of what she was seeing for even a moment.

"Oh, thank God." Lt. Plumber lay next to her, clutching her left hand.

On her other side, Mrs. Richardson knelt with one leg twisted under her and her skirt hiked to her thighs. She held Ginger's right hand so tightly it ached. The rest of the circle sprawled on the floor, half seated, half kneeling, as if they had lunged from their seats when she pulled free.

Why hadn't they let her go?

Helen shook her head, panting. Tears glistened on her cheeks. "It's not your time. I know . . . oh, sweet girl. I know it hurts, but you have to stay here."

Ginger closed her eyes. She had told Ben that she'd expected him to report in someday, but she'd lied. He could not be dead.

"But I am." He knelt by her in the spirit realm, carefully not touching her or anyone in the circle.

"Can you hear my thoughts now?"

"No." He cocked his head. "But your aura is like . . . it's like a book in a language I'd forgotten I knew."

Helen asserted control of the circle. "Let me take your report, Capt. Harford. It's not good for her to have you here."

"No—" Ginger struggled to sit up. "I can do it."

"You can listen." Helen's voice was ragged. "Then you are going off duty. I'm not having your death on my watch."

Ben leaned in. "If you die because of me . . . I'll never forgive myself, and never is a very long time. Do you really want to leave my soul trapped in that memory?"

Lifting her hand, which Mrs. Richardson did not release, Ginger wiped her eyes on the back of her arm. "You aren't playing fair."

"All's fair in love and war. We're in both." His grin was just as jaunty as it had been in life, and belied the deep purple of his grief. "Let me make my report."

Ginger nodded and sat huddled on the floor. The room was so cold. She shivered. Even her hands, clutched tightly by Lt. Plumber and Mrs. Richardson, ached like ice.

Ben stood, brushing the wrinkles from the memory of his uniform. "I was at camp 463, smoking, when I died. It was past midnight, I'm guessing maybe two or three in the morning."

"And someone strangled you." Helen grimaced. "We saw when you pushed Ginger back into her body. Do you know who that was?"

He rippled, and for a moment the memory of grappling with the garrote at his throat was juxtaposed over the image of him standing in front of the circle. Then it was just him again, tall and lean, hair escaping from its pomade, even though pomade did not exist in the spirit realm. Ben stroked his mustache as he thought. "No. His hair was light, but whether it was blond, white, or grey, I can't tell you."

"Are there any other details we should know?"

"Not if you saw it . . ." He faltered. "I'm sorry. I mean—you lived it. I am sorry that you had to feel that."

Next would be the last message. Ginger sank further into

herself. He'd give his message and then be released, and she would never see him again in this life. She rocked back and forth. There had to be more questions to keep him just a little longer. "What about Merrow? Do you think he saw anything?"

Ben shook his head. "I couldn't make any sound, and with the guns . . . I doubt he heard a thing."

Helen sighed, and then lifted her head. "Do you have a last message?"

"Tell my parents that I love them and I am so sorry that I won't be home for the holidays. Merrow has their presents. Give him my thanks for his service." He swallowed and looked at Ginger. His brows turned upward. "And tell Ginger that I love her so much and that she has to live to be an old woman. It is the only thing that could make this bearable. Please . . . please, Ginger."

She had to remind herself to breathe, and only just managed. Biting her lips, she nodded.

"Is there anything else?" Helen asked.

Ben shook his head. He took a breath that he did not need and straightened his shoulders with determination. "What happens now?"

"You should see a light." Helen glanced around the room at the other soldier ghosts waiting. "Most people report that it is golden."

Ben revolved in a slow circle. His feet did not move. "And . . . if I don't see it?"

Ginger tightened her grip on Lt. Plumber's and Mrs. Richardson's hands. "Do you . . . do you feel as though you still have something left undone?"

"God, yes. I want to find the bastard who killed me. I—" Ben stopped, going white and crystalline with shock. "I always thought that was a metaphor. I won't—I won't be able rest until I stop him."

★　★　★

It had taken some work to get Ben past the salt line that ringed the working area, but Joanne had solved it by brushing her foot across the line to break it for long enough for him to slip out. The other circles had seen Ginger's despair, and knew that Ben was dead, but the massive influx of souls had kept them busy.

It was a small mercy. Ginger did not think she would have survived their sympathy. Nor was she sure she wanted to.

She now sat on the narrow bed in her room, propped against the wall at its head. The circle was crowded into the small room on chairs they had dragged in from other parts of the old asylum. Mrs. Richardson and Lt. Plumber sat on either side of her, holding her hands. They could not quite see Ben, although they could hear him.

Helen could see the spirit world clearly. She kept looking between Ginger and Ben, her aura filled with dark skeins of worry.

Ginger had told him the exact words that Capt. Norris had overheard before being murdered. Then she'd moved on to her suspicion that the explosion was to flood the Spirit Corps with useless deaths. He had flickered with agitation, changing posture without moving. "Can you find out about Merrow for me?"

"Of course. It will be in the records if he . . . and if he hasn't, we'll check the hospitals."

"Thank you."

Wetting her lips, Ginger leaned toward Ben. "In your letter, you said there was a traitor in the command structure, but you didn't say who. Could it be the same person?"

He froze. His image stood unnaturally still save for a flicker of silver confusion and orange frustration. The orange flared brighter, and Ben shuddered. "Maybe. I had figured out that it was someone in the command structure because of the direction and type of information that was leaking. Who? I don't think I knew."

Ginger watched him with some concern. Ben's memory of his life was already starting to fade. "When did you figure it out?"

"The other day. It was. . . ." The orange danced over him in flames. "We were in . . . we were in Amiens. There were some prisoners of war I was interviewing."

"We?" Helen asked.

"Merrow and I. I mean—he was with me, but not doing the interviews, so . . . so he wouldn't know who—" Ben held his head. "Why can't I remember what day? No. Scratch that. It's because I'm dead. Gah. I thought that would take longer."

There was an inexorable fading of memory that afflicted all ghosts who remained for too long on this side of the veil. It was usually slower than this, but it was inevitable. Ginger shivered, and Mrs. Richardson squeezed her hand. That gentle pressure and the flood of concern from the entire circle made her chest tighten with tears. Ginger inhaled slowly.

With the circle linked like this, it was a pretence that would fool no one, but she still tried for a cheery and rueful tone. It would be easier on them. An outward display of grief was more difficult to ignore. "I'm not sure you can blame it on being a ghost, since you always had to make notes while you were alive to keep track of things."

Ben looked up, brightening. "Ha! Notes. Maybe there's something in my notes."

"I thought you said you didn't know who it was."

"I don't." He grimaced and paced in the middle of the circle.

"But the fellow who killed me apparently thought I did. If I go to my billet I can go through my notes."

Helen said, "If nothing else, familiar surroundings might help."

In the hall, there came the rapid patter of a woman's heels running toward them. They clattered to a stop outside the door, the handle rattled, and then the door flew open, framing Lady Penfold.

"Ginger, my poor sweet dear. I just heard—" She stopped and stared directly at Ben's spirit. "Oh, my."

He bowed. "Good morning, Lady Penfold."

She looked back to Ginger. "Am I correct that Ben is haunting you?"

Haunting? That evoked images of ghosts who had not crossed over, memories evaporating until there was nothing left except a single traumatic event. Yet there was nothing else to call it. "He still has unfinished business."

Surveying the circle of people surrounding Ginger, Lady Penfold stepped into the room. She looked into the hallway before shutting the door. "Then why are you here, instead of at Potter's Field?"

"He was—" Her voice broke, and Lt. Plumber tightened his grip on her left hand. Ginger swallowed and tried again. "He was strangled by a British officer. We don't know who."

"Good lord." Stripping off her gloves, Lady Penfold crossed the room to stand behind Helen's chair. "May I join in?"

Helen raised her eyebrows, meeting Ginger's gaze. The question in her aura was clear enough that Lady Penfold could probably see it. Ginger nodded. "Thank you, yes."

Joanne started to stand up. "You can have my chair, Lady Penfold."

"Oh, no, no, Miss Burrows. You have all been working far

too hard. And I don't intend to do this for terribly long, so I shall stand right here, if Helen doesn't mind."

"That's fine, my lady."

"Good. Good." She put her hands on Helen's shoulders so that the tips of her fingers touched the other medium's neck. With a little sigh, Lady Penfold lowered her chin and settled into the circle. In the spirit realm, she looked at Ben and *tsk*ed. "I suppose you are set on finding who killed you."

"I am."

"And you cannot be persuaded to rest, if we promise to complete that task for you."

If he did that, then he would be gone truly. No. No—tremors shook Ginger's body and pulled her attention from the circle. She bit her tongue, trying to focus enough to stay steady in the spirit realm. The bed shifted under her as Mrs. Richardson slid closer, so that the warmth of her body was pressed against Ginger. Waves of compassion poured through their connection.

Ben turned from Lady Penfold, and his brow creased. "Maybe you should go out of the room, Ginger. There are two mediums here now."

"No."

"It is distressing you."

"The fact that you are a ghost is distressing." Even to her own ears, her laugh was utterly unconvincing. "Conversation about how to deal with that fact is not. I will be fine."

"Well." Lady Penfold frowned. "Well. It seems to me that the first thing we must do is to speak to Brigadier-General Davies while Ben is still a coherent entity. I'm terribly sorry, dear, but you do know what will happen to your memory, and I only mention it hoping that you will reconsider whether or not you might be able to rest."

"It's not a choice." He held up his hands. "Not that I'm being stubborn, but . . . the idea just makes me restless. Like . . . like I itch all over."

Lt. Plumber cleared his throat. "Begging your pardon, ma'am, but it's occurred to me that until we see who it is that Capt. Harford suspected, maybe we shouldn't go telling anyone. Just in case it's the wrong anyone."

"Are you suggesting that it might be Brigadier-General Davies? I've played bridge with him and his wife once a week, when we are all in Town, for the past two decades." Lady Penfold sniffed. "Utter nonsense. I refuse to believe he's a traitor."

Ginger nodded. "And he was here. When Ben was . . . he's been here the whole time."

"They aren't working alone—" The frustration still flashed across Ben's aura, the oranges deepening in places to bloodred anger. "Brilliant. I know that much, but not who specifically. I can't say that I approve of my facilities as a ghost."

"I can't say that I approve of you being a ghost." The gallows humour came reflexively from months of working with the dead, though she felt anything but witty.

More than one traitor. Of course there must be, disheartening as it was. Thinking that in the entire British Army there was only one person who could be seduced by promises of money or power would have been hopelessly naive. Of course, before the war, Ginger would not have been able to believe, seriously, that anyone could betray their country.

Ben's aura jagged suddenly into darkness, then flashed back to red.

Ginger sat up. "What is it?"

"Lady Penfold . . . how did you know I was dead?"

"I was having tea with Mrs. Davies. There! Aha. There you have it. The brigadier-general himself came to the house to tell me, thinking my niece might need comforting. By his aura, he was quite shaken by it, which I think suggests that he could not be involved."

"Damn. I'm regretting that I reported in." He grimaced and shook his head. "Not that I had much choice—and it's damned strange, I'll tell you that. Like being sucked into one of those vacuum things. But the point—the point is, the fact that I reported in has already made its way to . . . well."

Lady Penfold tossed her head. "You need not be coy. It has made its way to the biggest gossip in the Army. My dear, I know my reputation, and I know that it is earned, but I am in fact capable of keeping a secret when necessary. If you tell me not to share that you have reported in, then I won't."

Ginger said, "Well, my behaviour was hardly discreet. I think the news would circulate among the Spirit Corps and the intelligence department regardless."

"When you write the report, you have to say I didn't see anything, but that I thought it was a German." Ben seemed to expand, looming over the group. "And, particularly, you must not tell anyone that I am still around."

"Why?" Helen asked.

A wave of understanding and fear rolled out from Lt. Plumber. "Because . . . if whoever killed him knows that there are now eight living witnesses to the captain's murder, then we're all in danger."

Chapter Eight

★ ★ ★

The bounds of propriety, even in wartime, meant that Ginger had never been to Ben's room before. She had not even been certain where he stayed in town. Ben lived—had lived—on the third floor of a private home, owned by an elderly Frenchman. He let the rooms out to different British officers and their soldier-servants. When Ben passed into his room at Ginger's side, he rippled with grief.

"Are you all right?"

"I think it just hit me." He held up his hand and passed it through a small desk set under the window. "This isn't a game."

"No."

He sighed and then laughed, wiping his face. "I'm not certain why I keep sighing. I'm fairly certain I'm not breathing."

"It's very common. Sighing, I mean." He was a collection of memories, including the physical ones.

"Well . . . well, I've fantasized about inviting you here, although in my dreams it was rather tidier."

The room was small, and likely had once been a servant's quarters. A narrow bed sat in the far corner next to a tall bookshelf. The shelves were crowded with books and stacks of paper tied into bundles. The desk was similarly buried beneath papers.

"I have, in fact, been plagued with curiosity about your life as a bachelor."

The door to the room's wardrobe hung open. His uniforms hung neatly pressed, but the bottom of the wardrobe was covered in unwashed clothing, and a sock lay upon the ground.

"Perhaps it would be better not to satisfy that curiosity."

Ginger picked up the sock and stuck her finger through the hole in the toe. "Please tell me that this is not the usual state of your socks."

"Well . . . sometimes they've been soaked in invisible ink."

"Invisible ink?"

He nodded and stood over the desk looking at it. "It's a death sentence to be caught with a bottle of invisible ink, because then you're clearly a spy. So we soak our socks in it and then extract it in water at the other end."

"That seems remarkably clever. And I thought our cipher was good."

"Book ciphers are one of the better ones. Unbreakable without the book. There's a whole set of ways to pass information. Ciphers like ours, advertisements in the newspapers . . ."

"Holes in socks?"

"Heh. Not quite. Though . . ." He cocked his head to the side and stared into the distance. "I wonder if that would work."

"I can darn them for you . . ." Not that it mattered what his socks were like now.

Ben cleared his throat. "I don't think that would make a difference in how the ink works. It all comes out in the wash."

"Have you ever really washed anything?"

"Merrow does. If not for him, the room would be in even worse shape." Ben crouched next to the bookshelf, his head tilted to the side to read the titles.

"Anything coming back?" Though his notebook had been with him in the field, there was the possibility that familiar surroundings would help.

"Nothing useful. My mind has offered me a few lines of poetry, which is not at all helpful. *Down the blue night the unending columns press*." He put his hand on a book, and it passed through. Ben cursed under his breath. He crouched there, with his head bent and his aura bright with fury. But then he turned and smiled at her. "Could I ask you to pull this out for me?"

"Of course." She knelt and pulled out a small volume of Rupert Brooke's poems. She opened the book and thumbed through the pages. "Is this important?"

"No . . . But it is bothering me that I can remember part of the poem and not the whole thing. I won a badge with it at speech day back at Uppingham School."

"I see how handily you slipped in that boast on your oratory." Shivering, Ginger turned back to the table of contents. Brooke had not written the poems until he was at war, which was a good ten years after Ben had attended Uppingham. His memory was already starting to blend events. "Which poem?"

" 'Clouds.' "

She flipped back to poem and held the book open for Ben to see it. He went amber with satisfaction. " *Down the blue night the unending columns press / In noiseless tumult, break and wave and flow, / Now tread the far South, or lift rounds of snow / Up to the white moon's hidden loveliness.'* Thank you. It was going to bother me that I couldn't remember that, and I don't need more unfinished business to keep me here."

"Finding out who—who killed you is quite enough."

Ben shook his head. "It's more than that. Whoever killed me probably did so because I was close to figuring out who was targeting the Spirit Corps. I need to stop him."

Ginger walked over to the desk and picked up a piece of paper. It was a bill for groceries. "If we work through the question, perhaps we can rebuild your line of thought. You were at the same camp that had the explosion. Might you have stumbled upon the saboteur instead?"

He steepled his fingers together and tapped them on his lips. "Perhaps . . . either way, we know it was an officer with light hair."

Ginger closed her eyes, trying to think of the man. "I can't recall seeing his uniform clearly enough to tell rank."

"No. But I felt braid on his cuffs when I was trying to pull his hands free."

"Shall we presume that he survived the explosion?" She sorted through the papers on the desk, looking for anything useful.

Ben nodded. "I think we have to. Which means we need to look at the roster to see who survived and is a fit for the description."

"Will hair colour be listed?"

"On their enlistment cards . . ." Orange frustration obscured him for a moment. "But I do not know how you will convince command to let you look at them or the roster."

"I could ask Brigadier-General Davies . . . if you are certain that it's not him."

"I'm not." He gripped his head and grimaced. "It seems as though it gets fuzzier all the time."

"You said you wrote it down." Ginger pulled open a drawer. "Where would your notebook be?"

"It would be with . . . with my body. I keep feeling like I can go back. To my body, I mean. Like this is temporary."

A flicker of hope caught Ginger. "Is there a chance that you aren't . . . might you have simply lost consciousness and come unmoored?"

"No."

"But it might explain the feeling that this is temporary."

Ben greyed with sorrow. "No, darling. Do not . . . I am—I am quite certain."

She nodded and bent her head. Her eyes burned as her vision blurred. She picked up a packet of envelopes, without seeing it clearly. When she blinked her eyes clear, the handwriting on the envelopes was her own. "You saved my letters?"

"All of them." With a rakish grin, he cocked his head. "Am I to understand by your surprise, Miss Stuyvesant, that you did not save mine?"

"Don't be absurd. Of course I did." Ginger wiped her eyes with the back of her hand. The sense he had described of being sucked toward the nexus at Potter's Field . . . it was designed to catch their soldiers on the verge of death, so it was, in theory, possible that his body had recovered from the strangulation. She flipped through the letters. "The last few are missing."

"Nothing sinister. I carried them to the front with me. They'll be . . . they'll be in my breast pocket."

"It sounds as though we should go to the front."

"No!" His image stuttered, flashing between standing by her and huddling in a crouch. Black fear swirled around him. "It's not safe."

"But since your notebook is there—"

"No. You can't. No. No. No." He shook his head, which was

almost lost in the darkness surrounding him. "You can't go. You can't. No. No. Nonononoo—"

"I would be careful."

"Don't. No. No, don't." Without a body to anchor him, dread distorted Ben's form. He sank into a crouch under the weight of fear. Great black sheets of it spread out from him, waving like seaweed at the bottom of the sea.

"Sh . . . sh . . ." The tendrils of fear stretched out and brushed against her. So cold. Ginger's heart raced. She swallowed, trying to catch her breath. "Ben—Ben, look. I am going to read you some poetry."

He stared at her without comprehension. The temperature in the room dropped until Ginger could see her own breath.

"I am—I am going to read. What shall I read?" Shaking, she fumbled as she picked up the book of Brooke's poetry. "Shall I read the poem you memorized?"

"Yes." The fear receded a little, but Ben still crouched as if sheltering from a bomb. "Yes. That would be good."

She sank onto the bed and pulled his rough wool blanket around her. "Here. Listen."

> DOWN the blue night the unending columns press
> In noiseless tumult, break and wave and flow,
> Now tread the far South, or lift rounds of snow
> Up to the white moon's hidden loveliness.
> Some pause in their grave wandering comradeless,
> And turn with profound gesture vague and slow,
> As who would pray good for the world, but know
> Their benediction empty as they bless.
> They say that the Dead die not, but remain
> Near to the rich heirs of their grief and mirth.
> I think they ride the calm mid-heaven, as these,

In wise majestic melancholy train,
And watch the moon, and the still-raging seas,
And men, coming and going on the earth.

She finished that poem and moved on to the next, and the next. As she read, Ben gradually calmed down, until he came to sit on the bed beside her. Outside, the sun had set. Ginger became aware again of her ever-present fatigue. She yawned until her jaw popped.

Ben looked over. "You're tired."

"Yes."

"You should sleep." He plucked at the quilt, frowning when his fingers passed through it.

Even if she were to go to the front, which seemed a necessity, she would not go tonight. She tried to joke, hoping it would distract him further. "Shall I sleep here? In your bed? My heavens, Capt. Harford, that is rather forward of you."

He gave a shy smile. "Sleep here? Please?"

Despite her fatigue, Ginger rather doubted she would actually sleep. But with luck, a night in familiar surroundings would help him stabilise, and then tomorrow—tomorrow she could try to make him see reason. But for now, she would try to sleep.

Ginger is pretending to sip a glass of champagne, just touching the liquid to her lips. Ben sits down and leans against her, a warmth against her shoulder.

He bends his head and murmurs in her ear. "I'm trying to decide if Miss Porter needs a rescue from FitzWilliam. Pretend I'm trying to wheedle a kiss?" His breath is warm and smells of the champagne, mown grass, and honey.

"Am I to take it that I shan't get one?" She raises her glass again and turns her head demurely.

He chuckles, low and throaty. "At the first opportunity."

She shifts so that her thigh touches his and the silk of her dress shushes against the black wool of his trousers. It has been so long since she has seen him in evening wear that she had almost forgotten how elegant white tie is. Which does not make sense, of course, as he wears white tie to dine every evening, just as all the gentlemen in their set do.

There is something she is supposed to remember . . . a nagging sense that she is supposed to talk to Ben about something. But if she talks to him now, she will disturb whatever it is that he is listening to.

She concentrates, trying to hear the conversation over the chatter and bright laughter of their peers. There is something else.

"Ginger?"

"Hmm?" She turns her head and meets Ben's gaze.

"Can you hear me?" His eyes are bright and fixed upon her.

"Of course I can." She lifts her hand, but the champagne flute is gone. "You are sitting right in front of me."

"Yes . . . but are you aware?" He puts his hand in hers, and a gentle current of electricity coursed up her arm to her chest.

Ginger inhaled suddenly, breathing in the understanding. "Are we lucid dreaming?"

"Thank God. Yes." Ben lifted her hand and pressed his lips against her fingers. They were warm and soft, with the slight tickle of his mustache. "I am so very sorry about earlier."

"Earlier?" He meant something while she was awake. He had been frightened or frightening. She could not quite recall. "It doesn't matter."

"I think I might be more fully present than you." He turned her hand over and kissed the inside of her wrist. "Certainly, I feel more . . . more myself right now."

Ginger bit her lower lip and caught her breath. "That would make sense, wouldn't it?"

They were outside, sitting under a flowering apple tree. Bees buzzed around them, mixed with the scent of mint tea. The sun dappled them and crystallised in an amber aura around Ben. Ginger sank into it, letting her own aura expand outward to brush against his with the shush of silk on wool.

Here inside him, she found radiant trust and vivid green-gold confidence—there was the haze of fear, but inside, the reasons were clear. He was afraid for her—not because he thought she was weak or foolish, but because he was all too aware of the dangers her abilities would place her in.

Evergreen and cinnamon memories brought the security of sitting by the fire and watching snow fall. She nestled deeper, trying to drive out the cold of the snow. Ben opened more deeply, flowing around her with the crackle of embers. Her soul trembled, breathless with longing.

"Oh, God!" Ben suddenly fractured into panic and pushed her away. "You have to wake up."

"Why?" Nothing appealing awaited in the waking world. She could touch him here, but, awake she would have only a rough wool blanket and a cold room to face. "Stay with me."

"Wake up." He shoved her, then jerked back. "Damnation. Ginger, you have to wake up. Please, dear God, wake up!"

Ben flurried away, soul sparkling out of sight. She pushed deeper into the dream, trying to find him. The thought of returning to her own body was enough to make her weep. There was no reason to go back.

A thump tugged at her attention.

Ginger paused, floating in a half-dream. A sudden pain in her shoulder intruded itself in her consciousness. Trying to shrug it off, she spun away, but she was not so deeply asleep as before.

Something slapped against her ribs. Then her upper arm. Her legs.

A sudden jolting flurry of hard corners slammed against her. Something wood crashed.

Ginger tumbled against the floor, awake. Books lay scattered around her, and the bookshelf rested at an awkward angle against the wall. It had knocked the bed over when it fell.

Her body was cold. She gasped, breath wheezing into her empty lungs.

She had stopped breathing. Coughing, she sucked in another breath, and her lungs ached with the cold air. She must have been too far out of her body. Shaking, Ginger rolled onto her side.

"Ben?" Her throat ached with even that single syllable. Ginger coughed again and pushed up to sit, braced on her arms. "Ben?"

Taking in a deep breath, Ginger let her soul slip a little free of her body so she could see him more clearly. The spirit realm hissed around her as veils of energy flowed past one another. In the corner, under the bookshelf, a shadowy spot of cold wavered. He must have projected into the mortal realm to knock the shelf over and exhausted himself.

"Ben?"

The door flew open, bouncing against the wall. Merrow stood in the doorway.

Chapter Nine

★ ★ ★

Merrow was dressed except for his jacket. His sleep-mussed hair meant he had probably arrived in the night and slept in his clothes, in the manner of soldiers at the front. A plaster covered a large abrasion on his forehead. His jaw fell open as he stared at the mess.

Ginger cleared her throat. "The bookcase fell over."

He flinched physically and in his aura, which folded in on itself. "Why—why are you here?"

"I was sleeping." Ginger pushed to her feet, struggling not to trip on her skirt. She had to brace herself on the wall to fend off dizziness.

"Did you—did you do this?" He stared in horror at the room, which gave every appearance of her having had a tantrum.

"No—" Ben had said not to tell anyone he was still around as a ghost.

Merrow's aura spiked with alarm. "Someone . . . someone trashed the captain's apartment?" He wiped his hand over his mouth, eyes darting about. "I need to ask you to leave."

"Perhaps I can help tidy."

"It's not—not appropriate for you to be alone in the captain's room." He tugged at his collar. "At night."

"There can hardly be anything inappropriate about it, since my fiancé is dead." She had meant it as a joke, but it drove home the reality again. Ginger pressed her fingers against the rough plaster wall and bent her head. Breathing was as difficult as it had been when she had first woken. "My apologies. That was a coarse joke to make."

"We did that—that sort of thing all the time. Jokes about death, I mean. At the front." The young man's aura was thick with fear and grief.

"Why are you here, instead of at the front?"

He stepped into the room, collecting packets from the floor and stacking them on the desk "I'm here to—to pack Capt. Harford's belongings and return them to his parents."

The cold spot that was Ben rose from the floor. She could almost see him in the shape of his aura again. He drifted toward Merrow, going a silvery blue-green with curiosity.

Ginger rubbed an incipient ache above her right eye. "You've come from the front. Did you bring his things, by any chance?"

"No. There—there was an explosion . . ." He picked up the packet of Ginger's letters, flipping through the envelopes.

The idea of him, or anyone other than Ben, reading those intimate words soured Ginger's insides. "Those are mine."

He stopped and looked at the letters again. "They're addressed to the captain."

"Yes, but I wrote them." Ginger held out her hand. "I would like them back, please."

"I'm sorry, Miss Stuyvesant. The captain's orders were very clear." He turned the packet over in his hands, frowning at the disorder in the room. "If anything happened . . . I'm to—to collect all of his papers and send them to his parents."

"Please." Ginger took another step closer.

The papers on the desk rattled in a breeze.

"I wouldn't feel right making—making that decision for them, ma'am." He tucked the packet under his arm. "I'm very sorry."

The breeze rose into a wind, swirling in a vortex around Ben. Visible in a flurry of paper, the wind flung itself at Merrow. The young man was shoved back.

He cried out, raising his arm over his face to stop the papers that pelted him. In the spirit realm, Ben stood between her and Merrow, responding to a perceived threat to Ginger. He rose over the young man, back arched forward. His form was deep grey shot through with molten red. He grabbed a book and threw it at Merrow.

Each manifestation into the physical world sapped his energy. She had to stop him. As weakened as Ben was, his spectral form could wind up trapped in its fear and anger, unable to complete its task.

Merrow staggered back under the onslaught, and, despite the fear wrapped around him, shook his head. "What is—I don't understa—oof." A book slapped him across the mouth.

Supporting herself against the wall, Ginger pushed a little farther outside her body. Distantly, she felt her knees begin to buckle and paused to tighten them. She took a breath. Turning her attention to the spirit realm again, she called, "Ben, leave poor Merrow alone."

The reds and blacks ground against each other, scraping like gravestones.

"Ben! Darling, please listen to me."

He swarmed forward, his figure distorted so that it was barely human, only an amalgam of emotions.

"Ben!" Something . . . there must be something that would call him back to himself. Helen had tried evoking a memory of a happier time with Ginger. "You promised me a kiss!"

He slowed, but the wind did not stop whipping through the room.

"Don't you remember? We were in the Lake District at that ghastly house party, and you thought Miss Porter needed to be rescued from FitzWilliam. And you were right; you went and spilled champagne on him. You promised that I should have a kiss later, but—"

"I did, though." He turned.

"Not that one." Ginger shook her head, though truly, she did not keep track of which kiss was which. "Kisses of greeting, teasing kisses, romantic kisses, kisses of farewell, but not the deferred one from when you rescued Miss Porter."

He swayed, staring at her without the memory of blinking. "Didn't I?"

"No." She wet her lips. "In fact, there was another deferred kiss just last week. So leave Merrow alone, please, because I require your full attention."

"But he has your letters."

"It is my prerogative to give them to whomever I like." She paused, remembering to breathe. "Merrow may have them to give to your parents."

"Oh." Ben scrubbed his hands through his hair, but it stayed unmussed and perfectly pomaded. The wind stopped.

With a rattle, all the paper dropped to the ground. Well. She should have tried giving the letters to Merrow sooner.

Ben stared at her, confusion flickering over him. "I can't kiss you, though. That will hurt you."

"Not now, sweetheart. No." Ginger pulled back into her body. Cold and numb, she shivered as she leaned against the wall.

Merrow straightened slowly. He stared at Ginger as if she were the ghost. "Is he . . . is the captain? He's . . . ?"

"A ghost." They had planned to keep it a secret, but with Ben poltergeisting, there was little point in it.

"I thought—" Merrow dropped Ginger's letters and jumped when they hit the ground. Horror surrounded him. "I thought we only had to report in to the Spirit Corps, and then we were released. We have to keep working even after we're dead?"

"No—oh, God, no." Ginger pushed away from the wall, holding her hand out to soothe Merrow. "Nothing like that. Ben was . . . Ben was murdered. By a traitor."

"Not—" Merrow's voice cracked. "Not in the explosion?"

"No." The poor thing. Merrow must have slept until the explosion shook the camp, then gotten caught in the horror of that. Before the war, she could have imagined few things as awful. There was one, though, that required no imagination. Ginger took a breath and faced him directly. "A British officer strangled him when he went out to smoke."

Merrow's aura flooded with guilt. "I told him . . . I told him that smoking would be the death of him."

"Well . . ." Ginger swallowed and studied the papers on the floor.

"Sorry, ma'am." Merrow stooped and picked up her packet. "I reckon he's made it clear that he wants you to have these."

Ginger took them, shivering as Ben came to stand beside her. "Thank you, Merrow."

"Are you—are you all right, ma'am?" He shifted his weight. "Forgive me for saying so, but you look . . . you look a little done in."

Ginger crossed the room to the chair, which stood by the now bare desk. She sank into it, feeling the weight of her mortal form pressing down upon her. "May I ask you to find Helen Jackson and have her to bring our circle here? It would be most helpful. I need help to stabilize Ben."

"Circle . . . you're a medium. They're *all* mediums?" He blinked, a violet shock shooting through his aura. "The Spirit Corps is here. In Le Havre."

They had put so much effort into misleading the troops about the location of the mediums, it had never occurred to her that Merrow would believe it as well. She had assumed he would know, as Ben's batman. She tried a partial truth. "All mediums? Heavens, no. Though I am, because they needed one to serve as a liaison from the London branch to the brigadier-general. The main point is that I need help, and Helen will know how."

"Certainly." He stood a little straighter, as if coming to attention. "Where do I find her, ma'am?"

"She should be in the billet at the old asylum." Ginger glanced out the window. It was still full dark, but she wasn't sure she could trust herself to sleep again. "Please convey my apologies for waking her."

★ ★ ★

While she waited on the circle, Ginger tried to restore some order to the room. Not because the chaos bothered her, but because she was fairly certain that she would lucid dream again if she fell asleep.

Joanne arrived first. She pattered up the stairs, rosy cheeked and smelling of cigarette smoke. Edna followed close on her heels. Both wore party frocks, as if they had danced all night.

Joanne put her hand on her chest, her breath steaming in the cold air. "Lord. I thought we'd be the last here."

Edna crossed the room and took the papers out of Ginger's hand. "Here, ma'am. Sit. Let us do that."

"I'm afraid I'll fall asleep, and . . ." Admitting it aloud rankled, but they would all know as soon as they linked into a circle. "I'm in danger of coming unmoored."

Ben leaned against the wall, disturbingly clear to her sight— if she weren't so glad to see him, it would be a dangerous sign of how "loose in her skin" her soul was.

He tilted his head and looked at Joanne. "Will you tell Ginger she has to get some rest? I won't come anywhere near her."

"They can't hear you." She had spoken aloud without realizing it, until Edna looked at her wide eyed. "Sorry . . . that was to Ben."

Joanne said, "Pvt. Merrow said Capt. Harford needed stabilising, but it seems more like you do."

"You aren't far wrong."

Edna put her hands on the bookcase. "Help me with this, Joanne?"

Brushing her hands off, Joanne gripped the edge. "Ready? Go." In moments, they had the shelves up and settled. Joanne laughed. "I don't think you needed me at all for that."

Edna ducked her head and shrugged. "It's easier than wrangling a sheep."

The bustle had masked the sound of the rest of the circle arriving, with Merrow close behind them. Lt. Plumber watched Edna and nudged Merrow, in that way men have of sharing admiration. "That's a woman, see? One who isn't afraid to lift things."

Merrow cleared his throat a couple of times and looked at the floor. "If you say so, sir."

Helen took one look at Ginger and her aura went poison green with disapproval. She strode straight to the narrow bed and yanked on the frame to turn it upright. She pointed at Ginger. "You. Lie down." Then she spun on Ben. "And you—are you trying to kill her?"

"No!" Ben went grey with horror. "No, no, no—"

"Ben!" Ginger held out her hands to him. "I'm only tired; I'm not going to die." At least not today.

"Only tired!" Helen barked a laugh. "I've seen dead people that got more energy than you. Now lie down."

"But Ben is the one who needs to be stabilised." Ginger was exhausted, yes, but if Ben lost his sense of self, giving him a resolution would be markedly more difficult.

"And part of what is making him unstable is thinking that you are in danger. Lie down."

Ginger sank onto the bed.

"Good." Helen sniffed and turned to the circle. "Mrs. Richardson. Lt. Plumber. I want you to form a small circle with Ginger and anchor her so she can sleep. Everyone else will link up with me, and we'll work on Capt. Harford."

Ginger shook her head. "But you won't have a full circle."

"I'm going to add Edna and Pvt. Merrow—if they'll agree to it." With her hands on her hips, Helen did not appear predisposed to accept a refusal.

"I—I've never . . . I wouldn't know how, ma'am." Merrow ran his hands through his hair, making it stick up like random pieces of straw.

Mr. Haden clapped the young man on the shoulder. "She'll

guide us. It's that easy, it is." He sighed and stared at the floor. "Except for us not having any chairs. Getting off the floor will be harder for these old bones than being an anchor."

Helen knelt and held out her hands to either side, gesturing the others to sit. "I'm afraid I need you, Pvt. Merrow, because you know Capt. Harford best."

His Adam's apple bobbed, and Merrow nodded. "Yes, ma'am." He sank to the floor with the others. "My mum would be . . . well . . . she always thought mediums were . . ."

"The devil's work?" Joanne dropped carelessly down beside him. "Poo. It's a blessing what we do. You'd know so if you heard some of the messages our boys send home."

From her spot on the bed, Ginger watched with some bemusement as the circle sorted itself out. Lt. Plumber limped to stand beside the bed, staring at it with his lower lip caught between his teeth.

Mrs. Richardson plopped herself down at the head of the bed and arranged her skirts in her lap. "There now, poor dear. You just lie back and rest your head in my lap." She looked up at Lt. Plumber. "You sit by me."

"I'm not sure . . . is that proper?"

"Well, I don't think you'll threaten my virtue."

He chuckled and sat, leaning his crutch against the wall. "I suppose not." Setting the stump of his leg on the bed, he grinned. "And I don't take up as much room. Unexpected benefits."

"You are both very odd." Ginger glanced away from them again, and over to the other circle. Ben had drifted to the middle, but she could not quite see him. She started to stretch out of her body and was stopped by a sharp poke in her shoulder. "Ow!"

Mrs. Richardson held her knitting needles in one hand, poised to deliver another jab. "Don't you go out of your body, missy. Now lie down and sleep, like Helen said."

"Yes, ma'am." Ginger lay down with her head in Mrs. Richardson's lap, feeling as if she were a small child with her own grandmother.

"Good." Mrs. Richardson took one of Ginger's hands and one of Lt. Plumber's.

The soldier took Ginger's other hand. Cradled between them, the combined weight settled Ginger deeper into her body. She sighed. The closeness of her flesh was familiar and repulsive at the same time. It would be so much easier to slip free entirely.

But not yet.

Chapter Ten

★ ★ ★

23 July 1916

Ginger awoke to sunlight falling across her face. She felt, if not entirely rested, more secure in her own skin. A minute clicking sounded above Ginger's head. She shifted and looked up.

Mrs. Richardson had a pair of knitting needles working. She beamed down from over the length of blue-grey wool. She whispered, "There you are."

Lt. Plumber rested a hand on Mrs. Richardson's shoulder to maintain contact while she knit, but he still held one of Ginger's hands. He gave it a little squeeze and yawned at the same time. In a low murmur, he asked, "Feeling any better?"

"Thank you, yes." She squeezed his hand before releasing it to sit up.

The other circle had moved and was now crowded together by Ben's desk. Merrow sat at it, with Helen standing behind him. Her eyes were closed and her hands rested on his shoulders. The other members of the circle made a link around them. Merrow was sorting the papers, tilting his head from time to time as if he was listening to someone. Ben's aura, in muted blues and yellows, stood over his shoulder.

Ginger pushed out a little, just past her own skin. Ben snapped into focus. He was leaning over Merrow's shoulder, looking at the papers as the young man sorted them. "File that. Garbage . . . garbage . . . wait—no. It's my notes on a cipher . . . mm. Burn it. The message wasn't relevant to this, but I'd rather someone not reverse engineer the code."

He looked more like Ben than he had last evening. His features were regular, and while there was a line of concentration between his brows, he no longer had a haggard, inhuman appearance. The colours playing around and through him were muted shades of steel blue concern and a lemony orange aggravation. The haze of fear had not vanished entirely, but lay beneath the other veils of emotion.

Ben straightened, looked around, and caught sight of her. He smiled, and amber rippled across him in an aurora of happiness. "Thank God."

Helen's spirit turned to face Ginger, while her body's hands remained firmly on Merrow's shoulders. "I was worried you wouldn't listen to reason."

Ginger raised her eyebrows. "I'm not that stubborn."

Ben barked a laugh. Helen snorted. Mrs. Richardson coughed.

The nerve of the lot of them. She was really not as appallingly stupid as they seemed to think she was. Aside from almost losing herself the night prior. "I *did* send Merrow for help."

"True." Ben rubbed the back of his neck. "Although the need to do so was my fault."

"But only because I—"

"Lovebirds." Helen cleared her throat. "The point that we should focus on is that there are certain realities you both need to accept. The longer this takes, the more coherence Capt. Harford will lose."

Ginger shuddered. At her back, Mrs. Richardson lay a steadying arm around her shoulders. Swallowing, Ginger nodded. "So we need to find the man who killed Ben as quickly as possible."

"Not for me—" Ben held up his hands. "Yes. Yes, the whole coherence conundrum. But they are targeting you and the other women of the Spirit Corps. I can't let that . . . I have to stop them."

"I think . . ." Ginger slowed, watching him for signs of distress. "Last night you became upset when I proposed this, but I think it is the only choice. Whatever you found is at the front. We need to retrace your steps."

"I don't want you to go." The layer of fear rose to his surface, turning the other colours a murky grey.

"But, Ben . . . you cannot go by yourself without completely losing your memory of your purpose."

"I'm not . . . I'm not tied to you, am I?" He turned to the other medium. "Helen? Tell Ginger she can stay here."

Shaking her head, Helen looked between the two of them. "I think you are—or rather, I think your fear for her will distract you to the point that you will forget everything else."

Ben's image flickered so he stood simultaneously at attention, and also half bent with his hands buried in his hair.

Biting her lip, Ginger waited on the bed while the other circle projected comfort and security at him. The waves of soothing pinks and ambers washed through Ben until he shuddered and stood at ease again.

With one hand, he stroked his mustache as if nothing had happened. "I take your point."

Lt. Plumber said, "How were you planning to get there, ma'am?"

"I—" She had not put any thought into it. Yet. "I thought I might borrow some of Ben's clothes and take the train."

Ben and Lt. Plumber both laughed, and even Merrow showed a shy grin. Ben said, "Darling, no one would mistake you for someone of the masculine persuasion."

Mrs. Richardson cleared her throat. "If I might . . . Ginger will need an anchor, am I correct?"

"I can hardly travel with a full circle." Even if the Spirit Corps didn't need every suitable person on duty, a large group would be conspicuous.

"You would only need one or two." Helen appraised Mrs. Richardson with narrowed eyes. "And if you planned to do a full séance, you could recruit any mundane who was willing."

"Exactly, my dear." Mrs. Richardson nodded over her knitting. "I was thinking that I might go with you. That way you could still travel as a young woman, and I could play your chaperone. Not that you need one."

Joanne wrinkled her nose. "But wouldn't it make sense for it to be one of us? The younger ones, I mean? Those regular Spirit Corps girls, the ones who just do the hospitality huts, are always travelling in pairs."

"Ah . . . but an elderly woman has a great deal of leeway in the world." Her eyes twinkled as she looked at Mr. Haden, and she winked. "We can get away with murder—oh, dear. That's probably not in the best taste. The point is, I can do almost any shocking thing and people will go out of their way to help me."

He guffawed. "Aye! That's true enough."

Gratitude rolled out of Ginger, and for a rare moment she could see the edges of her own aura in a golden incandescent haze. Her breath caught in her throat. "Thank you. That is really lovely of you."

Ben turned back to his desk. "Merrow, if you'll open the bottom drawer, it has a false back. I have some travel documents that should—no, wait. I've got nothing for a lady."

"I'll go." Merrow turned from his place at the desk, shoulders still held by Helen.

Ben opened his mouth and then shook his head. "Thank you, Merrow. But I think we can ask Lady Penfold to help procure documents, and you've done enough, already."

"Even so, sir. It's my duty." The young man straightened his shoulders and looked, more or less, at where Ben stood. "I'm assigned to you while you remain in the service of His Majesty's Army. I don't reckon death has stopped you, so I'm still your man, sir."

★ ★ ★

After the circle discussed options, it seemed as though Ginger would have to speak to the brigadier-general before leaving. While not, strictly speaking, part of the army, the fact that she served as the liaison for Lady Penfold made it necessary for her to formally take leave. Besides, Ben wanted to see Brigadier-General Davies.

She stood outside Davies's door, with Ben hovering next to her as a whirl of aura and cold. She could sense him more than see him.

She tightened her lips and pushed her soul a little out of her body. Unless she pushed further out than was strictly safe, she would not be able to speak to him without her body repeating the words. So she did not push that far, just skimmed past the surface of her skin so she could see him more clearly.

Ben cocked his head. "You probably shouldn't do that."

Without a circle, in the fragile state that she was in, her danger of losing her grip on her body was much increased. But she couldn't let him wander without someone to anchor him, and they had to find out who killed him. "I'll need to be able to hear you while we're in there."

He groaned a little. "I would much prefer it if you weren't right."

"But, darling, I always am. It would be a difficult habit to break now." She raised her hand and knocked on the door.

"Enter!"

Ginger pushed the door open, feeling as though she should hold it for Ben, but he passed through the wood and entered at her side.

Brigadier-General Davies stood and came around his desk. "My dear girl, I am so terribly sorry for your loss."

Those simple, trite words stopped Ginger. She put her hand over her mouth and could not inhale. She had to turn from the brigadier-general before she burst into tears. Why now? Why did a banal phrase from a man she did not like gut her?

"He was the best of us. So clever—well. I hardly need to tell you that." Davies sighed, and it sounded so genuinely full of remorse that Ginger turned back. She had a duty and a reason for being here. His aura was dark sorrow cut with anger.

Ben grunted in her ear. "I'm trying to decide if he is upset and angry because I was killed or because I reported in."

Ginger wiped her eyes with both hands. He had a point. Auras told emotions, but not the reasons for them. Her priority now was to be able to help Ben with his investigations. "I am here on two matters. The first is that we believe that the explosion at Amiens was to flood the Spirit Corps with the reports of soldiers who do not have strategic information."

As succinctly as she could, Ginger explained the problems the attack had created. Brigadier-General Davies grunted several times and asked pointed questions. When she finished he sighed. "There *was* a push by the Germans immediately after that. If it happens again—which seems likely—then let us know the moment it becomes apparent. It won't be much, but knowing that we should have the other troops go on alert might help."

"I will pass that along." Ginger wet her lips. "Which brings me to my next point . . . I would like to take a leave of absence."

"To mourn, of course." Davies frowned, and resettled his glasses. "My problem is that I can't really be retraining someone for your position right now. With Harford gone, there's not a one of us that really understands how the Spirit Corps works."

"Aside from all the women in the Spirit Corps, of course."

"What? Yes. I suppose so. Not the military application of it, but certainly the minutiae of the work."

"I was going to recommend that Helen Jackson serve as the liaison in my absence."

"Who?"

"The second in my circle."

"The Negress?" His brows went up in surprise.

Ben drifted around the brigadier-general. "Shall we place a wager? I say that he won't go for it. If I win . . . you have to read poetry to me."

Ginger tilted her head, trying to keep her eyes on Davies rather than Ben. "She is a very talented medium."

"I am certain that she is, but that is neither here nor there."

"Mm . . . if you win . . ." Ben reached out and passed his hand through Davies's chest. The man shuddered. "If you win, then I shall provide relief from the heat by hanging out over your bed."

Ginger blushed at the very idea of him being over her in bed, which was likely his plan. Bless him for trying to tease her out of her temper. Still—the matter at hand stood. "Helen is the best choice among the available mediums." She very much wanted to tell the brigadier-general that Helen had been instrumental in creating the binding for the soldiers, but that piece of classified information was out of bounds as a tool. So she deployed her aunt's title. "And she's a favourite of Lady Penfold."

"It is not possible, and if you were in a better frame of mind, I am certain you would see that."

"Because she is a woman of colour." Even as she spoke, Ginger was uncomfortably aware of how she had viewed Helen when they had first met. Spending time wrapped in another person's emotions and thoughts quickly wiped away all of her preconceptions about the West Indian troops who had volunteered to serve in this bloody war.

"There are regulations." He turned back to his desk and tapped a thick *Manual of Military Law*. "It says that people of colour, and specifically Negroes, 'shall not be capable of holding any higher rank in His Majesty's regular forces than that of a warrant officer or non-commissioned officer.'"

"But the mediums are not part of the military. The Spirit Corps is a voluntary organization, so those regulations do not apply to us."

"They do when we are discussing a liaison who will be privy to confidential information."

"And yet Captain Keatley is part East Indian."

"His *mother* was Anglo-Indian, but his father is old British stock. It is not the same thing at all."

"Oh . . . of course. Because his *father* is British. May I point out that Helen is also a British citizen? I am not. She is, in fact, a more experienced medium than I am."

"I have already said no."

"With absolutely no grounds and in admitted ignorance of what we do." Her heart raced and her knees shook with anger.

Davies let out a heavy sigh and walked back around his desk. He dropped into his chair, leaving Ginger standing in the middle of the room. He picked up a paper and peered at it through his glasses. "I will speak with Lady Penfold and get her opinion. Assuming she will deign to come to a meeting."

"I truly do not think you understand the requirements of our job."

He slammed the paper down on the table. "I am making allowances because you have clearly been made hysterical due to Capt. Harford's death, but the answer is still no. It will continue to be no. And if you insist on carrying on in this manner, I shall have you committed for your own health. Do I make myself clear?"

Ginger drew herself upright. "Completely."

"You may at least satisfy yourself that I will grant your request for leave. You are not fit to serve in your present state." He shuddered and pressed his hand to his temple, where Ben had slid his forefinger into the man's head. "Dismissed."

Turning on her heel, Ginger stalked out of the office and slammed the door behind her. Childish? Absolutely. But that awful, insufferable man could have exactly the behavior he expected. He wanted to see hysteria? By God, she would show it to him.

Ben passed though the door and circled in front of her. "So . . . you'll be reading me poetry?"

"I am not certain that I have a sense of humour today."

"Sorry." He glanced back at the office. "It's not often that I wish to lose a wager."

"Well . . . I suppose you have to be right occasionally."

Chapter Eleven

★ ★ ★

Ginger walked down the impossibly steep stairs from her room on the upper floor of the old asylum, carrying a small rucksack she'd borrowed from Ben. Her own valise was too bulky and awkward for a journey to the front. While she packed, Ben had stayed back in his apartment with the full circle to anchor him. He'd wanted to come to help her pack, but in a building full of mediums, he wouldn't be much of a secret.

As she crossed the cramped lobby of the former asylum, the worn carpet muffled the click of her boot heels. One of the mediums had bargained for the carpet in an effort to give the narrow space some sense of home. They'd each added their own small touches, desperate to have a refuge. Ginger eyed the beleaguered fern that she'd rescued from the ballroom when it had become a hospital. She hoped someone would remember to water it while she was gone.

"Miss Stuyvesant? Are you leaving us?" Near the front door, Lady Winchester lowered a week-old copy of the *Times*.

"Not for long." Explaining the circumstances seemed impossible, and yet for all Ginger's disdain for her before the war, Lady Winchester *had* volunteered and been a ready pupil here. "I've been given leave for . . . for personal reasons. Lady Penfold will let you know who is in charge while I am away."

"Oh. I had heard . . . I so hoped I was misinformed." She folded the paper and stood, reaching out a hand. "You have my sincere condolences."

In the narrow lobby, it would be impossible to leave without passing her. Ginger swallowed, pressing the tears back down her throat. She mumbled something as Lady Winchester pressed her hand in sympathy. The room spun about her.

Ginger wrenched her hand free and stumbled out the front door. She nearly collided with Aunt Edie.

Her aunt clapped her gloved hands together. "Oh, thank heavens you have not left yet."

"Did you get my note?" Ginger swallowed and pretended to fuss with the strap on the rucksack.

"Yes, yes." She handed Ginger an envelope. "This is the best I could do. It won't get you everywhere, but the transfer papers will at least get you on trains. And I will *absolutely* listen to Helen, but I doubt that even I can sway the brigadier-general on that point. Now—is Ben with you?" Lady Penfold waved her parasol over her head. Her aura was positively vivid with worry. "No? My dear girl . . . I come with the most troubling news— come, sit in my car, so you have a tiny bit of privacy."

"You alarm me."

"I intended to, so that is all to the good. I only wish it were not absolutely necessary—absolutely. I cannot allow you to go without telling you—oh! Listen to me, about to tell you everything on the street. Come. Come." Lady Penfold turned, still waving her parasol, and led the way down the stairs to where her private automobile waited, idling on the broad drive. The aged Frenchman her aunt used as a driver stood by the door, waiting.

Looking at her watch, Ginger hesitated only a moment. They had plenty of time to make the train to Amiens, especially if she could convince Aunt Edie to give her a ride in her car to the station. "I only have a few moments."

"Yes, yes." Lady Penfold patted the seat by her. "The girls told me—although I asked them not to tell me *where* you are going, only that you have a train to catch."

Ginger ducked into the cool interior, tossing her bag onto the seat at her side. A line of white crystals sparkled by the door. "Is that salt?"

"Yes." Lady Penfold leaned out of the car and spoke to her chauffeur in rapid French that was more fluent than correct. She sat back, shutting the door.

"Why do you have salt lining the car, Aunt Edie?"

"Because—a moment." Lady Penfold closed her eyes and slid her spirit a little out of her body. Then she pulled back in. "I needed to be certain that we are alone."

Ginger's chest tightened. "What is wrong? Is it Ben?"

"In a manner of speaking." Her aunt reached out and took both of Ginger's hands in hers. "Recall that you had asked me to talk to Brigadier-General Davies about the murdered man? Well, I did. The reason that he did not wish to speak to you about the murder is that they . . . they found Ben's hat in the baths."

She jerked back, but Lady Penfold's grasp stayed firm. Ginger shook her head. "That can't be. I heard the men talking. Neither of them had Ben's voice."

"I know, darling girl. There's more. . . . Brigadier-General Davies had concerns because Ben's grandmother was German."

"The king is German, by that measure!" Ginger wrested her hands free. "You cannot tell me that you seriously believe that Ben—whose soul you have touched—would kill a man in cold blood. . . ." Except, of course, that she knew he had. But that had been a traitor.

"And this is why the brigadier-general did not want to tell you. Because he knew it would upset you and that you would tell Ben before they could question him. Of course, now an investigation is somewhat beside the point, but . . ." Lady Penfold fished a pocket handkerchief out of her clutch and offered it to Ginger. "But I thought it absolutely vital that you know what the brigadier-general thought before you left."

But Ginger *knew* that neither of the men there were Ben. "He did not kill Capt. Norris. His cousin—Ben has a cousin who is a captain, and they have the same surname. Reginald Harford. He's here in Le Havre. Mightn't it be his hat?"

"Yes." Aunt Edie nodded and lowered her hand, still holding the kerchief. "But it might also be Ben's. So either the murderer is still corporeal and at large, or he is inhabiting your dreams. Either way, you needed to know. I will trust you to do with the information what you will, but I would have felt terribly remiss if I did not tell you. Was I wrong?"

"I—no. Thank you. You were correct."

"Good." Lady Penfold flopped back into her seat. "That poppy-headed man. He thought you were too delicate—now, I'll grant that you probably could not have been trusted to not warn Ben, but, really . . . that is entirely understandable. Fragile? Ha!

He does not know my niece. Now. Where shall I drop you? Oh! And have you a gun?"

★ ★ ★

Between Lady Penfold's travel documents, and the papers that Merrow had pulled from Ben's desk, they had no problems securing a seat on the train to Amiens. Ginger leaned her head on the window, crowded against it by Mrs. Richardson, who was in turn crowded by Merrow. Around them, the train was sea of khaki uniforms. One or two other civilians provided spots of colour amid all the drab.

"I was thinking about the time in London when we did the charity circus." Ben leaned against the wall, with his arms crossed over his chest.

Ginger smiled at the memory. Pretending to sleep, she could murmur to him, without everyone on the train thinking that she was mad. "You were very dashing in your loincloth."

He threw his head back with laughter. "That is kind. I mostly recall being very cold."

"I think that is how most of us felt. Do you remember poor Miss Porter's moment of horror when she realized what wearing a skirt on the trapeze meant?"

"You were very kind to trade acts with her." Ben winked. "I will grant that some of my appreciation was because you did not trouble with a skirt on the trapeze."

"I do have the most delightful memory of your face when I came out for rehearsal." She had been terrified of having her legs exposed, but also a little thrilled. Watching Ben's jaw drop had been more than enough reward for her daring. "You made a valiant effort to look only at my face."

Ben suffused with pink embarrassment. "Well . . . I was only successful at that when you were facing me." He swallowed and wet his lips. "It is a good thing we were already acquainted, or my motives might have been susp—"

"There! That's finished and not too shabby, if I do say so myself." Mrs. Richardson's voice made Ginger jump in her seat. The older woman had been occupied with her knitting since they left Le Havre. She held up an olive green muffler. "I've made you a new muffler, Pvt. Merrow."

"Oh . . ." The young man tugged at the ragged brown wool wrapped around his neck. "Thank you but . . . but this is—fine."

Mrs. Richardson frowned. "My dear . . . I know that servicemen don't make much money, and in these times there's not much opportunity to rekit."

"It's just . . ." He plucked at the muffler, which had loose stitches dangling from it. "It's just that my niece made it. To bring me luck, she said."

"Oh. Well, that explains the—" Mrs. Richardson broke off, but Ginger could still see her opinion of the shoddy knitting as a sour patch on her aura. Still, the older woman smiled and patted Merrow on the knee. "How about some socks, then?"

"Thank you, ma'am." He ducked his head. "That—that would be very kind."

"Good. Now to find a home for this." Mrs. Richardson sat forward and tapped the soldier sitting in front of them on the shoulder. Doing so, she reached through Ben, and, with the reminder that no one else could see him, the few illusions Ginger had been able to create about the nature of their trip snapped. "Excuse me, young man? I noticed you shivering. Would you like a muffler?"

The soldier turned, his brows drawn together in confusion. "A muffler?"

Ben appeared to lean against the wall in front of Ginger.

Until Mrs. Richardson had asked the soldier about his shivers, Ginger had been able to pretend that the man in front of them was simply cold. But in July, his chills came from the parts of Ben that passed through him.

Ginger stood. "I am going to stretch my legs."

Surrounded by the flower of Britain, all these young men who were alive while Ben was not, was too much. Before she began to scream, she had to move. She did not wish any of them dead, and yet . . . and yet.

She pushed into the aisle, stepping over the rucksacks that leaned against the seats. How many of these men would speak to Helen, or someone else at Potter's Field, by the end of the month? By the end of the week? Tonight?

The cool breath of Ben trailed behind her. Ginger braced herself against the swaying movement of the train as she worked her way back. If she could just stand on the platform, the fresh air would do her some good.

In Potter's Field, the soldiers came in reconciled to their deaths due to the nature of the conditioning that had been laid upon them. But none of these men had any real concept that they would die, and, given the course of the war thus far, probably only a handful would see England again without a wound.

A man stood up in front of her. "Pardon, ma'am. You're in the Spirit Corps, aren't you?"

"I—why do you ask?" She took a step backward before she could stop herself and shivered as Ben enveloped her. The man wasn't asking if she was a medium. The mundane version of the Spirit Corps had hospitality huts all through the arenas of war. Potter's Field was the only one with mediums. She was wearing her Spirit Corps uniform still, so there was nothing sinister in his question.

"I know you ladies just serve tea and all, and . . . this is an imposition, but it would mean a lot to me. I didn't get to kiss my sweetheart good-bye." He rubbed the back of his neck. "Can I close my eyes, and have you kiss my cheek? And pretend?"

All the deferred kisses this war produced, and most of them would never be collected. "Of course."

He closed his eyes and turned his head, holding on to a seat for balance. Ginger rose on her toes to kiss his cheek. It was lightly stubbled and smelled of cheap soap. He was taller than Ben and had straight hair of an in-between brown.

Ginger whispered, "Be safe."

"Thank you." His voice was hoarse, and he turned away without looking at her, but not before Ginger saw that the rims of his eyes had grown red.

"Me, too!" Another man popped up out of his seat. Skinny and with freckles under close-cropped red hair, he winked at Ginger. "Just plant it right here." He leaned toward her, laying a finger on his cheek.

"I'm next!" Behind Ginger, a soldier tapped her on the shoulder. Built like a bulldog, he had an upturned nose that wrinkled when he grinned at her.

A breeze ruffled the bulldog's tie. Ginger glanced into the spirit realm. Ben stood with his hands clenched into fists, twice the size he usually was, with red shuddering out of him.

"Please don't." She put out her hand as if that could stop Ben. If he poltergeisted here, she did not have the circle to calm him again.

"I would very much like a body." Ben growled and shoved his hands through one of the men.

The soldier who had asked first stood up again. "Hey—hey, fellows. Leave the lady alone. She was just being nice."

"I just want her to be nice to me too," the freckled soldier said.

The bulldog nodded and glanced around the car. "A kiss is all we want, right, fellas?"

A roar of agreement went up around Ginger. She ground her teeth together. Of all the stupid things. Where the devil was their commanding officer? No doubt riding in the first-class cars.

The first man shook his head. "Come on—"

Chuckling, the bulldog glanced around him and other men from his unit stood.

"Gentlemen, I am but one woman." She held out her hands in placation. "Please understand that kisses are outside our normal purview. When you arrive in Amiens, my fellow sisters of the Spirit Corps will be happy to make you feel welcome in any other way."

"Going straight to the front."

"That's right."

"You're our last chance."

"Then I'm afraid that, with behaviour like this, you have no chance at all." Oh, but her tongue was going to get her into trouble someday. Likely today. Ginger tried to slide past the bulldog so she could return to her seat.

"Hey." He put his arms across the aisle and held on to a seat on both sides. "I asked nice."

At the front of the car, Pvt. Merrow stood up. He straightened his coat and walked back to Ginger. "Let—let her pass."

The bulldog glanced over his shoulder. His aura did not even flicker at the sight of Merrow, who had to be two stone lighter than him at least. "Beat it, kid."

"No." Merrow licked his lips and swallowed. "This is your only warning. Act like—like a gentleman and let her pass."

The bulldog and his fellows laughed. Oddly, Ben laughed too. "They have no idea . . ."

No idea about . . . ? And then Merrow moved with a speed and fluidity that astonished Ginger. It was not boxing, or any other sport she had ever seen. Two quick strikes with the edge of his palm broke the bulldog's grip on the seat. Another strike with a flat hand spun the man, whose eyes had widened as his aura flared with red anger.

Merrow grabbed the bulldog's arm, pulling the man toward him, and then flipped him over his shoulder and dropped him over the bench, in the laps of his fellows. They went down in a tangled mass.

Straightening, Merrow tugged his uniform until it was tidy and stepped to the side, blocking them long enough for Ginger to pass. As the men began to stagger to their feet, the other soldiers, who had been content to watch, filled the aisle and stopped them from reaching Ginger and Merrow.

She sat down, shaking a little, between Mrs. Richardson and the wall. The older woman gave Merrow a hug when he sank into the seat. "Oh, well done, young man."

"I've never seen anything like it." Ginger glanced to the back of the train. "How did you do that?"

"It's—It's called bartitsu. I . . . I read about it in a Sherlock Holmes story, and then it turned out it was a real sport, so I found a teacher and . . . I'm a little guy. This . . ." He spread his hands, which were shaking, and gave a shy grin. "You didn't—you didn't think Captain Harford kept me around for my looks, did you?"

Ben leaned against the wall, aura unruffled again, and grinned. "Tell him I kept him around for his pluck. The bartitsu was a bonus."

Chapter Twelve

★ ★ ★

When they disembarked from the train in Amiens, Ginger realized how much the sound of the engine had been masking the guns. She had been able to hear them, of course. Even in Le Havre, the battery range had been like distant thunder.

Here though, her very bones vibrated. Mrs. Richardson flinched at a particularly loud explosion, although her aura did not show any alarm.

The soldier to whom she'd given the green muffler paused by them. "That's one of ours. Nothing to be worried about."

"Thank you, dear." Mrs. Richardson patted him on the arm and winked at Ginger. "Now, do take care of yourself, and if you write to me, I'll mail you some socks as well."

Ginger stifled a smile, as the older woman had deftly detained him as a shield while the bulldog and his cronies disembarked. There had been no more incidents on the train, but the crush of the platform would make a casual shove very easy. Ranks of smartly uniformed men disembarked from the train, clean and ready for duty. Standing on the platform waiting to board were bedraggled rows of soldiers covered in dirt and smoke, unshaven and unwashed. Amid these unwashed masses wove an unexpected scent of musk and honey.

Beside her, Ben suddenly stiffened.

"Miss Stuyvesant, is that you?" Familiar aristocratic tones cut through the hubbub in a timbre strikingly like Ben's. "By Jove, it is."

With a smile, Ginger turned to meet Reginald Harford. "Captain. How do you do?"

"Very well indeed, if you're here." The tall blond man peered past her toward the train. His hair was perfectly pomaded, and his cheeks shone as if he had come straight from the barber. "Where's Ben? Off struggling to manage all your luggage?"

She had thought to break the news gently, but his comment changed her mind. "He's dead."

Reginald gave a laugh and then stopped. His aura went white with shock. "You're serious."

Ben leaned close to Ginger and murmured, as though anyone else could hear him, "Don't tell him that I—well, not survived exactly, but that I am a presence still."

She hadn't planned to. It didn't matter how shocked Reginald's aura looked, she didn't trust him further than she could throw him. "The explosions at camp 463."

He reached up as though to pull a hat from his head in respect, but his head was already bare. "Devil of a thing." Reginald glanced around the platform. "And you are here to . . . forgive me if this is indelicate, but there won't be a body to view."

"I . . . I know." Ginger plucked at the strap of her rucksack. "His parents asked me to collect his belongings."

Reginald scowled. "I hadn't realized how little they trusted me." He brushed the words out of the air, though he could not erase the discontent from his aura. She could hardly blame him. It had not occurred to her until just that moment that Reg might receive Ben's belongings. "Forgive me. That was unnecessary. Of course they would want you to have his things. And I would be a cad if I let you carry on alone."

"I'm not—"

"Johnson!" Reginald stepped to the side and called past Ginger. "Escort Miss Stuyvesant to HQ and then— Where are you staying, Miss Stuyvesant?"

"At the . . ." She trailed off. The solder, Johnson, was the bulldog from the train. "At the Spirit Corps lodgings. And truly, I have Ben's batman with me, so I shan't need a guide."

"That runt, Merrow?" Reginald barked a laugh. "Ben would want me to look out for you."

"No, really. I wouldn't." Ben ran a finger down Reginald's back, making him shudder.

"I am well provided for already."

"It's war, Miss Stuyvesant. I know that all you Spirit Corps ladies see is the dancing and tea in the hospitality rooms, but trust me. You'll want a man with you. I'd come myself, but I have to get these misfits to the front."

"Then, please, take all of your men with you. I do not require Johnson in the least."

"I insist."

"And yet, I have already declined." Ginger offered her hand. "I wish you the best at the front, Captain."

Chuckling, he bowed over her hand. "The red hair should have been a clue that you'd be a firebrand."

Ben circled his cousin. "God. And he's going to inherit the estate. He'll run it into the ground by the time he's thirty."

"Captain . . . where is your hat?"

"What?" Reginald straightened, a hand going to his head. "Never wear the thing, if I can help it."

It occurred to Ginger that if Ben's grandmother on the Harford side was German, then so was Reginald's. And she had a very good idea of where his hat was.

★ ★ ★

Ginger left Mrs. Richardson at the lodgings for the Spirit Corps volunteers and went with Merrow to the camp. The streets of Amiens alternated between picturesque canals, seemingly unmarked by the war, and others that were ruined wastelands. On one street, the entire front of a building had been reduced to rubble, leaving the rest untouched, so that Ginger could see inside it like a dollhouse.

Though there were some civilians, most of the people were soldiers. Frenchmen in their "horizon blue" uniforms and Algerian tirailleurs with soft red caps passed British soldiers in their khaki. A group of West Indian soldiers sat on the roadside, cleaning their rifles. Their rolling accents brought Helen to mind.

She had left Lady Penfold with a list of possible mediums to pair Helen with in the circle. The challenge was that it had to be someone absolutely trustworthy, since Helen carried the knowledge of the binding in her mind. While another medium wouldn't automatically sense it, the risk when linking minds was that memories could cross the boundaries. Whoever it was would have to be approved by the powers that be.

To the side of the road ahead, long rows of peaked white tents stretched to the edges of the field. Men in khaki walked among them, or sat in the shade of their tents. They were all so young. Suddenly, Merrow did not look quite so much like a boy.

It seemed that there was barely a man over five and twenty among them.

At Ginger's side, Ben sighed and stared with flutters of lavender wistfulness at the tents.

"Are you all right?"

Merrow glanced around at her voice, and Ginger gestured vaguely to the air beside her. "I was—Ben. Sorry."

His eyes widened, and he bit his lower lip. "Just—you just pretend I'm not here, ma'am."

"Thank you."

Ben watched Merrow increase his pace a bit to give Ginger a modicum of privacy, though he didn't go so far as to be out of reach should she need him. "He's a good man."

"So he seems. Now . . . why did you sigh?"

"Oh—just, I never thought I would miss those." He nodded to the tents. "But they make me feel a little homesick."

"What? Did you and your family go camping?"

"Nothing so rustic." He shoved his hands in his pockets. "Truth be told . . . disturbingly, it feels more like home here than in London, which I barely remember. Even before . . . this. Dying, I mean. I don't know why it's so hard to say. . . . But even before that, London—hell, England seemed like a dream."

How ironic that being on the Western Front actually made Ben more stable, because he had such strong emotions associated with it. If not for Potter's Field calling British souls to the nexus, it would be littered with ghosts. And, likely, if she went into the areas held by the French or the Central Powers, the air would be cold with them.

Past the tents, the field dropped away into a series of scorched pits. Scattered pieces of wood lay like kindling. Scraps of fire-blackened cloth fluttered among the rubble.

Ben stopped abruptly. "Ginger. I think you should go back."

"Please tell me we are not going to have this argument every time I try to do something." She followed Merrow another few feet, until the familiar coolness of Ben's ghost faded. Ginger stopped and turned to face him. "Are you coming?"

His aura fluctuated with uncertainty. "I can't imagine anything useful surviving."

Behind Ginger, Merrow called, "Anything the matter, Miss Stuyvesant?"

"Ben doesn't think anything could have survived." Ginger forced a smile for the young man, looking over the devastation. A smell of charred meat lay over the field. "I'm not certain how you did."

"I can—I can show you." Merrow pointed to the edge of the craters. "We were in a cabin, not—not a tent. Part of it is still standing."

Now that she knew what to look for, she could see that one of the piles of rubble was the remnants of a building. Nearly an entire wall, and part of another, leaned together like a pair of drunk old men.

"Merrow, you can't take her. . . . He can't hear me." Ben stared at the sky. "I do not think I shall ever get used to this."

"That makes two of us." Ginger turned and began to pick her way over the rubble at the edge.

"Wait—" Ben pressed his fingers to the bridge of his nose. "Will you please point out to Merrow that they are still clearing the site?"

"I feel like a telegraph operator." Ginger stumbled on the uneven soil, and Ben put out a hand to catch her, but passed through her arm. She waved him off. "I'm fine, dear. Private Merrow? Ben says that they are still clearing—"

She stopped and understood, finally, what Ben had recognised that she had not. The scraps of cloth that fluttered in the field were from uniforms. Corpses. Ginger dealt every day with the dead, in the form of souls, but not bodies. The soldiers were still retrieving the bodies of the dead.

Merrow looked back over his shoulder. "Ma'am?" His expression changed abruptly, as his aura sprouted burgundy spikes of alarm. He scrambled back up the crumbling slope and passed Ginger to stand on the road. Ben spun at his passing and similar protective spurs erupted from his form.

"Damn. Ginger, darling. Do be so good as to go stand behind that brick wall, won't you?"

She had no intention of doing anything of the kind. Ginger turned, as the men had done. Coming along the road toward them were Johnson and five other men.

Ginger sighed. "I see." The stupidity of men never failed to astonish.

With something like a growl, Ben started walking to meet them and then flowed streaming over the ground. He circled them in a whirlwind, kicking dust up. Johnson coughed, raising his arm against the debris.

Merrow jumped a little and glanced over his shoulder at Ginger. "Is that . . . ?"

"Yes." Ginger could not put Ben back together again if he exerted himself too much as a poltergeist. She balanced on her toes in a moment of indecision. Which would defuse the situation? If she removed herself and hid—no. Johnson and the men would fight Merrow and then come find her.

Ginger walked forward, trying to recall how she used to move to make the lines of her silk gowns sway and draw attention to the curve of her corset. In the heavy blue linen of a Spirit Corps volunteer, it was difficult to do, but the movement still caught Johnson's eyes.

"Miss Stuyvesant—" Merrow scrambled after her. "I don't—I don't think this is a good idea."

Ben whirled back through the air to hover in front of Ginger. "One of his friends said that he's going to challenge Merrow to a fight. If Merrow looks like he's winning, he's going to shoot him. Either way, he's going to have his way with you. You have to go."

"Nonsense." Still, she wasn't so foolish as to come within grabbing distance of the men. If Merrow were close enough, she would touch him so that he could hear Ben as well. Although, truly, Johnson's intentions were painfully clear. "Lt. Johnson. What a pleasant surprise to find you here."

With a grunt, the man lowered his arm, still squinting against the dust. "Capt. Harford wants to make sure you're taken care of." He jerked his head toward the other soldiers. "I brought some help along."

"So I see." Ginger swallowed, painfully aware that "taken care of" could have more than one meaning. "That was very kind of him."

"I thought so too." Johnson smirked and flexed his fists. "Gave me an opportunity to pay my respects to you and your fellow."

"What did you have in mind?"

"It depends on how cooperative you are."

Merrow stepped in front of Ginger again—this time, square into Ben. The sudden chill made him shudder. "You won't touch a hair on her head."

"It wasn't the hair on her *head* that I was interested in, kid." Johnson pulled off his coat and handed it to one of the other men. "But if you're asking for a rematch . . . I lost my balance on the train. Don't intend to do that again."

"Wait—" Ginger tried to step around Merrow, but he doggedly

stayed between her and Johnson. "This was about a kiss. I regret declining."

"I'm sure you do." He cracked his neck.

With no more warning than that, he rushed Merrow. The young man crouched a little, bracing himself for impact—

—and then Johnson was on the ground, so swiftly that Ginger did not see how it was done. Merrow was kneeling on the man's chest, holding one arm across his throat.

Ben shouted, "Gun!" and flung himself back toward the other men, highlighting a man with blond hair who aimed a revolver at Merrow.

Ginger pointed at it. "Merrow, watch out!"

Merrow flung himself back into the dirt of the road, as the small crack of the revolver added its noise to the greater thunder of the front. He rolled to the side, dropping into the cover of the ditch. Ginger fumbled with her bag and pulled out the gun that Lady Penfold had given her on the way to the train station.

Small, with intricate chased gold patterns and a mother-of-pearl handle, it looked like a toy compared to the revolver in the blond man's hand.

Shaking, she pointed it at the man with the gun. "That is quite enough."

Johnson sat up, laughing. "Do you even know how to fire that?"

She did not, in fact. Her family had never been the sort to chase a fox, or even go shooting for birds. It wasn't the done thing in New York, and when she'd moved to London, it had been all about the pleasures of Town with only occasional forays into the country for a house party. Still, her aunt had shown her the basics in the car, and they seemed straightforward enough.

"Stay where you are." Ginger took a step backward. "Pvt. Merrow, come with me, please."

Johnson waved the blond man forward. "Go ahead, Lyme. She doesn't know what she's doing."

Ginger looked around wildly for Ben. He was clad in plates of red fury, like armour, with spikes of deep-burgundy alarm. He knew how to fire a gun, but could not touch it.

And she could. Just as she could hold a pen and channel a ghost so they could draw on a map. "I can shoot a gun as well as if I were channelling Ben Harford."

Ben's head whipped around with a flash of crystal blue understanding. "Are you certain?"

Johnson stood and advanced toward Ginger. She squeezed the trigger, and the gun only clicked. He laughed again. "Saftey's on."

"Yes. Please, yes." Ginger looked at Ben and opened the doors to her soul.

"She's asking for it, boys." Johnson winked. "They always do, in the end."

Ben kicked dust up around them, raising a field of dirt and leaves and blood-covered fabric. He barrelled back and sank into Ginger's embrace.

He is behind enemy lines and, God help him, the route back to their own trenches has been overrun. He's wearing one of the Huns' uniforms, and his German is good enough to pass, thanks to his grandmother, but he doesn't know the passwords for this unit. If they challenge him . . .

If they challenge him, there's nothing to be done. He checks his revolver and makes sure there's a round in the chamber.

He starts forward, then stops before he rounds the corner into their section of trench. Crouching by a British corpse, he grits his teeth and shoves his hand into the man's pooling blood, then wipes it across his forehead, letting it run down his cheek.

Slinging his rifle off his back, he makes sure it's loaded but the safety is on, then he uses the gun as a makeshift crutch. Limping, he staggers around the corner.

"Hilfe! Hilf mir!" *He points back the way he came.* "Die Briten—die verdammten Briten durchbrochen."

The young man on watch is scrawny, with dark hair and circles under his eyes. He looks as frightened as British Tommies do and probably wants to be home just as badly. The blood and the limp act as a password.

He is past the sentry and limping down the trench. There's a sign lying in the mud. St. Vincent St. *All of the trenches have names from back home. He knows this one. Around another corner, and then . . .*

"Kennwort."

"Die Briten—"

"Kennwort."

The limp and the blood were only going to get him so far. He raises the rifle and snaps the safety off. The recoil slams against his shoulder.

Ginger stared at the pistol in her hand. Smoke curled from the muzzle. Her arm ached. Why did her arm ache? God, but she was exhausted and cold. So cold. Someone was screaming. The sentry that she had—no, that Ben had shot—no.

It was Johnson, and he was on the ground clutching his knee. The man with the gun . . . he was on the ground too, but holding his hand. Both of them were bleeding. Had she . . . ? Of course she had. That was why she had let Ben use her body.

"Ben?"

Wind circled her, tugging at the hem of her skirt. "Here."

Oh, thank God. She almost lowered the pistol with relief, but there were still four other men. Merrow had re-emerged from the ditch with a fresh cut on one cheek. He had his gun in his hand as well.

Ginger addressed those of Johnson's men who were still

standing. "I think you gentlemen should take your colleagues and go back to Amiens."

"I'll see you thrown in jail," Johnson shouted from the road. "You can't just shoot a British soldier and get away with it."

Ginger tried to keep the gun steady. "And if you tell them that I shot you, they'll ask why. Did you really think this through?"

"So maybe you don't go to jail. Maybe we take care of you in Amiens."

"You are an idiot. You were trained to report in when you die. You think you can just kill someone and not have anyone know?" But, of course, someone had done just that. Ben's murderer had to be someone who knew how the Spirit Corps worked.

Ben slid around her in a gust of wind. "Truck."

She looked past the men. A truck trundled down the road toward them, kicking up dust in its wake. Merrow saw it and stepped back. "Come—come on, miss. We can make it to—to the walls and—"

"And what!" Johnson screamed. "I'll bloody well tell them where you are."

The truck had closed half the distance, and the people in the front were just visible through the dust-spattered windshield. A member of the Indian Army drove, his white turban creating a marked contrast in the world of khaki. Next to him sat an elderly white woman.

An elderly white woman wearing the blue of a Spirit Corps volunteer.

Ginger lowered the pistol. "Mrs. Richardson?"

The truck slowed to a stop on the other side of the cluster of men. Mrs. Richardson leaned out of the passenger side door. "Oh, hello, dear! I saw these nice young men following you and thought you might need a ride after your chat. So I found Cpl. Patel, and he was good enough to bring me along."

Ben brushed against her again, the breeze almost like his hand at her back. "Go."

She edged to the side of the road, where Merrow stood with his jaw hanging open. He shook himself and followed her to the truck.

Johnson was still screaming from the ground. "I'll tell the captain about this!"

"You do that." Ginger lifted her skirt and climbed into the cab beside Mrs. Richardson.

Merrow paused. "She's done you—you a favour. That wound she gave you is a Blighty one. You get to go home."

Ah . . . the wound that every soldier seemed to yearn for. Just severe enough to get you shipped back to England. But she hadn't done it; Ben had. She was almost surprised he hadn't killed the man. Ginger looked at the gun she still held. She had no memory of firing it. Not as herself.

"There you go. Cpl. Patel, do you think there's space to drive around them?"

"Yes, ma'am." He gave a jaunty grin beneath his thick black mustache. "Though I would not mind driving over him. He is a nasty man, that Johnson."

"That's just what I said, dear." Mrs. Richardson beamed over her knitting needles. "I'm so glad that you happened along."

Ginger cleared her throat. "And . . . how did you two become acquainted?"

Cpl. Patel patted the grey muffler wrapped around his throat. "She made me a very kind gift. Most of the Indian Army was sent back home, because it is so terribly cold here. If we had a hundred Mrs. Richardsons, we would all have stayed, I think."

"Such a dear." Mrs. Richardson looked around to Merrow, who was crowded into the back of the truck. She leaned over to Ginger and murmured, "Did you get what you came for?"

Ginger shook her head.

"Mm. Well . . . where to now, then?"

Ben slid between and around them, mixing with the wind of their passing. "POWs."

Ginger nodded. "To the POW camp next, I think. He came out to question them, so hopefully we can rebuild what he learned."

If she could just rebuild Ben, that would be a start.

Chapter Thirteen

★ ★ ★

Cpl. Patel dropped them off just down the road from the POW camp, which was a bleak place surrounded by metal fences and barbed wire. British soldiers marched around the outside in crisp parade fashion, guns held at correct angles on their shoulders. By contrast, the Germans inside the wire were hunched and ragged men. Their shoulders stooped in a perfect match for the heather grey of defeat.

Ginger sat in the shade of a small shrubbery, holding hands with Merrow and Mrs. Richardson, so they could hear as she spoke to Ben. "And you have no recollection of who you spoke with?"

Ben stood in the middle of their tiny circle and flickered between standing at perfect attention and with his hands buried in his hair. "I don't remember . . . did I know their names?"

"You had a list, sir." Merrow shifted, and his aura reeked of failure. "In—in your notebook. I'm sorry I never saw it."

"Not your fault . . . gah." Ben spun in place, all orange with frustration. "Who was it . . . ?"

"Perhaps the guards will recall who you asked for?" Ginger looked down the lane to the camp. "If we begin querying people again, mightn't it jog your memory?"

"Maybe." His face was drawn into a deep frown.

Thank heavens his ghost had a face again. He had lost energy after she had channelled him, but had not appeared to lose his sense of purpose as he had when he poltergeisted. She could only assume that using her corporeal form helped anchor him somewhat.

"Then let's give that a try." She squeezed the hands of Merrow and Mrs. Richardson before releasing them.

Still in tune from being in the circle together, they stood as one—or, rather, they began to, but Mrs. Richardson struggled a bit getting up from the ground. Merrow put a hand under her arm and steadied her as she rose.

She patted his hand. "Thank you, dear. These old bones aren't as spry as they used to be." She raised an eyebrow at Ginger. "Now, don't go looking all alarmed. I can chase after seven grandchildren at once, so I'm perfectly capable of this. Just a bit stiff is all."

They walked down the middle of the lane to the POW camp. A guard spotted them almost at once, and spoke to his partner. "Pvt. Merrow! What're you doing back so soon?"

Ginger grimaced. Of course he would be recognised, since he'd been here with Ben.

Gesturing over his shoulder at Ginger and Mrs. Richardson, Merrow said, "I've been sent to—to escort these two ladies. Charity work." He stepped forward, tugging at his muffler, and showed the guard one of the papers Merrow had taken from the hidden drawer in Ben's desk.

The guard barely glanced at it. He gave an odd whistle, and an officer emerged from the guard hut. "What? What? Oh! Um . . . ladies."

Ginger took a step forward to meet him, but Mrs. Richardson murmured, "Best let me, dear. He'll think I'm in charge because I'm older."

Biting her lip, Ginger let Mrs. Richardson toddle forward. "Good afternoon, Lt. . . . ?"

"Thackeray, ma'am." He wiped a handkerchief over his florid face.

"Lovely. I am Matron Appleton, and this is Miss Cowen." She rattled off the pair of false names as if she had been born to spycraft. "We've been sent on a charity mission to visit your prisoners. Our idea is that a demonstration of English hospitality will make them think more kindly of us when it comes time to being questioned."

He snorted and spat in the direction of the prisoners, and then flushed with embarrassment. "Sorry—sorry. That was coarse. Forget what it's like to be in the company of ladies. I was just thinking that what makes the Huns feel charitably toward us is that we didn't shoot them." Thackeray barked a laugh. "Didn't shoot them, what?"

Mrs. Richardson cleared her throat, and the man's laughter wound down like a clockwork toy. Favouring him with a smile again, she held up her bag. "I suspect some good mufflers and socks would do more for them, don't you?"

"As to that, my boys could do with some clean socks."

Ginger gave one of her society smiles. "But of course, we have some for them too. We mustn't forget our boys."

After some more chat in which they were pressed to take tea

with the lieutenant, who was nervous to the point of sweating about having ladies at his camp, Mrs. Richardson and Ginger were at last given leave to speak with the prisoners.

Ben passed through the wire fence as though it weren't there and circled through the prisoners. Anyone watching would have only seen the eddy of dried leaves he left in his wake. "They don't look familiar. I think . . . he was tall. Yes. I should still be able to recognise who I questioned. Right?"

Ginger nodded. It would be so much easier if she could speak freely to him, but with the guards standing right there, it was not advisable, unless she wanted them to doubt her sanity. He saw her affirmation and sighed.

"Now then . . ." Mrs. Richardson eyed the air by Ginger's left shoulder as if Ben were there and gave a little wink. "Let's see who seems to be in the most need . . . Miss Cowen, what do you think?"

"I'm considering." She bit her lower lip, watching Ben sift through the POWs. He stopped next to a tall man with a ratty scarf and greasy blond hair.

Ben looked over at her. "Thank God. This is the man—we talked . . . God. I can't—he knows. He knows about . . ." He fractured into five versions of himself, then came back into a single man. "I'm sorry. It's about the gas? I think—or, no . . . no, that's the man I'm supposed to meet in the trenches. This is . . . this is about the traitor."

Ginger pointed at the man, who stood amid a cluster of other men, each with their shoulders hunched against the setting sun. "What about him?"

"Oh, yes!" Mrs. Richardson beckoned to Thackeray. "Do fetch that fellow out, if you would be so kind?"

"Peter Schmitt?" Thackeray shook his head. "Do you know him?"

"To be sure, I do not."

"Oh."

"Oh?" Ginger raised her eyebrows.

"Ah . . . um. It's just that he's a popular man this week. Guess it comes of being a defector. Fourth time he's been asked for an interview, as it were."

"Really?" Ben had conflated things before. Might this be his contact from the trench? "Who else?"

"Eh . . . ma'am. I shouldn't say. Bit indiscreet, as it were, what?"

Ginger shared a glance with Mrs. Richardson, who gave a firm nod. "Well . . . we'll follow the lead of our betters. Let's definitely start with him."

★ ★ ★

In the small interview room, Ben shifted in anxious eddies around Ginger, raising the hair on the back of her neck. He stopped in front of her while Mrs. Richardson got the German fellow seated. Ben's form fluctuated with tension. "I don't like this. I don't like you being in here with him."

Mrs. Richardson beamed over her knitting needles. With her glasses halfway down her nose, she looked like someone's granny, which of course she was. The German fellow, a very tall and slender tow-haired man in his midtwenties, seemed to relax at this unexpected visitor. He had a heavy bruise over one eye, and his lip had been split. It made Ginger even more curious about who, besides Ben, had visited Peter Schmitt.

Schmitt glanced over to Ginger, and she smiled demurely at him. She had been spending so much time with her soul just past the surface of her skin that she had to make no adjustments to see his aura. He was plagued by despair and some fear, but a slight beam of amber satisfaction wound through it as he sat down.

"You poor thing." Mrs. Richardson lowered her knitting needles and *tsk*ed. "Look at the state of your muffler."

Merrow took up a position at her side to act as a translator. His work with Ben had required him to know German, for which Ginger was profoundly grateful. She had French, which had been useful in Le Havre, but was not here.

After Merrow repeated her words, Schmitt looked down at the knotted mass wrapped around his neck. "This?" he said through Merrow. "I made it myself from scraps."

It was more poorly knitted than Merrow's, which, was impressive even to Ginger's eye. There was also something . . . off about his aura.

"Well . . . I admire your ingenuity, but why on earth did you have to resort to that?"

"They stopped outfitting us. It's why we deserted. Not enough food. Sick. All the time, we are sick." He tugged on the scarf and grimaced. He wasn't lying about that, at least not if his aura was anything to judge by. "There is nothing noble about this war."

"I completely agree." Mrs. Richardson put her knitting down and reached into her carpet bag. She pulled out a grey muffler that would have gone well with Schmidt's uniform when it was new. "May I offer you another?"

He hesitated, fingering his own muffler. There was that flash of satisfaction again, and . . . why deceit? "Don't know why it feels like I'm betraying Germany, when they betrayed us first."

Ben crouched next to Ginger. "This is different from what we talked about. Ask him why he felt betrayed."

It might have been easier to just let Ben have her body again, but Ginger repeated his question to Merrow, who then repeated it to Schmitt.

"The entire war? Why? All of us dying to avenge the death of some nobleman who died in a country we're not even attacking. It's stupid." He peeled off the muffler and flung it on the ground at Merrow's feet. "It's all stupid."

"I suppose that's why you defected."

"At least you feed us."

Mrs. Richardson held the new muffler out to him. "I wish I had brought some cake instead."

Schmitt glanced at Merrow for permission before he reached out to take the muffler. "That is very kind of you, madam."

"But I hope your other visitors have brought you something to eat besides whatever dreadful thing they serve here."

"Other visitors?"

"Lieutenant Thackeray told me that three other people have been by this week." Mrs. Richardson took up her knitting needles again. "I thought we were being so original when we came to do some charity work."

"The others . . . they were not exactly charity." He tapped the bruise over his eye.

"Oh!" Mrs. Richardson nearly dropped her knitting. If Ginger hadn't been watching her aura, she would have thought the other woman was genuinely shocked and outraged. "That will not do. Not at all. There are conventions about how you should be treated. Tell me who did this to you, and I will make certain he is reprimanded."

Amusement rippled across his aura. "I don't think you will, ma'am. No offense."

Ben edged closer and slid his finger across the man's back. Schmitt shivered and glanced behind himself, then froze. His aura spiked with alarm.

Ben shot backward, arms spread wide. "Damn it all."

Schmitt turned back to Mrs. Richardson and studied her.

Cursing to herself, Ginger pulled all the way into her body. The man was a medium.

She reached for any pretty image she could to cover her panic. Kittens. Puppies. Afternoons walking in the park with Ben. The smell of his cologne when he had just come down for dinner, all dashing in his white tie. Not something she would ever experience again. For a moment, the grief crashed over her again and she had to close her eyes against it.

The German man made a small, sad exhalation that needed no translation from Merrow. "Who did you lose?"

Ginger wiped her cheeks. "My fiancé."

"My condolences." He looked down at the muffler that Mrs. Richardson had given him. "I think I had better go back now. If I stay here too long, they will wonder what I am saying. They already wonder."

"Of course." Mrs. Richardson gestured to Merrow. "Do you mind, dear?"

Schmitt stood and bowed, clicking his heels, with his arms stiffly at his side. "Thank you for the gift."

Ginger waited until the door shut behind him before she relaxed her grip on her body and slid outside her skin. "Ben, what in heaven's name . . . Ben?"

He was not in the room. Ginger jumped to her feet. Surely—surely he could not have completed his unfinished business without telling her good-bye. No. No, that was foolishness. Most likely he had simply followed Schmitt back to the holding cells.

Mrs. Richardson looked up at her with alarm. "What is it, my dear?"

"Schmitt—he was a medium."

"Are you certain?"

"He saw Ben. That's why he stopped talking." Ginger paced around the room. "I don't know if he saw my soul extended, but he almost certainly spent the last few minutes reading our auras."

"Oh . . . well, he would have seen a great deal of deceitful satisfaction in mine." Mrs. Richardson shook her head. "I know it is unbecoming, but I must say that I very much enjoy this spy work. So much more rewarding—not that I mean to slight the work we do normally, but . . . I sometimes do rather feel like an interchangeable cog in a larger machine."

"You are indispensable." Ginger crossed and took the older woman's hand. "Truly. You are one of the joys of my day."

"Bless me, child, but your hands are like ice."

The door opened and Merrow re-entered. Ben was not with him. Ginger inhaled sharply. It was fine. Schmitt could not actually harm Ben . . . not directly. Not without a circle. But forming a circle only took one medium, as long as he had mundanes to anchor him.

She ran out the door, dashing past Lt. Thackeray. In the gathering dusk, shadows cloaked the prisoner encampment. A cluster of men stood together, arms linked. Schmitt walked toward them, with Ben close behind him. He reached out his hands to join them.

"Ben!" It did not matter if people thought her mad. The same rituals that she and her fellow mediums had used to clear the asylum of restless spirits would work on Ben.

At her cry, he soared up and away from Schmitt. His aura flared into a glory of burgundy alarm. Like a meteor, he blazed down to land in front of her. "What is it? What's the matter? Are you hurt?"

"Miss Cowen?" Lt. Thackeray hurried down the path behind her. "What is the matter?"

And what could she say to that? *Pardon, but I thought the ghost of my dead fiancé was about to be threatened by these men in the wire cage? We're all spying together.* She stopped and shook her head. "He forgot the socks that Mrs. Richardson had made."

Thackeray mopped his face with his handkerchief. "But you said 'Ben.' Who is that?"

"I—Did I?" Ginger used her society laugh. "Oh, how silly of me. I think I just used my French by accident, but *bien* wouldn't make a bit of sense to a Hun, would it?"

"Likely not. Uncivilized savages, the lot of them." He pursed his lips as if he were about to spit again. "Well . . . who do you want to see next?"

She glanced at Ben as discreetly as possible, hoping he would follow her. His entire countenance was dark and eddied in response to unseen currents. She turned toward the house. "I should consult with the matron."

Ben said, "Ask for the man with the tawny sideburns. When Herr Schmitt came back in, he asked if 'she was one of our skirts.' And he used the English word for *skirts*."

Skirts. Just like the men that Capt. Norris had overheard before he was drowned. Ginger turned back on the path. "I should ask, I suppose. Who is the man with the tawny sideburns?"

"That's Amott Zitron. He's the one who encouraged this lot to defect and brought them in." Thackeray broke off and glanced past her to the lane. "More company? My, this is a busy week."

A car kicked up dust as it rolled toward them. Ben zoomed past, zipping over the ground in a cloud of red and black to circle the car. Ginger glanced towards the prisoners, and yes, Schmitt was watching Ben, too. Damn.

Even faster than he had gone, Ben reappeared at her side, almost without a transition between the two places. Useful, but also a bad sign that he was forgetting his humanity.

He stood between her and the car, armed with anger. "It's Reg. He doesn't look happy."

Chapter Fourteen

★ ★ ★

At Ginger's news of Reg's imminent arrival, Merrow quickly snatched up their things.

Mrs. Richardson frowned and glanced to the door. "Since I'm unknown to the man, mightn't it be useful for me to stay and see what I can learn from him?"

"We are clearly travelling together." Ginger threw her rucksack over one shoulder. "I suspect Lt. Thackeray will draw the link, even if Reg doesn't."

"But, dear, that's why I gave him assumed names. He doesn't know I was travelling with Miss Stuyvesant."

Ginger tugged on her hair, ruffling her auburn locks. "I rather doubt there are that many redheaded women in the Spirit Corps."

"Oh . . . bother." Mrs. Richardson sighed and bundled her knitting up.

From the door, Merrow watched the car drive up. "We need—need to go. Now."

Ben chewed his lower lip, his face stark white with concentration. "I can stay behind to eavesdrop. Reg hasn't a sensitive bone in his body."

"That's all well and good, but how will you find us after?"

Surprised, Merrow turned from the door. "I wasn't—oh. You were talking to . . . right." He went back to looking out the door. "We *really* need to go. They're parking the truck."

"Sorry." Ginger hurried to the door and glanced back at Ben.

He gave a crooked smile. "I'll always be able to find you. You're like a . . . a magnet made of fire."

"You always say the sweetest things." Ginger paused before she ducked out the door. "Don't go anywhere near the prisoners. I don't trust Schmitt for an instant, and I'm certain he's taught the mundanes to form a circle."

★ ★ ★

Ginger paced along the hedgerow with her hands tucked under her arms. Behind her, Mrs. Richardson and Merrow sat hunkered at the base of the hedge, talking in low voices. They had been hiding here for nearly two hours. Why was it taking Ben so long to rejoin them? Yes, his incorporeal form had seemed to provide a brilliant opportunity for spying, but there was no telling what the German medium could have done if he'd gone too close to Schmitt. She would really like to have placed a line of salt around Schmitt and his fellows to keep their souls confined to within the camp, but they'd had to flee too quickly with Reginald's arrival.

Truly, she wasn't sure how she could have salted the earth without giving herself away as a medium. And since she was in her Spirit Corps hospitality blues . . . that would be less than discreet. Oh, please, please let Schmitt not have seen her when she was outside her body.

The hedge rattled in a cool breeze. Ginger shivered and turned. "Oh, thank heavens."

"Hullo, darling. Did you miss me?" Ben leaned against the hedge in an attitude of studied nonchalance. His aura, though, was agitated and left shadows of himself shuddering among the leaves.

"I was beginning to worry, yes." It would be more fair to say that she had been worried since before they left the POW camp, but sometimes accuracy was best not shared.

Down the hedgerow, Merrow and Mrs. Richardson had stopped talking and stared at her. She must have looked a sight, talking to the empty air. Ginger nodded toward them. "Come on. Let me link with Merrow and Mrs. Richardson so they can hear what you have to say."

"By all means." Ben tipped his hat and gestured for her to lead the way.

Mrs. Richardson wrapped up her knitting and tucked it into her bag. "I take it your young man is back?"

"Indeed." Ginger settled in the grass in front of them, tucking her skirt under her legs. She held out her hands. "I thought you would want to hear what he had to say."

"Oh, yes. Very much so." Mrs. Richardson took her familiar place at Ginger's right hand.

With Merrow on her left, Ginger closed her eyes on the corporeal world and stretched out to link with Mrs. Richardson, feeling the link pass through her to Merrow and back to Ginger. She slid a little out of her body, sighing with relief as her mortal weight lessened.

Mrs. Richardson squeezed her hand. "Not too far, dear. I won't be able to anchor you well without a full circle."

Ben stood among them, his face earnest. "Agreed. I don't want to risk you."

"There is no risk." Ginger shook her head with exasperation. "If you were suddenly going to pass beyond the veil, then yes, I would need a full circle to keep me anchored. But just here?"

Ben's disapproval rolled out in a sheet of flat green. He cleared his throat. "So. Reg did ask about—wait. Heh. I don't have to give an oral report, do I?" He covered his mouth for a moment. "I think . . . can I just show you the memory of what I saw?"

"Yes." How could she have been so foolish as to not consider that? She took reports like this multiple times a day from ghosts. "Yes, of course."

"I mean—is it safe?"

Ginger bit her lip. "I will be a little tired after, but no more so than at any day of work."

Ben watched her for a long moment, his form going hazy around the edges. Ginger felt very much like a book being read. He nodded, resolution snapping him back into focus. "Well then . . ." Ben held out his hand. "Welcome to my head."

Ginger stretched a tendril of her soul out and touched him.

He is floating in an eddy of memories. Flashes of emotion light the landscape around him.

He left Ginger. He should not have left her. It wasn't safe. He should go back to her—wait. He tightens into a ball, squeezing tight in an effort to remember. No. He was going to her later. Now he needs to listen. Listen to what?

Reg. That bastard.

The anger helps him remember his purpose. Right . . . right. He is spying and needs to listen to Reg in order to make sure Ginger is safe. One of the dim grey smudges is yammering on the other side of the veil. He reaches out and parts it, pushing through a little so he can hear better.

Reg is sitting in a chair with his feet up on a desk. "I have it on good authority that Miss Stuyvesant came here."

The plump lieutenant—what is his name?—Thackeray, like the author. He has always liked the author even though his schoolmates had hated studying him in—

Focus.

Thackeray wipes his face. "There's been no one to visit by that name. We had Matron Appleton and Miss Cowen here, and several male visitors, but no one else of the gentler sex."

Reg laughs. His soul is the dark emerald green of greed. "She's not gentle. Not by any means." Squinting, he stares at Thackeray until the man takes a step back. "Let me ask this. Did either of them have red hair?"

"Oh! Oh, yes. Miss Cowen did. Lovely red . . . I mean. Yes, sir." His aura is dark with fear.

"And she had Merrow with her?"

"Um . . . yes, sir. I thought, being Capt. Harford's—I mean, Capt. Benjamin Harford's man, that she was, they were, well, on official business. As it were."

Reg sits forward in his chair, dropping his feet. "That Merrow is a weasel and a traitor. I'll see him hanged."

"I . . . um . . ."

"Where are they now?"

"They . . . um . . . they were in the visiting cells, but . . . um." Thackeray tugs at his collar. "They aren't now."

"So. Find her. A little slip like that can't have gotten far." He waves Thackeray off with one manicured hand. "Don't hurt the

old woman, but, Merrow . . . I won't blink if you shoot him on sight."

Thackeray scurries out of the room, and Reg turns to one of his men. "You say she had my cousin's batman with her on the road? No one else?"

"That's correct, sir. Not until the old lady arrived in the truck." He shrugged. "An Indian fellow was driving it, but not a sahib. Don't figure he matters."

"Well. The old lady is clearly with Stuyvesant and Merrow. Find out who Matron Appleton is—only don't be stupid enough to think that's her actual name. Find the Indian. We need to know how involved he is." He smoothed his hair with that smug little smirk he always wore. "And I'll want to talk to Zitron."

Slipping through the currents, Ben circles his cousin. Always a bully. From the time they were kids, he had always been a bully, but he'd picked his targets carefully. Never hurt the heir—he had to stay in his uncle's good graces just in case. But the stable-master's son? He had been an easy target.

He slid his hands into his cousin's throat. The man shuddered. Ben had stopped Ginger from breathing by accident. Why couldn't he do it on purpose?

Ben jerked his hand away. "Sorry—sorry. I didn't—I'd rather you didn't . . ." He crouched under a blanket of shame and stood amidst rage at the same time, both images woven into the ether. "I forgot that you got emotions with the memories. My apologies."

Ginger's chest ached. Mrs. Richardson squeezed her hand and was a warm and comforting weight. Merrow seemed dull with shock. Ginger sucked in a breath, shuddering. "It's fine."

"Yes . . . well. My head—not the carefree place it used to be. Just think, if I'd passed earlier, you'd have jolly memories of cricket matches to live through."

"Then I should have perished of boredom and joined you."

"And this is when I curse your father's American blood."

Ginger blew him a kiss. She forced her body to take another breath. "Did you hear what Reg and Zitron talked about?"

"He asked if you'd spoken. Zitron said no. Then it was just innocuous things about the weather and the camp facilities. And nothing about skirts. I can only assume they were speaking in code, but damned if I could figure it out." He gave a wry grin. "Even if I weren't . . . scattered, I wouldn't have been able to sort it."

Mrs. Richardson asked, "Are there really codes based on the weather?"

Ben laughed, and a bubble of amusement floated up from Merrow. Ben said, "The weather. Fish. The number and length of pauses you take in a sentence. I once knew a fellow who could stammer in Morse code. It was quite impressive. Another woman used the length of stitches in her dresses to carry messages. I used to carry cigars that had onionskin paper tucked inside. Lived in fear of grabbing the wrong one and smoking my secret message."

Merrow said, "Remember the baker, sir?"

"Right!" Ben rubbed his mouth, grinning. "We had a live drop who signalled that he had a message waiting by the number of pastries in the window. You had to let him know you were the contact by ordering a specific grouping of pastry. Damn good pastries. Pleasantest password exchange I've ever had to do."

"All of which are lovely," Ginger said. "But the question that I want to bring us back to is what Reg wanted with Amott Zitron."

Ben spread his hands. "I don't *think* Reg does intelligence work, but he might. We don't all know each other."

"Hmm." Ginger could not shake the feeling of Ben's distaste for his cousin. "Is it . . . is it possible that Reg had you . . . had you killed for your inheritance? And that it's totally unrelated to the Spirit Corps?"

"No." Ben shook his head. "Absolutely not."

"He is blond and an officer and stationed here."

"He also smells like a cologne factory. I would have recognised him by that."

"But . . . but you couldn't breathe. Would you have been able to smell his cologne?"

Ben hesitated and then shook his head again. "Well . . . he's had ample opportunity before. Why now?"

"Because it would be easy to disguise as an accident of war."

He froze in thought, his edges just flickering with arrested motion. Then he shook his head again. "If I had been shot in battle, perhaps. Although . . . as much as I don't trust him with money or anyone I care about, I don't think he would actually stoop to those depths." He held up a finger to stop Ginger. "And—I was strangled. So whoever did it knew the camp was going to explode; otherwise my death would have been too obviously a murder. It's best to proceed with the idea that it's related to my investigation into the leak."

All of which made sense, but none of which, in Ginger's mind, precluded Reginald from being the culprit. "So what do we do next? Go to meet your contact in the trenches?"

"What?" Ben radiated confusion.

"Earlier today." She grimaced. His memory was slipping more. "When you were trying to remember what you'd spoken to Schmitt about . . . you mentioned a contact in the trenches. Something about the gas."

"I did?"

"Yes, sir." Merrow shifted next to Ginger. "I mean, I—I

didn't hear you say that today, but that was the plan we had before . . . before the explosion."

Ben stared at Merrow with something like horror. "That was . . . I did? What else did I say?"

"Um . . . we'd planned to—to go back to Le Havre. You wanted to talk to Miss Stuyvesant about something. I—I don't know what. But you'd had a letter. From her, I mean. And then we were going straight back to the trenches."

"The captain who was murdered." Ben sagged with relief. "Right. Right. I remember, I wanted to talk to Ginger about Norris. And if I wanted to do so before going to meet my contact . . . that means that I thought they were related. And—damn."

"Why is that bad?"

"Because I don't remember where in the trenches."

Merrow brightened. "I know that, sir. Because we've been there before."

"The Baker Street trench? The 11th Lancashire Fusiliers. Right." Again, a wave of relief rolled off of Ben. "Well. Thank God I remember some things."

"Oh, lovely." Mrs. Richardson brightened. "If only Sherlock Holmes were there, we could ask for a bartitsu demonstration."

Chapter Fifteen

★ ★ ★

24 JULY 1916

Merrow managed to find nurses' uniforms for Ginger and Mrs. Richardson. When she'd asked where, he gave a shy grin and ducked his head. "I have a—a friend."

Mrs. Richardson had given a delighted chuckle at that, and nudged the young man with a wink. "Say no more."

The red cross on their arms gave them freer movement into the trenches than their blue Spirit Corps uniforms would have, and the wimple of a nurse covered Ginger's distinctive red hair. It could not mask her flinches at the constant sound of the guns.

Or the ghosts. She had not thought about the effect of going among so many old ghosts. The British troops had been conditioned to report in and then go to their rest. But these trenches had been held by the Germans, then the French, and then the Germans—trading back and forth with the price of soldiers' lives. Thousands of memories crowded in with every thundering concussion, each one saying that this was the last sound he had heard before dying. Ginger's chest was tight, and she could take only the shallowest breaths. The brimstone-scented air burned with reminders of death.

She was not dead. These were not her memories. She kept her gaze fixed on Merrow's stooped shoulders as they walked down the narrow earthen trenches. Mrs. Richardson followed behind her, from time to time patting her on the back.

Ben stayed at her side, slipping through the ghosts as if this had always been his natural environment. "It is all right, darling. These are deep trenches. You aren't going over the top. It's all right."

With her head down, she doubted any of the soldiers they passed could see her lips. Certainly they could not hear her over the din. "I am fine."

"Your aura—"

"Damn my aura." Ginger knotted her hands into fists to stop their trembling. "I cannot help my feelings, but I can bloody well control the way I act about them."

Ben pulled back a little. "I am so sorry I brought you here."

"It was my choice."

Merrow had stopped and was speaking with a lieutenant who seemed too bookish to be in a war. Merrow showed him one of the documents from Ben's drawer and gestured back to Ginger and Mrs. Richardson. The lieutenant stroked his mustache and then beckoned them forward.

"Lt. Tolkien'll get us set up."

The lieutenant touched his helmet and nodded to Ginger. "Thank you so much for visiting us, sisters. We've a couple of chaps as could use looking after. I told Private Merrow to put you in the dugout and I'll send them round to see you once you're settled."

"Thank you." Ginger smiled demurely. "We must all do our part."

Mrs. Richardson patted her bag. "And we have good clean socks too, which should help with trench foot."

It was uncharitable, but Ginger rather hoped they would be gone before then. She had trained as a nurse in the early days of the war, before they put the Spirit Corps together, and knew how to treat various ailments of the feet. It was not the thought of dealing with trench foot which made her wish to be gone, but rather the constant boom and hum of shells flying overhead.

Most of the soldiers sat in their bunkers, or leaned against the sides of the trenches looking as though no sound was occurring. How did they manage it? She knew, intimately, the crushing fear that most of these men carried inside them, and yet watching them, she would not have been able to tell that they were afraid without their auras. All of them had an air of desperate confidence.

The small dugout that Tolkien directed them to had been carved into the clay walls of the trench. It was not tall enough to stand in, even for Merrow, and had only rough planks laid for a floor. Steel water tins served as stools. Little clots of dirt shivered free from the ceiling in time with the impacts.

Merrow wiped off one of the tins with his handkerchief and turned to the other. "Just give—give me a minute."

"Thank you." Ginger looked back out into the trench. "Where was he to meet the spy?"

"There's a listening trench off the Baker Street trench. It's almost all the way to the German lines. Tolkien's in charge of signals, and he says it's clear."

Ginger nodded and brushed the sweat off her palms onto her skirt. "How much time do we have before the rendezvous is scheduled?"

Merrow checked his watch. "Another hour and a half before the window for contact opens, but it'll take a while to worm down the listening trench."

"Well, we should probably go before I lose my nerve."

"It's only big enough for one." Merrow stopped. "I should be the one to go, ma'am."

"You can't hear Ben." Ginger straightened her cuffs. "It would be different if you could."

"Maybe he could—could he possess me?"

Ben harrumphed. "I'm not a demon."

"No. If you were a sensitive and supported by a full circle, you could maybe channel him, but as it is . . ." Ginger smoothed her skirt, which was covered with dirt at the hem. "I am here because it needs to be me, and I can go down the listening trench as well."

"I don't think—" Ben started, and stopped abruptly as Ginger turned on him.

"If you are going to say that you don't think I understand what a listening trench is, then I will be forced to remind you of how many men have reported in from them. I know exactly what it is and what I am volunteering to do." But that did not mean she relished the idea at all. Still. It needed to be done. "Mrs. Richardson, will you be all right waiting here?"

"Oh, you know I can occupy myself anywhere." The older woman held up her bag and pulled her knitting out of it. The ratty, badly knitted scarf that had been Herr Schmitt's tumbled out of her bag. She picked it up and frowned at the offending item. Then she smiled up brightly at Ginger. "Besides, I have these poor soldiers to attend to. Go along, you two. I shall look forward to your report."

Biting his lip, Merrow stepped out of the dugout and gave Ginger a sturdy nod. "Let me at least show you the way to the listening trench."

"Thank you."

They went along through the trench, with Ben spinning in circles around her. "I don't like this. I don't—I don't . . ."

"Weren't you the one telling me it would be all right?"

"Yes." He pulled in some of the dark sheets of fear that flapped behind him, wadding them up. But each one shredded in his hands and frayed into a dense mist around him. "Yes. But that was before we decided that *you* were going into a listening trench. I don't like it—"

"Here we are, ma'am." Merrow stood next to a narrow channel carved into the earth at right angles to the rest of the trenches. "It'll get shallow really fast. You have to crawl on your belly, and—whatever happens, do not lift your head above the walls."

"I won't." Ginger shook out her skirt. She should have worn men's clothing—even if it wouldn't have fooled anyone, it would have been more practical for this. "Will you wait with Mrs. Richardson? And look after her?"

"Of course, ma'am." Merrow swallowed, a ball of tight anxiety. "Be careful. Or the captain will—will haunt me for the rest of my days, I should imagine."

Ben laughed and clutched his head. "He has that right, but don't say so."

"He says he won't blame anything but my own pigheadedness." She offered Merrow her hand. "Thank you."

He stared at it for a moment, then drew himself up and offered her a salute. "I see why he loves you, ma'am."

Loves. Present tense. Ginger turned her head away so the tears that pricked her eyes would not trouble Merrow. Nodding to herself, Ginger started down the trench. The sides brushed against her skirt, and she had to turn sideways to keep from rubbing her shoulders. A step up made it so shallow that she had to crawl with her skirt hiked up to her knees.

Gradually it became more shallow, until she had to creep along on just her elbows and toes. The dirt was shattered and torn by successive blasts. The smell of ozone and burned flesh took up residence in her nostrils. Ginger's shoulders ached from the unaccustomed posture.

She stopped to catch her breath and rest, with her forehead pressed against the earth. Ben lay next to her, half in the dirt wall at her side. "Are you all right?"

"Yes. Of course." Ginger wiped her face on the back of her sleeve and left a streak of dirt across the fabric. "Conserving my resources is not a sign of weakness, just prudence."

She raised herself onto her elbows again and squirmed forward. The uneven, shallow trench had been dug in a hurry. She and the other sappers had needed to speed out under the cover of darkness to make this trench, praying the Germans wouldn't see her or Basil as they was digging. Hard it was, digging in the dark and trying to be silent and every second sure that you were about to be shot.

"Ginger!"

She blinked and shook her head. "I'm fine." That had been someone else. Not her. She set her teeth and crawled on.

Ben floated beside her, trailing a long cloak of worry behind him. "Did I ever tell you about the time I scored a century and took a five-for in the same match? I'd have carried my bat, except for this very athletic chap at silly mid off."

"Are you attempting to calm me with cricket stories?"

"I thought something innocuous might take your mind off things."

"Innocuous or dull? I am not yet that desperate."

"I thought you admired me in my whites!"

"Appreciating fine tailoring is not at all the same as having an interest in the game." Ginger crawled grimly forward. "It was part of my full disclosure when you proposed."

"Along with the fact that you favour Dvořák over ragtime, which I continue to be baffled by."

"That is because you had a misguided impression of American girls based on the newspapers. You, on the other hand, are predictably British, and—oh! God."

Ginger yanked her hand back from the corpse that lay partially in the trench ahead of her.

"Ginger! Stay down. Do not—"

"I am *not* going to stand up screaming like an idiot." Ginger wiped her hand on the dirt. "Honestly. I deal with dead people every day."

"But not . . . not their bodies."

"No." Fortunately, she was not a squeamish person. The body in front of her had belonged to a German who had been dead for several days. The biggest problem was that she was going to have to move it in order to continue forward. "Thank heavens his ghost did not stick around. *That* I couldn't have borne."

"And this is part of why I love you so very much."

Ginger wriggled forward and rolled onto her back for better leverage. "You do pick the oddest time for declarations. Though . . . I suppose this isn't any more peculiar than your proposal. Not really."

"You look charming when covered in dirt."

"Oh! Is that the theme?" She took hold of the corpse by the lapels of its uniform and tried to work it backward, to little effect. "I had rather hoped it was when I was rescuing someone."

"I was not in need of rescue."

"Excuse me?" She paused, the corpse's head leering down at her. "Your motor was stuck in the mud, and you weren't exactly making any strides pushing it out on your own. We would have been there all night if I hadn't gotten out to help."

"Speaking of pushing . . . do you want me to . . . ?" He slid closer to the corpse and ran a hand along its back. The fabric rippled in a cool breeze.

"Don't you dare poltergeist." Watching him wear himself to shreds again . . . it was not something Ginger could manage. She wet her lips, set her shoulders, and gave a jerk to the side.

The corpse slid over, not completely out of the trench, but lying more to the side. Another push and she should—

A machine-gun burst slammed into the corpse. It jerked and flopped as if having a fit. Bits of rotting flesh spattered the trench around her. Ginger stiffened and lay still, staring at the smoke-filled sky. Her heart raced in her chest, but she set her jaw and tried to be calm. As long as she did not lift her head, she would be safe in the trench.

Ben crouched over her, as if the red plate armour of his alarm could protect her.

When the machine gun had stopped, Ginger whispered, "Can you see the gunner?"

"Indeed." He tilted his head. "He's still watching the corpse."

Ginger craned her neck to look down the trench toward the listening post. The machine-gun fire had actually shifted the corpse enough that she thought . . . "I can get past it."

She had to press against the arm and shoulder of the dead man to wriggle past, and the fluid-drenched soil stank with the contents of his innards. She held her breath as she pushed past him, waiting for another machine-gun burst.

Once past, she rolled onto her belly again and resumed the relentless crawl forward.

After what seemed like another quarter hour, Ben soared up overhead, stretching his arms out and spinning, before zooming down next to her again. "Darling, from here on, be very quiet. We're only a few metres from the German line."

Ginger nodded and continued her slow creep forward until the trench ended in a slightly wider, deeper depression. It was just deep enough to sit in, if she kept her head low. She leaned against the side and rubbed her throbbing shoulders.

Ben hesitated and put one hand on her shoulder; the cool of his presence seeped through the cloth and into her skin. "Does that . . . does that help?"

She nodded. It was like having a living ice pack—or not. Not living. Ginger smiled and gave him a thumbs-up.

"You can whisper." He frowned. "I think . . . I don't think I'm exactly hearing your voice. I mean—I know I can't hear your thoughts, but no matter how much other noise is around, I don't seem to have any trouble hearing *you*."

She tried the experiment of just mouthing the words. "Well, that's one improvement in your new state, then."

"Hey!" He laughed, ruffling her hair with a breeze. "I always heard you. I just may not have always *listened* to you."

"Ah. Well, then . . . that hasn't changed after all." How was she supposed to keep on without him? "So. What am I to do now? I mean—here. How do we make contact with your person?"

"We wait. The window for contact is two hours, so we just have to wait until he comes in. If you sit against that wall, you should be able to hear tapping. When you do . . ." Ben trailed off, soul fuzzing around the edges with uncertainty. "Just let me know."

"Will you need me to write it down?"

"Yes—yes, I will." He ran his hands through his hair. "Thank you."

She pulled out a pad of paper and a pencil she had tucked

into her pocket, and shifted to sit with her back against the wall closest to the Germans. It gave her a view down the long trench she had just crawled through. She had barely been below the surface for most of the way here. The sappers who did this didn't do their job proper. Didn't she know it was hard. Her hands, bleeding from all the blisters as was on them from the shovel. And all the while, digging half crouched, as if that would make a difference if the Huns decided to start shooting. And then the steady tapping of German sappers, crawling beneath—

No. The tapping was here and now. Ginger bit the inside of her lip and tried to steady her breathing again. Her hands weren't blistered. She hadn't dug anything. Ben crouched in front of her, cloaked in worry again.

"Tapping." Ginger mouthed and laid her head against the dirt wall.

Ben slid against the wall to sit next to her. He tapped back on an exposed piece of stone, but his hand passed through it. Ginger scrabbled in the earth to find something—anything hard, and came up with a spent shell casing. She placed it against the stone and raised her eyebrows in question.

Ben nodded and repeated his taps. Ginger matched his movements.

The tapping paused and then resumed, but in a different pattern. Ben said, "Morse code."

She nodded and began to record the tapping that the other person was sending to them. It was a series of numbers, obviously a book code, but she had no idea what the book was. It continued until she had filled the page with:

(112 3 5) (4 1 8) (38 7 3) (206 9 3) (53 5 9) (98 9 8) (136 4 5) (60 38 8) (63 7 44) (3 3 51) (78 21 18) (47 6 3) (51 7 3) (226 2 7) (38 37 8)

(38 2 4) (50 4 7) (40 9 41) (39 8 4) (30 15 4) (25 44 2) (202 3 8) (49 55 9) (63 7 5)

(58 4 3) (62 34 3) (34 8 73)

(50 35 1) (73 25 3) (67 44 7) (266 6 6) (77 64 2) (88 8 10) (99 68 8) (95 5 8) (68 49 3) (48 74 5) (74 1 1) (54 8 3) (67 12 5) (90 7 8) (27 64 6) (88 5 5) (30 7 3)

And then the tapping started to repeat. Ginger followed along, making sure that she had recorded everything correctly. As she did, Ben slipped through the wall, disappearing into the earth.

He reappeared after a few moments, shaking his head. He gestured to the rock and mimed tapping. Ginger matched him, using the shell casing again. It was only a few short taps, but whatever they signalled was met by three single strikes and then silence from their correspondent.

Ben gestured to the trench. "After you."

Ginger raised her eyebrows. She'd rather expected to be out here longer, though truly she did not mind getting away. Tucking the paper and pencil away, she began the long crawl back out of the trench. She waited until they were past the German corpse before she spoke to Ben.

"So. What does the code say?"

"I have no idea." He bit his lower lip, frowning.

"I think that I somehow thought I was the only one who had to struggle to translate book codes and that you were a crack genius at it."

"Alas. No. We need to get a copy of *The Story of an African Farm* to read it."

She had left her copy in her room at the asylum. It had not even occurred to her that he would use the same book as in their private cipher, but it made sense to limit the number of books he had to carry. "So what did you see when you went through the wall?"

"Hmm? Oh. The fellow who was sending the message is a German *oberstleutnant*. We met in a café in Berlin when I was doing some intelligence work there. I was just making sure it was really him." He scratched his head. "He had some paper, besides the notes about the message to me, but I couldn't see the whole thing. *Gespenstiger Spione über Salz gestoppt werden* . . . Ghost spies can be halted via salt . . ."

"The relationship between salt and spirit is not exactly a secret."

"Hopefully he talks about it in the message." Ben spun to look back behind them. "You know . . . being a ghost is so useful for spying that maybe I'll stick around after we find my killer."

Ginger's stomach turned. She did not want to lose him, but the longer he stayed here, the less of himself would remain. She would lose him just as surely as when he crossed behind the veil. "Please don't think me rude, but—"

The ground shook with an explosion, louder and closer than any had been yet. Ginger curled into a tight ball, heart pounding. Dirt rattled down. Clouds of hot dust billowed past, choking her. And over the guns and her own coughing came the hoarse screams of wounded men. The screaming was real this time, not a memory.

Ben soared up and then shot back to her. "That was the Baker Street trench."

Chapter Sixteen

★ ★ ★

When Ginger scrambled out of the end of the listening trench, the sandbags and retaining walls on one side had collapsed in a great wave of earth. Soldiers scrambled across the earth, blood spattered over them. They dug frantically with helmets or spades or their hands. Limbs emerged from the dirt like sickly tubers.

She remembered drowning in mud.

Ginger pressed her fingers into the wall of the trench. The dugout had been in the wall that collapsed. "Mrs. Richardson and Merrow."

"I'll find them." Ben dove into the mound of dirt as if it were no more solid than water.

Wiping her face, Ginger stepped into the chaos. Soldiers lay against the stable wall, away from the collapse, covered in dirt and blood. As men were dragged from the dirt, they were carried down the trench.

A soldier spotted her and beckoned. "Miss! Can you help?"

She had been trained in nursing for the war, and had spent the first part working in hospitals as an assistant. She could wrap bandages and change a dressing or hold someone steady. She knew exactly what happened in the trenches when a shell hit, because she'd experienced the deaths of so many who died this way. But these men needed real medical care.

And where was that to come from?

Ginger went to the soldier, stumbling over the uneven dirt. He was kneeling next to a man whose leg ended below the knee. He'd tied a crude tourniquet with his belt, but the wound still oozed blood.

She knelt by him. "My supplies were in the dugout, but I'll do what I can. Is there any water?"

"I'll see what I can find, and—Miss Stuyvesant?" The man laughed and slapped his knee. "Well this is awkward, what?"

Ginger stared at the soldier for a moment before his features resolved themselves. His usually blonde hair had been dyed to a dull brown. "Capt. Axtell. What . . . ?"

"Classified." He winked at her. "And call me Sgt. Meadows. Got a bit of a concern with this company. Don't tell a soul you saw me. Not even Harford."

"He's . . . he's dead."

Axtell blanched and looked past her to all the dirt. "In that?"

"No—before. At the camp 463 explosion."

"The what?" He snorted and shook his head. "That's what comes from being out in the field. Miss all the news. Sorry about Harford. Now, about these men. Can you help them?"

The sheer joviality of his tone made Ginger's throat tighten with revulsion. When they had been in meetings together, his laughter had seemed an inadequate mask for the constant anger in his aura. Here the juxtaposition was beyond macabre. She shifted a little away so that the thick fury of his aura did not touch her. Swallowing, she focused on the task at hand. "I'll need cloth for bandages, if there is anything even remotely approaching clean." She glanced down the line of men. Some of them were already soulless husks. None of them, so far as she could see, was Merrow, nor wore the distinctive grey uniform of a nursing sister. "Has someone sent for the medics?"

"The communication lines are down. Bad luck, that." He chuckled. "But Lt. Tolkien's sent a runner, so it shouldn't be long."

"I'll try to make do until they get here. Find me those bandages." Without waiting for Axtell to leave, Ginger went to the next patient.

This one had the braids and pips of a captain and could not be above five and twenty. His blond hair was crusted with blood. He might even have been the man who had killed Ben. Ginger pushed his sleeve back and felt for his pulse. The beat was strong and regular, so he was merely unconscious, though she had no real way of knowing how bad his head wound was. She brushed his hair aside and was rewarded with the sight of a length of split skin and a large contusion, but the skull beneath seemed sound.

How was she supposed to do anything for these men? She did not even have bandages. And Merrow. And Mrs. Richardson. Ginger's breath shuddered as she exhaled. She would be in the way if she tried digging. Ben would find them, and then she could decide what to do.

And on the subject of decisions, even if she couldn't bandage anyone yet, she could at least decide priorities. Ginger went down the line, looking at the wounds. Some of the soldiers were conscious. Some would have been better off if they weren't. Some were clearly not going to live much longer.

God forgive her, but some of them were going to report in very soon.

Feeling like a vulture, Ginger picked one who was struggling but still alert. He must have been near the blast, and his right shoulder was gone. His breath strained and bubbled red on his lips. Ginger knelt by him, and his clear blue eyes focused on her with horrible clarity. She wet her lips. "I am so sorry. There is nothing I can do for you."

He gave a small nod and—God help her—he winked, as jaunty as anything.

"Do you remember your training? About reporting in when you die?"

He nodded again.

"All right . . ." Ginger took a breath and focused on him. "When you reach Potter's Field, you need to report to Helen Jackson—that will make sense when you get there. Tell her to relive your last moments, and that I said you were very brave."

Ginger glanced over her shoulder, but none of the other soldiers had time to spare for the wounded, as they continued to try to find more survivors. "Helen, there is a German medium named Peter Schmitt at the prisoner of war camp near Amiens, and he's formed a circle with the prisoners there. I don't know if they have German ghosts reporting to them, but just to be on the safe side I recommend putting salt barriers around all the camps. Ask Lady Penfold to look into Capt. Reginald Harford again. He followed us to the POW camp, and his men attacked us on the road. He seems to know the prisoner Amott Zitron, and Ben thinks they were speaking in code to each other."

A couple of small tin first aid kits thumped onto the earth beside her. "Best I can find. That'll do for a start, what?"

Ginger jumped and glanced up at Axtell. When had he dyed his hair dark? It seemed as if half the people in the army fit the traitor's description. She popped a kit open and pulled out the roll of gauze inside. "Thank you."

"How's Royston?"

"Not going to make it, I'm afraid." Ginger stood and turned away from Royston. "When did you dye your hair?"

"By God! How like a woman to wonder that in the middle of a war." He grinned. "You'd like the name of my hairdresser next, I suppose."

"I suppose so." She turned her back on him and walked to the next man in the line. "Please, go help with the digging."

He laughed again, shaking his head. "Oh, there's no point. Anyone they haven't found is dead by now."

She inhaled sharply and then coughed on the dust in the air. Wiping her eyes, Ginger looked back at the mound of dirt. Merrow might be mixed with the other survivors, but nearly anonymous in his khakis. But Mrs. Richardson . . . surely there would be no missing an elderly woman among the bodies pulled from the earth.

She fixed Axtell with a glare. "If you are supposed to be incognito, you might pretend to care."

For a flash, his ever-present smile hardened to match his aura. And then he laughed again. "Right-ho. Off I go!"

Someone so obviously callous could not be the traitor who killed Ben, but beyond that, Axtell had nothing to recommend him. Shuddering, Ginger knelt by the next soldier.

This was someone she could, in fact, help. He had a long gash down one arm where shrapnel had torn his skin. He held the edges together with one hand and sat against the remaining wall of the trench, shaking. Dirt covered him, masking all sign of rank on his uniform.

Ginger still had the packet of gauze in one hand and the tin kits in the other. She set the kits down. "Let me see."

He did not respond, so she tapped him lightly on the shoulder. The young man jumped. He stared at her with wide brown eyes. "I can't hear."

He must have been close to the blast for the sound to have hurt him. If he had received no more damage than a cut on his arm and the loss of his hearing, he was lucky indeed. *Please . . . please let Mrs. Richardson be all right.*

Ginger patted his shoulder and gestured to his arm.

He held it out. The damage was more severe than it had first looked. He'd likely lose the use of some fingers. She gritted her teeth and tore off some of the gauze. Using that, she wiped away what blood she could. He stiffened but did not cry out, though his aura was filled with pain.

Wrapping the remaining bandage around his arm, Ginger tried to draw the edges close enough together to stop some of the bleeding. Why wasn't Ben back yet?

And where was Merrow? Ginger stood and moved to the next soldier. He had a broken leg, and there was nothing she could do besides telling him to be brave.

Brave.

What a word to use when facing pain. These men were already brave, just to be here. The bold smiles and nonchalance with which they greeted her was not matched by their auras. She did not know how anyone could survive with the amount of grief and fear and pain that these men carried.

"Ginger!" Ben appeared at her side. She almost answered him, despite the soldier sitting right by her.

Excusing herself, Ginger stood and turned so that her back was to the wounded. "Did you find—"

"I can't make him stop. I mean, he can't hear me, so of course I can't." Ben shook his head and stopped. Inhaling, he closed his eyes and then met her gaze again. "Sorry. I get confused when I'm away from you. Merrow is still trying to dig, but—and I am so, so sorry. More sorry than I can express, but—"

"Mrs. Richardson is dead." The words had no meaning.

"Yes." He gestured through a deep purple morass of grief back to the mound of earth. "The dugout collapsed with the blast, and. . . . but Merrow. Can you make him understand?"

Ginger nodded and walked toward the mound of dirt. Mrs. Richardson was dead. She ought to feel something, but there seemed to be a hollow spot within her. She did not actually believe it was true.

Scrambling over the loose dirt, Ginger worked her way to the other side of the mound and tried to keep her head down below the range of German snipers. Ginger had expected Ben to die in the war, especially after the reports from the dead started coming in, and the death toll became clear. In some ways, she had begun mourning him the first time she saw him in uniform. But Mrs. Richardson? She had mufflers to knit and Mr. Haden to flirt with and Ginger to admonish and grandchildren to chase, and it was not possible that she was dead.

And not even dead for a higher cause. Simply a chance shell landing on the trenches. A stupid, stupid, meaningless death.

A death that was inescapably Ginger's fault.

She slid down the far bank, skirt coming up around her knees. Tugging it down as she stood, Ginger found the same scene on this side that she had left on the other. Wounded men lay along the side of the trench with their comrades attending them. A few still dug at the mound itself, but their work seemed more in line with clearing it than with saving anyone.

Only one man still dug with energy. Merrow had his helmet in hand and was using it as a makeshift shovel. Kneeling, he dug a helmetful of dirt and flung it to the side, widening a hole as if he were going to rebuild the dugout. Dirt covered him. It caked his hair and crusted his uniform.

"Merrow?" Ginger came up behind him.

He kept digging.

What was his first name? She had never heard it. He was always just Merrow or Pvt. Merrow and nothing beyond that. "Merrow—" Ginger put a hand on his shoulder.

He flinched and jerked around, raising a fist. His aura was terrible, all terror and guilt and guilt and guilt. Tear tracks ran through the dirt on his cheeks and left behind startling white lines of skin. His eyes were red with weeping. "Miss—she's—I have to . . ." The young man turned back to the hole and dropped to his knees again. Digging. "It's my fault. I stepped out, just for a minute, to talk to Sam. I shouldn't have left her."

"Merrow, I'm so sorry." Ginger watched him dig without any sign of hearing her. "You couldn't have done anything if you'd been there."

He kept digging, with his shoulders hunched forward over the hole.

"Dear, you have to stop." Ginger knelt by him and put a hand on his arm. "Ben has looked for her."

He flinched again, turning toward her. A line of blood dripped from his ear. Ginger caught his chin and turned his head to the other side. There was blood at the other ear as well.

She released him and waited until he looked back at her. "Merrow, can you hear me?"

His brows turned upward in confusion.

Merrow stared at her mouth as Ginger repeated herself. "Can you hear me at all?"

He touched his ear and brought his hand away to look at the red stain. Then he started to laugh.

Chapter Seventeen

★ ★ ★

Ginger sat outside the field hospital with a cup of tea, waiting for them to finish treating Merrow. The nurses—the real nurses—had taken a single look at her and declared that she was "shell shocked" and of no use without a rest. Shell shock. A nervous condition caused by exposure to intense trauma. By strict definition, she had been in that state for over a year, as had most of the Spirit Corps.

God. What was she going to tell Mr. Haden? Mrs. Richardson wouldn't even be able to report in and send a last message, because only British men were bound with the ID discs. The nexus wouldn't pull anyone else to it.

Ben flickered around her in the ghostly equivalent of pacing. He would take two recognisable strides and then be five paces away, without transition.

Ginger turned the cup in her hand. "I wonder where Axtell got to."

"What?" Ben was at her side in an instant. "He should be in Berlin by now."

For a moment, she thought it was another sign of his memory slipping, but Ben hadn't seen Axtell. He had been looking for Mrs. Richardson under the earth, and Axtell had already moved on by the time he came back. She said, "Well . . . that may be where he was before, but he was in the trench just now."

"There wouldn't have been time for him to get to Berlin and back."

"Maybe he didn't go? He said something about investigating that company. Of course, I wasn't supposed to tell you." She turned the cup again, just warming her hands against it. There were times when it seemed she would never be warm all the way through. She should ask Mrs. Richardson for some . . . no. There would be no more fingerless gloves or mufflers. "I find Axtell inherently unpleasant, so I don't miss him. Just wondered where he went."

Ben hunkered down in front of her, frowning. "You're certain about that."

"That I find him unpleasant?" She raised an eyebrow. "No . . . no, I know what you meant. Yes. He had dyed his hair brown, and he said he was going by Sgt. Meadows. He told me not to tell anyone, including you, that I'd seen him there."

"That's . . . that's not right." He stroked his mustache in thought, looking past Ginger toward the trenches. "Will you be all right waiting here for Merrow if I go look for Axtell?"

"Of course." She reached out, as if she could take his hand, and caught herself. "What is bothering you?"

"I am not certain, to be honest. I can't tell if it's something I've forgotten or something that I have yet to put together, but—" He shook his head, grimacing. "Something seems . . . off. Will you be all right? Truly?"

"Yes." She glanced at the hospital. "I'll see if can find a copy of *The Story of an African Farm*."

"You like it that much?"

Ginger stared at him, not quite certain if he was joking. "Well . . . I thought I might try to translate that book code. From the message we just got?"

He froze, confusion binding his limbs in place. "Ah. Right." He swallowed and tried to shrug off the braids of murky silver confusion and orange frustration. "Carry on, then."

"I will." Ginger smiled at him, knowing her aura must be blue-black with dismay. Did he not remember that they had taken a message from the listening trench, or had he forgotten which book was associated with it? For that matter, she had no way of knowing if Axtell was really supposed to be in Berlin, or if Ben had mixed up another set of memories. "Are you certain that you can go and come back?"

He stood and gave her a wry grin. "I'm more confident in my ability to return to you than I am in my ability to do anything else." With a wink, he stretched up and soared away, leaving the air dismally warmer with his absence.

Ginger stood and faced the field hospital. It had been a manor at some point, and the nurses who were not working were housed in the servant quarters. She would start there. *The Story of an African Farm* was popular enough, and such a slender volume, that one of them might have brought it along with her books. It was worth a try.

★ ★ ★

Ginger rubbed her forehead, trying to ease the pain behind her right eye. It did nothing to make the words on the page any more sensible. One of the chauffeuses had brought a copy of *The Story of an African Farm* with her and had been delighted to find someone who appreciated it as much as she did. The theme of the rights of women had been part of what had inspired her to join up to drive ambulances. Ginger had lost a good twenty minutes chatting about the book with the girl before she managed to escape with it to sit at a garden table in the sun.

At the moment, she was desperately hoping that the book was a different edition than the one that she and Ben had used. If it was the same edition, that meant she had missed a number somewhere, because the message made almost no sense.

THE WATCH THE LADY HAD BEEN TURNED

BRING ME AND MADE ANY OTHER LOVE TOUCHED IT ON YOU

YOU MAY WORK OF DEATH'S FINGER POINTING DOWNWARD

AS MUCH AS WITH AN ADROIT MOVEMENT HE

SO A BEGGAR FEELS WHO AM ONLY WHEN A PIECE OF

HE CAME CLOSE NOW.

It must be that she missed a number and made the entire sequence go off, because the first line made a sort of sense. . . . *The lady had been turned* seemed as though it had to be about the mediums. Did it mean that a *medium* had turned traitor? But the rest . . . Ginger groaned and dropped her head to the table. She'd gone over the numbers twice and couldn't find one that she'd dropped. She needed to rest her eyes for a minute.

When Ben got back, she would make him help her figure out where she had gone wrong. Or maybe the message would make sense to him. Or he would agree that she was working from the wrong edition. She would just rest her eyes.

Only for a moment.

★ ★ ★

Ginger is sitting in a box seat at the Met, only it is not the Met but Ben's box at The Queen's Hall in London. She is in London, not New York. She doesn't know how she could have mistaken the two. The symphony is wonderful, even if the seats are too close to the tympani. Still, she loves the New World Symphony *by Dvořák, and the percussion is a substantial reason why. The music always makes her nostalgically homesick for New York.*

Ben leans over and hands her a handkerchief.

She smiles and takes it, wiping her eyes in the dark. He always knows. She lowers the muffler he handed her and admires the work that Mrs. Richardson did on it. Mrs. Richardson . . . Ginger begins to weep anew.

Ben pulls her close to him. "Oh, beloved. I am so very sorry."

"I shouldn't have brought her." *Which is odd, because Mrs. Richardson would love this symphony. Only no . . . no, that isn't right.*

Ginger inhaled and straightened. "Is this a lucid dream?"

"Yes, but I'm keeping an eye on your breathing this time. And no kissing." *Ben kissed her forehead.* "At least not on the lips."

"Mrs. Richardson is dead."

"I know." Ben brushed her hair back from her face, and his fingers were warm. "I can't express my regret deeply enough."

"Forgive me—I'm still orienting to being awake—or asleep, but alert. Lucid. I'm adjusting to being lucid, though I'm not terribly lucid, am I?"

"I suspect this is why it is useless for spying."

"At least you seem more coherent here." She frowned. "Actually, I'm surprised you can dream as a ghost."

"I'm not. I just entered yours." Ben pulled her a little closer and rested his head against hers.

"Ah. And I suppose my brain is filling in the gaps in your behaviour. So you could, in fact, be wildly erratic."

He gave a crooked grin, dimples winking at her. "That was what my mother always complained about."

"She always told me you were a well-behaved child."

"Well, she wanted you to marry me. She wasn't about to tell you what I was really like." Ben traced a circle on the inside of Ginger's wrist and sent warm shivers into her centre. "But you knew I was a scoundrel by the time you said 'yes.'"

"Humph. I thought that was my corrupting American influence."

"Which I loved very much." Ben cleared his throat. "But there are some things we should talk about, and I am a little more coherent here. I found Axtell. You're right: he dyed his hair."

"Did you think I couldn't tell the difference between blond and brown?"

"No, no. But I thought it might be a wig. Which is damned odd."

"Why? I thought disguises were part and parcel of the intelligence department."

"Yes, but Axtell has been on assignment in Berlin because he can pass—better than I can—as a German. I can't see why Davies would have him dye his hair, which will make his previous aliases useless." He scrubbed his face. "I feel like I am missing something."

"If Axtell didn't go to Berlin . . . would he have been near camp 463?" She twined her fingers through Ben's and settled back against the sofa.

"Maybe. . . . He's not as highly placed as I think our leak is, but . . ." He ran his thumb in circles around the base of her neck. "Don't forget to keep breathing."

"Yes, dear."

Ben kissed her on the forehead again, pulled her closer, and recited:

> "Now that we've done our best and worst, and parted,
> I would fill my mind with thoughts that will not rend.
> (O heart, I do not dare go empty-hearted)
> I'll think of Love in books, Love without end;
> Women with child, content; and old men sleeping;
> And wet strong ploughlands, scarred for certain grain;
> And babes that weep, and so forget their weeping;
> And the young heavens, forgetful after rain;
> And evening hush, broken by homing wings;
> And Song's nobility, and Wisdom holy,
> That live, we dead. I would think of a thousand things,
> Lovely and durable, and taste them slowly,
> One after one, like tasting a sweet food.
> I have need to busy my heart with quietude."

Ginger shivered again as he finished reciting. "That is lovely. What is it?"

"Rupert Brooke—goddamn it." Ben squeezed his eyes shut, face twisting into a mask of pain. "I hate this."

"What?"

"The gaps in my mind. The cipher—it's not The Story of an African Farm. It's Rupert Brooke's poems."

Ginger sat up with a gasp, shocked into wakefulness. Across the garden table from her, Merrow jumped, nearly dropping the novel. She had no idea when he had arrived. His face was pale, and cleaned of dirt. It seemed odd to see him without his niece's scarf tucked about his neck. His uniform—

He wore "hospital blues" and had a piece of paper with the letter *E*, for *England*, pinned to his uniform. At Ginger's side, Ben sucked in a breath of dismay.

Setting the book down, Merrow ducked his head and rattled the paper, which represented the order to ship him home. "They say—they say this is a Blighty one. At least for a while."

"What did they say about your hearing?"

He lifted his head and squinted at her. "Try again?"

Ginger touched her ear. "Your hearing?"

"Right ear is a lost cause. I might—might get some back in the left." He tugged his ear lobe. "I expected—I expected deafness to be quiet, but it sounds like—like bells underwater."

Ginger reached across the table and took Merrow's hand. She squeezed it in lieu of the words of sympathy he couldn't hear her say. As awful as it was to have him hurt, she was glad of it. He would go home and be safe. If she had insisted on coming alone, then Mrs. Richardson would still be alive and Merrow would have his hearing. And yet . . .

Ben shook his head. "Maybe you should have me exorcised, so no one else . . ." He trailed off. Merrow was staring at him. "Can you hear me?"

"Yes." Merrow blinked rapidly and turned his head to look in the general direction of Ben's ghost. "Yes, sir, I can. H-how?"

"Psychic vibrations." Ginger swallowed as he turned to look back at her. "You can hear me too, can't you?"

"Yes, ma'am. But—but I couldn't earlier." His aura took on the lavender-rose of cautious hope.

Ginger released his hand. "But not now, am I right?"

The rosy glow crashed into a deep grey violet and Ginger grabbed Merrow's hand again. "It's because my soul is a little outside my body to talk to Ben. So you are feeling that connection and able to hear just as you would in a circle. Your hearing is damaged, but your soul isn't."

Ben said, "After the war, I'm not sure any of us can claim to have undamaged souls."

"True enough, sir." Merrow rubbed the back of his neck and looked down at the *E* again. Then he touched the page with the numbers that Ginger was struggling with. "I could stay. And help. I thought I wouldn't be much use with no hearing—but I could help."

Ginger looked at Ben, and almost pulled her hand away so they could speak privately, but it seemed cruel to cut that slender cord of understanding from Merrow. Even without words, Ben understood her question. Was it immoral for her to want to keep Merrow with her? On the one hand, he would be safe back in England. But on the other, when they were finished with this task . . . Ginger did not want to be alone when Ben left.

"I think . . ." Ben cocked his head and considered. "I think that all we need to do is decode that page. You remember how book ciphers work, don't you, Merrow?'

"Yes, sir." His aura lit with eagerness.

"Good." Ginger sighed. Decoding could not lead him to any harm, so long as they stayed away from guns. "Then we need to find a copy of Rupert Brooke's poems."

Chapter Eighteen

★ ★ ★

25 July 1916

Ginger walked back out of the nurses' quarters with her face still stiff from smiling at the ambulance driver who had loaned her *The Story of an African Farm.* She had the best collection of books at the hospital, but, alas, only fiction. Ben floated along at her side. "Chatty young lady."

"Indeed." Under other circumstances, Ginger might even have enjoyed the conversation. "I do like her taste in fiction, though I wish she had a taste for poetry."

"Let's hope Merrow had better . . . ah." Ben gestured ahead to where Merrow awaited them at the garden table with empty hands. "I suspect not."

Merrow was chewing his lower lip and frowning at a scratch in the table's surface. He did not look up until Ginger's shadow fell across the table. He offered a weak wave.

Ginger held out her hand, and Merrow sighed before taking it. His hands were rough with raw spots from where he'd been digging. She sat next to him on the bench. "No luck, I take it?"

"No." His shoulders hunched, and he shrugged a little. "There was one fellow who had his war poems, but Capt. Harford had said he used the collected works for the code."

"So back to Le Havre?" Ginger rubbed her brow with her free hand. She should have asked the nurses for an aspirin.

Merrow shifted in his chair. "Would it—would it save time if we went to Amiens? There's a bookstore—across from the bakery where we used to do live drops."

Breaking into a grin, Ben brightened. "Well done, Merrow. Excellent plan."

★ ★ ★

The young chauffeuse with the book collection gave them a ride back to Amiens along with two other nursing sisters who were going in for a bit of shopping. Ginger avoided mentioning that they were going to a bookstore, because otherwise the chauffeuse likely would have followed them.

Stepping into M. Pouliot et Fils bookstore in Amiens was like stepping back to a time before the war. Tall shelves filled the room. Books in rich leather and fabrics in every jewelled tone stood in orderly ranks. The very air smelled of contentment. Ginger stopped in the doorway and inhaled the heady aroma of leather and paper and ink. No chaos amid the gilt letters, only order and peace.

The soldiers who perused the shelves spoilt the illusion, but all of them had a more relaxed set to their shoulders than any she had seen recently. One French captain sat in a deep leather armchair, engrossed in a thick leather book. A British lance corporal had settled on the floor at the base of the shelves with his head bent over a slim volume of verses.

A mousy little woman in an elegant walking suit and shop-keeper's apron turned from a quiet conversation with a Frenchman and smiled at Ginger. She was neither M. Pouliot nor his son, but she seemed clearly proprietary, with a pair of pince-nez perched upon the end of her long nose. Only her hair, white wisps of which had escaped her bun, stood in a disorderly contrast to her shop.

"Good afternoon, sir and madam. And how may I help you today?" She laid a hand upon a stack of lavender clothbound books. "I have novels, which will transport you away from your labors here. Or should you like some philosophy?"

It was strangely tempting to let her recommend a book, some innocuous treat that would let Ginger escape and pretend the war was not happening. But flanked as she was by Ben and Merrow, pretending would be impossible, even if she had time. "Thank you, madame. I was hoping you had a copy of Rupert Brooke's collected works."

The little woman's face split in a beaming smile. "I do. I do, indeed. Very popular it is among the servicemen. And ladies, of course. I have it bound in leather and cloth. Which do you prefer?"

Ben drifted forward. "Ask if you can look at it. The edition is more important than the binding."

Ginger put her hand on Merrow's arm so he could hear her. "The book is for my companion. I have been extolling its virtues to him. Would it be possible to look at a copy to see if it is really to his taste?"

"But of course!" The bookseller beckoned them forward. "Here. I have a chair in which you can sit, monsieur. Rest yourself, and I shall fetch it for you." She bustled back into the shop and disappeared down another row of shelves.

"This would be easier if we could simply buy the book and find a private place." Her satchel with her funds had been buried when the dugout—Ginger had to turn from Ben and hold her breath. Oh—Mrs. Richardson. Smoothing her apron, Ginger put a smile on her face and turned back, but Ben's aura was the pale green of sea mist with sympathy. So much for hiding her distress.

Merrow at least pretended not to notice her reddened eyes. In a low voice, he said, "This is—is as private a place as we're like to find. Tucked back in a corner like this?"

Ben nodded in agreement and passed through a bookshelf, reappearing a moment later farther down the aisle. "There's no one in the aisle, and the other side is a wall."

"Well, you gentlemen are certainly more experienced in this sort of thing than I am."

Merrow took his cap off and twisted it in his hands. His hair stood up above the fresh white bandages wrapped around his head. "Still . . . someone should keep watch, because Capt. Harford—the other one. He's still stationed in Amiens."

Ben grimaced. "I can keep a lookout on the street. I can't stop them, but it would at least give advance warning. Will you be all right decoding on your own?"

Ginger nodded and murmured, "I should be, though my last effort was less than satisfactory."

"Entirely my fault. I told you the wrong book."

Merrow cleared his throat. A ruddy gold of nervous apprehension filled his aura. "Maybe I should be the one to . . . study the book? I can't hear. So. Being a lookout? But I could do this. The captain—he showed me how. Before."

He had a good, though unfortunate, point. Ginger glanced at Ben, who drooped with guilt. "Thank you, Merrow. Having two of us on the lookout is perhaps more useful. If you don't mind. . . ."

The shopkeeper bustled around the corner with a leather copy of the poems. Ginger couldn't help but notice that she had brought them the more expensive version to peruse. "Here you are, monsieur! The finest calfskin. Very durable in the trenches."

Ginger took the volume from her. "Thank you. I wonder that you are able to keep your shop going."

"Oh, yes. England has a special interest in making sure my books get through, which is very kind of them. Literature is so important to the health of the mind. And in these times . . . I should thank you, sir, for your service. Indeed, I should and I do. My own son went into the trenches." She gave a little shrug and a sad smile that told her son's fate. Likely her husband as well.

Merrow looked at the shopkeeper blankly, brow creased in frustration. He wet his lips and took the book from Ginger.

She rested her hand on Merrow's shoulder. "I'm afraid his hearing was damaged, but I hope this volume can give him some comfort."

Bending his head, Merrow opened the book to the title page, and held it so Ben could see. Clouds of blue-green relief fizzed off of Ben. "It's a later printing, but the same edition as mine. Good lord. Thirty-eight thousandth impression. Still, this should do."

The shopkeeper made a *tsk* of sadness over Merrow's condition. "I hope your people are sending him home."

Ginger nodded. "But I thought something for the trip would help."

"Of course. Of course. Literature is the best remedy for the heart and head." She took off her pince-nez and polished them on her apron. "The best remedy."

And now, Ginger needed to get the shopkeeper away from Merrow so he could decode the letter. "Perhaps you could show me the novels you mentioned?"

"Myrtle Reed! Yes, of course. Am I right that you are American? She writes the most lovely books. . . . And American too. I thought it would give you a taste of home."

Chattering happily, the shopkeeper led Ginger back to the stack of lavender and gilt volumes. The stack gave her a good view of the street through the front windows of the shop. Outside, myriad uniformed men gave a grim reminder that the shop was only an oasis—a mirage, really—in which one could pretend the war was not happening.

★ ★ ★

It took Merrow only half an hour to translate the message. Ben had drifted in and out of the shop. Ginger was not entirely certain if he was returning to check in or because he had forgotten why he was outside. More distressing, she suspected that Ben did not know either.

He was inside the shop when Merrow emerged from the end of the aisle with the closed book of poems in his hand. His aura was filled with jags of ruddy gold apprehension as he beckoned to her. Ginger set down the copy of *Flower of the Dusk*—which really was very good—and hurried to Merrow's side. Ben flitted around them, vibrating with anticipation. The tremors blurred the outlines of his form, making him appear even more tenuous.

Merrow led them back to his chair and pulled out the paper he'd been working on. "I—I checked twice. It's not—not good."

Ginger took the paper from him and offered him her hand so he could hear Ben. He slipped his hand into hers and the rough tracery of scabs from digging tickled her skin. Ben leaned over her shoulder, raising gooseflesh at the base of her neck.

MAKING SEA TEARS SHELL TO ENTRAP YOUR GHOSTS ON BATTLE FIELD.

RIGHT ABOUT LONDON TRAITOR.

TRYING TO RECREATES YOUR SOUL BIND FOR GERMAN SOLDIER.

SEEK GHOST TALKERS.

WILL SHELL CAMP HOSPITAL MEN ON LEAVE TO OVERCOMES WITH GHOSTS BEFORE BATTLE.

Ben snorted. "Well . . . that last bit comes a little late."

"At least we know it was not an isolated effort." She tapped the first line. "*Sea tears* . . . That must mean salt—a salt bomb?"

"Likely."

A barrier had to be an unbroken line, but if they salted the earth thoroughly enough it might work to constrain a ghost's movements. But to cover the earth that thoroughly would require multiple bombings, with salt spraying like buckshot everywhere. The mediums wouldn't survive. She ran a finger over the second line. "What does he mean about the London traitor?"

"I don't know." Ben smiled at her, standing at ease, and also crouched at the base of the shelves, grey and rocking with fear.

Merrow's brows drew together. "It sounds like—like you made a guess. About who the . . ." He paused and looked around, though no one shared their aisle. "You know."

Ben's smile grew more fixed, his lips drawing back impossibly far, so his teeth were like a skull's. "I know what it sounds like. But I don't know what my guess was."

"But, London," Ginger said. "That narrows it down, or at least tells us that it isn't someone in Le Havre."

"He wasn't working alone." Ben clutched his head, laughing. "Wonderful. I can remember that, but not who."

"Well, and you know it's a man."

"Oh. Well. That makes it all clearer. I suspected a man in London." The standing Ben turned in place; the crouching version of himself rocked faster. A sudden breeze rustled the paper in Ginger's hands. "Because lord knows, there are few enough of those in the military. Why the hell didn't I write it down?"

"You—you did, sir." Merrow shifted uneasily. "In your notebook. It's not your fault that—"

"Yes it is!" Ben flung a book across the aisle. It slapped against the shelves and dropped to the floor with a thud. "Mrs. Richardson is dead because of me." Another book flew off the shelves. "You are deaf because of me." Another book. "Ginger is in danger because of me." He yanked another book off the shelf.

The bookseller ran into the aisle and slid to a stop, staring at the book, which to her eyes appeared to float in midair. *"Mon dieu!"* Her gaze darted around and then landed upon the books splayed on the floor. "What have you done?"

Ben dropped the book, and the bookseller jumped at the noise. The little woman's aura went crimson with anger. "Out! Out of my shop."

"Madame, I am so terribly sorry." Ginger bent to retrieve the books. Even if the shopkeeper was a sensitive and aware of ghosts, it would not do to draw the connection in her mind between Ginger and mediums. "I do not know what hap—"

"No! Do not touch anything. Only leave. At once."

At the end of the aisle, one of the French officers appeared. "Is there a problem, Madame Pouliot?"

"They have been throwing books." She crouched to pick up one of the volumes, smoothing the pages.

Now the British officer also appeared. His uniform was crisply pressed, and he wore a monocle. He narrowed his eyes at Merrow. "One of ours, what? I can have him brought up on charges of disturbing the peace."

"Thank you, Maj. Westrup. That is not necessary, so long as they leave." The shopkeeper's earlier affability had entirely vanished as she gathered the other books.

Ginger rose and put her hand on Merrow's arm again. "He was recently wounded, and I was hoping that the poems might help. I misjudged. I am terribly sorry, and I will take him back to the hospital straightaway."

"That's for his CO to decide, now isn't it?" Maj. Westrup stepped past the French officer and came down the aisle, tapping his officer's cane against the floor with each step. "Come along."

Ben slid past Ginger and put his hands against Westrup's chest as if he could stop him. The man walked through, shuddering at the spot of cold. Ginger kept her grip on Merrow. "Please. Surely you have seen men in his condition before."

"If you are referring to the shirkers, who pretend to 'shell shock' so they can get sent away from the front, then yes. I have." He looked down his aristocratic nose at her, and Ginger doubted he had seen even a day of serious combat. "Now then. Am I going to have to have you both arrested?"

"Very likely." Ginger drew herself up straighter and mustered all the disdain she had ever used in setting down a presumptuous cad. "I am taking my charge and returning to the hospital. If you so much as lay a hand on us, I will write it up and report it to my MO. While you may not believe in shell shock, Sir Alfred Keogh, the Director General of Army Medical Services, very much does."

For the first time, a fracture of uncertainty flickered in Westrup's aura. "Well. So long as you leave Madame Pouliot's shop, it does not really matter. But do it promptly."

Which was clever of Westrup, because it made Ginger's haste to leave look like fear of him. She kept her back straight and a grip on Merrow's arm as she marched him out of the shop. The other patrons all turned to watch them leave.

Ben eddied around the room, ruffling pages. "Bad. Bad. Bad . . ."

It was. And stepping back out onto the war-torn street only confirmed that. Ginger steered them towards the train station. With the spy in London, it seemed as though the most sensible thing to do would be to go to Lady Penfold and have her arrange a meeting with Brigadier-General Davies. Even if the spy had compatriots, Davies could not be one of them, or the Germans would already have the answer to where the mediums were located. And if their path took them to London itself, they would have to pass through Le Havre to get there. Either way, the next step would be to catch the train.

Merrow glanced over his shoulder. "Damn—sorry, ma'am. Only, Westrup is following us."

Chapter Nineteen

★ ★ ★

Ginger only just managed to restrain the urge to look behind her. Ben, however, had no such need for restraint and zoomed back. She grimaced, hoping he would not do anything foolish to Westrup.

Ginger bent her head to Merrow, though he was hearing her through the spirit plane. "Let us hope that he is only following to ensure that we return to the hospital. Once we reach the train station, we will simply take the train toward Le Havre instead of toward the hospital."

"I can—I can knock him down, if it comes to it. But—but I'd rather not."

"And I would rather you didn't have to." What was Ben doing? That made her want to look around more than any desire to see Maj. Westrup. The station was at the end of the street. They just had to get on the train. Once they were back in Le Havre, she could get advice from Lady Penfold on what to do next, and . . . and it would give her a chance to tell the circle about Mrs. Richardson.

She dealt with death every day and knew, better than most, that there was life beyond this event, and yet the hole that Mrs. Richardson left behind was immense. Ginger blinked to clear the stinging in her eyes.

And then blinked again. "Oh, bloody hell."

Merrow jumped a little at her very unladylike curse and then echoed it when he saw the same problem ahead. Lyme, the blond from Reginald's crew, was standing outside the station holding a piece of paper and scanning the crowd. He had two military police with him.

"Ben, if you can hear me, please come back." She was less concerned with her own safety, because they would be looking for a red-haired woman in a Spirit Corps uniform. In her nursing uniform, her hair was thoroughly covered. But Merrow was a problem.

If Westrup was still behind them, then a deviation from course to avoid the train station would likely cause him to raise a complaint, and that would draw the MPs' attention. Either course would lead to them being apprehended. Ginger scanned the street, looking for some distraction. Fruit vendors, a butcher, a clothier, a small café, automobiles, nurses, soldiers, and more soldiers. Scattered among them were more red-capped MPs.

"We could split up and try to board separately." Merrow tugged his hat a little lower on his head.

Being in hospital blues might help, but Lyme would certainly remember his face. The trick, then, was to make sure that they didn't look at his face. Ginger eyed the butcher, and one of Ben's memories flashed through her head. "Have you any money at all? Enough to buy a bit of steak?"

"Um . . . yeah." He fumbled in his pocket with the hand she didn't hold. "I should've just bought the poems, but I didn't figure we'd need them that long. And, well, travelling light. And—why steak?"

"Or liver. That's probably got more blood in it, actually." She steered Merrow toward the butcher shop, hoping Westrup would think she was picking up something for the trip. "I want to adjust your bandages and add some blood to obscure your face. Ben did it once when he was behind German lines." Only he had used the blood from a corpse.

A spike of alarm punctured Merrow's composure for a moment, and then he wet his lips and nodded. "All right. A fellow ought to—ought to be used to blood by now."

As they reached the door, Ben appeared in front of Ginger and nearly made her stumble. "Sorry." He put out his hands to catch her, as if that would do any good. "What's going on?"

"Reginald has men at the station," she murmured.

His head whipped around to stare at the station, and his lips pulled back in a snarl. Great wings of fire and jet spread out, fanning the air with his protective rage. "I'll kill him."

"I'd rather you just find out what's on the paper, dear." Ginger risked a glance back up the street. There was the damned major from the bookstore. "Come along, Merrow. Oh, and could you cover your eye as if you've been punched?"

Ginger could not quite bring herself to walk through Ben, so she stepped a little to the side to go around him. With a hiss, Ben soared off down the street, trailing anger after him like the wake of a ship.

She pushed the door to the shop open. The trill of the little bell called the butcher to the counter, or rather the butcher's wife. The shop was spotlessly clean, and here, Ginger could see more of the effects of the war. They had very little meat for sale, and the prices were outrageous. Le Havre had better stores, but then they were the port where the convoys brought supplies into France. Here, so close to the front, most of the local provisions must have gone to the soldiers. What little was available had prices jacked up to take advantage of the officers fresh out of the trenches.

Still, she put on an efficient smile. "Good afternoon, madame. Do you have a scrap of beef? Something only fit for the dogs." Ginger glanced at Merrow, who dutifully had his hand clapped over his left eye. "He got hit by a cart, and I want to keep the swelling down."

The butcher's wife was a tiny woman with her dark hair pulled back into a severe bun. Lines of strain were etched under her eyes. She pursed her lips. "No scraps."

"I'm sure your cuts are of the highest quality." Though, in fact, Ginger had had kitchen staff to handle the butcher before the war, and she still wouldn't know a good cut from a bad one in the raw. "But this is only to—"

"I mean that there is no waste. The army." The butcher woman jerked her chin toward the door, as if that explained everything. And perhaps it did.

"Then your least expensive, please."

With a snort, the woman slapped a piece of waxed paper on the counter and reached into the cooler. She drew forth a fatty, gristly mess and dropped it into the middle of the paper. "Voila."

It was disgusting, and perfect. "Thank you. And might I buy your cloth as well?"

The butcher looked down at the bloody rag she was wiping her hands on. "This? Eh. I will get you a clean one."

"No, no—that one is perfect. No point in soiling a fresh one, since it will just get more blood on it."

She paid the outrageous price for the gristle and the rag, then sat Merrow down on the window ledge. With the efficiency she had acquired in her time nursing, Ginger wrapped the bloody cloth around his head with the gristle packed near his eye. A bit of it peeked out, which was gross and effective.

Ben pushed through the wall of the butcher shop just as she was finishing. He made a sound of revulsion that was, in the moment, deeply satisfying. "What the devil are you—oh . . . clever."

She glanced at him and raised her brows. With her head turned away from the butcher, Ginger mouthed, "What did you find out?"

He shook himself, settling the folds of his attention around his form. "Lyme has Merrow's picture, and yours." He ran his hand through his hair. "Specifically, he has my photo of you."

"Are you certain? I did have more than one copy made."

"And how many did you inscribe *To my dearest love*? I carried it in my breast pocket. Always." Ben glanced over her shoulder. "The butcher is starting to wonder why you're still here."

"Can you read her mind?"

"No, but I can read a scowl."

Ben slid toward the door. "I'll scout ahead. You two come slow behind me."

Ginger nodded and took Merrow by the arm. He was rigid under her grip, and his aura had gone dark with fear. With a nod to the butcher's wife, Ginger let Merrow hold the door for her, and then they both stepped out onto the street. The major from the bookstore was standing a little down the street, pretending, not very well, to be window shopping. Though what use he had for lady's handkerchiefs, Ginger could not imagine. Still, it meant he was not looking directly at them when they started down the street, so, hopefully he would not notice the alteration in Merrow's appearance.

Ben zipped through the crowd, causing a horse to shy as he brushed past it. He circled Ginger and Merrow, all spikes and plates of red armour. "There's a group of walking wounded, coming down the cross street. If you can bear over that way, I don't think the idiot behind you will be able to object when you join them."

"Thank you." And, of course, being in a group would make disappearing that much easier.

Ginger worked her way to the left side of the street, where another cut diagonally into the one they were on. Everything funnelled into the train station at this point. The stream of men in their hospital blues stood in marked contrast to the seam of khaki surrounding the station.

Her heart raced in her chest and sweat beaded the back of her neck, despite Ben's cool presence. This was oddly more nerve-racking than crawling through the listening trench. There, at least, she had the benefit of others' memories to know the exact range of things that might go wrong. Here, she had only her own resources—and, with luck, Ben's observations—to give her a bit of warning.

As they merged into the shuffling mass of wounded, Ginger tried to work Merrow closer to the middle of the group. Thank heavens they would not have to worry about tickets on a train bound for the hospital. Ben rose above the crowd and sank back down with some relief. "The major has stopped. He's still watching, but he's not following you anymore."

"It seems as if he really ought to have something useful to do," Ginger muttered. The hospital was in Étretat, which got them no closer to Le Havre. They would have to board the train and go straight through to exit on the far side. At least then they'd be inside the station, though she had no idea how long it would be until the next Le Havre train.

"Fellows like him never have anything useful to do." Ben chewed his lower lip and turned toward the train station. "I'll see if Reg is around anywhere."

Ginger nodded, none of her tension releasing now that they were in the line. The chances of Reg's men spotting them, disguised and in a group, were thin. She knew that she could relax a little, but her body would not unwind.

"Hallo, sister. Where did you come from?" A doctor in his midforties, with absurdly curly hair and a long scarf that would have made Mrs. Richardson faint, came alongside Ginger with his hands tucked behind his back.

Well, here was a good reason to still be nervous. Ginger let go of Merrow's arm, since there was no good reason for her to still be holding it. She concentrated and tried to sound less American when she answered. "I was at a casualty clearing station near the front. Sent back on leave, and then got pulled out almost immediately and reassigned."

"Oh. Don't I know how that is. I can't remember the last time I had leave." His long nose bent like a hook when he smiled. "Still. Glad to have you. Canadian?"

"Yes." Good enough for the moment. They were even with Lyme and the MPs. Ginger turned her head away from them to look at the doctor. "And you?"

"Oh, all over. I move from time to time, but you could probably tell that." He stepped forward and caught a soldier who stumbled, steadying him until the man could walk by himself. "Have you worked the trains before?"

"No. I'm really just transferring." Her back prickled as they walked into the station. *Please, please don't let Lyme spot us.*

"No such thing as 'just' transferring." He winked at Ginger. "But I'll put you in the car with the light wounds."

"That's very generous."

"Well, it's a pity you lost your leave. Still, at least Le Havre is a nicer place than the front."

"Indeed." Le Havre? That was unexpected luck. She had expected that the train would be going to the hospital in Étretat. Ginger glanced at the men around them and realized that they all had the fluttering letter *E* pinned to their uniforms. So this was a group of soldiers returning home. Maybe this would be the best possible thing. Merrow could just get on the ship with them and get out of this dreadful war.

A cool breeze announced Ben's arrival. "I think you're in the clear. No sign of Reg. Looks like he just has his men here."

The train stood ahead of them, with steam that billowed like an aura around its iron black body. It seemed to be made of fear and grief. Some of the cars were already full, and not even the bustle in the station could mask the moans of pain from within. The group of soldiers Ginger was with headed for the fifth car.

The doctor nodded down the line. "Go on to car eight. It's the lightest injuries there, so you shouldn't have to do much more than fetch water. Changing dressings on a train is a whole other skill."

"Thank you." Ginger reached for Merrow. "I've been looking after this fellow today. He can't hear."

The doctor eyed the bandages and *tsk*ed. "Looks like he might lose the eye too, judging by the blood. I'll take him into my own car. Don't you worry at all."

"Oh—" She could think of no plausible objections. "Thank you."

Ginger walked to car eight, praying that Merrow would be all right on his own.

★   ★   ★

Despite the doctor's assurances, Ginger spent the entire trip to Le Havre working. While the soldiers in car eight had very few physical wounds, their minds were not in good repair. One man spent the ride weeping silently with his head cradled in his hands. Another had chewed his fingernails to the quick and had to be restrained to keep from gnawing his fingers bloody. Ben paced alongside Ginger, but she had no opportunity to speak with him.

But she had time to think. It felt like she had so far done little but race from one place to the next since Ben—since Ben's death. They had thus far been assuming that the man who killed Ben was the same as the traitor that Ben had been after. But . . . if Ben was right, and the traitor was not working alone, then there was no reason that the murderer and the leak had to be the same person.

Indeed, it was far more likely that it was two different people, particularly given the message from the spy in the German ranks. Given what Ben said about Axtell, could he be the one? When did he dye his hair though? That was the question—Ben's murderer had light hair.

But the note said that the traitor was in London. If that was so, then an accomplice here had killed Ben. It seemed likely, to Ginger, that the accomplice would be one of the people involved in drowning Capt. Norris in the baths. Both murders had involved British officers.

And then there was the hat that Brigadier-General Davis had said was found at the scene. . . . Reginald had lost his hat, and it would have had the name Harford in it. He would have been able to go from Le Havre to Amiens without trouble. And certainly he had been dogging her steps. Turning up first at the train station, then at the camp. And leaving his men at the train station with her picture—

Ginger's thoughts skidded to a stop and she turned to Ben, almost speaking to him before she caught herself.

His brows went up in response. "What? What idea did you just have, my darling, beautiful girl?"

She clenched her jaw and looked about the car, but the other nurses were closer than she liked. Wetting her lips, Ginger moved a bit farther down the car and crouched next to a young man who was staring blankly out the window. Murmuring, hoping that it would appear that she was speaking to the young man, but that he wouldn't hear her, Ginger said, "You said you carried my picture in your breast pocket."

"Yes."

"So Reginald has your things." Of course he must. Why else would he have gone straight to the prisoners of war? "Ben, you said they hadn't finished clearing the bodies at the . . . from the explosion. So, if Reginald has my photo, where did he get it?"

He greyed, face sagging under the realization. "From my body."

She swallowed and forced herself to continue. "And your notebook. You always carried it—"

"—in the same pocket." He swirled in a storm cloud of frustration. "So we've escaped Amiens, when that's exactly where we need to be. Perfect."

Chapter Twenty

★ ★ ★

As soon as Ginger got off the train in Le Havre, she struggled back through the stream of soldiers disembarking from car eight to meet Merrow. Ben followed at her side, floating slightly above her head to look over the crowd.

"That doctor you were talking to is headed your way." He flitted forward and then back. "He hasn't seen you yet."

Ginger ducked her head and pushed through the soldiers to the side of the station. Chewing the inside of her lip, Ginger put her hand on her nursing veil. There were enough women in the station that she should blend in. The question was if looking like an on-duty nurse, with the veil, would get her more attention than removing it and the apron.

Well, she would need to have it off when they went to see Lady Penfold. Besides, it would make it easier for Merrow to spot her. Ginger uncovered her hair and took the apron off as she scanned the crowd.

In the hubbub, she asked Ben, "Do you see him?"

"Looking . . ."

The stream of soldiers thinned as they limped out of the station under the watchful eyes of the nurses in charge of them.

"Maybe he got out on the other side of the train?" Ginger folded the apron into a bundle around the veil.

"Stay here and I'll look." Ben zoomed across the station and disappeared on the far side of the train.

Ginger pressed against the wall, fidgeting with the loose strings of the apron. He must have gone past while she was helping the soldiers from her car disembark. Please, let that be all it was. Ginger wrapped the strings of the apron around it, pulling them tight just to have something to do with her hands.

She let her soul slip a little further from her body to see if she could spot Merrow's aura in the station, but the vast space was awash in a sea of murky colours. Picking out a single one would be impossible.

Except for Ben's. She would recognise his spark anywhere. He darted now from car to car, just visible through the train as a livid spot of alarm. He reached the end of the train and soared up to the high, vaulted ceiling of the station. Even before he sank to where Ginger stood, she knew what he was going to say.

"He's not with the soldiers. I don't see him anywhere near the station."

"Did you see him get on the train?" Ginger pressed her hand to her brow, trying to remember. "I was ahead, going to car eight. I didn't think to watch him."

Ben shook his head. "I was watching you."

"Do you think Lyme grabbed him?" She shook her head.

"I don't know why I asked that as a question. That's the most likely scenario, isn't it?"

"Damn it. Yes," Ben growled, the sound rolling out from him on a wave of vivid frustration and anger. "If Reg hurts him—"

"Let's keep that from happening." She rubbed her forehead, over the growing ache behind her right eye. "The train took three hours. If they got him, they've had him at least that long. So, we're going to my aunt's. She will make things happen, and we'll get him back." She hoped.

★ ★ ★

The Hôtel de Ville seemed impossibly grand after their days in Amiens. The daily grind of life at the front made the contrast between Le Havre and even Amiens stark. The hotel still had flowers on the tables in the lobby. With her head ducked, Ginger hurried across the lobby, feeling grubby against the opulent interior.

Ben flitted in front of her. "The way is clear up to your aunt's. Take the stairs, not the lift."

She raised her brow in question. Her aunt was on the third floor.

"In an elevator, you're trapped, and someone else controls your passage. Stairs are confined, but you have more options and control." He stared behind her, gaze flicking from the door to the street, to the people sitting in the lobby. "No one is following us, at least."

She waited until she was on the stairs and less exposed before answering him. "Do you really think Reg would be looking for me here?"

"Yes. I do." Ben's aura had pulled in tight around him, and fractures of murky red showed with each brittle movement. "If he has Merrow, then we must assume that Merrow has told him where we were headed."

"But Merrow wouldn't—"

"Given the right lever, any man will speak." Flakes of dry blue calm crumbled off of him as more fissures of apprehension cracked the surface of his aura.

She continued up the stairs, and Ben peeled away from her, floating up through the middle of the stairwell. He rotated slowly, eyes constantly moving around the space. Ginger's heart was racing from more than just the climb by the time she reached her aunt's floor. Ben gestured for her to wait at the top of the stairs as he sped down the hall.

Ginger leaned out in time to see him disappear through Lady Penfold's door. He reappeared a moment later and beckoned her. "It's all clear. Only the maid is here."

"No Aunt Edie?" Ginger knocked on the door, palms sweating suddenly.

"I didn't see her."

The door opened. Upon seeing Ginger, Bernetta, her aunt's maid, gave a little curtsy. "Pardon, mademoiselle. Your aunt is not in."

"When do you expect her back?"

"Not for some time. She has gone to London."

"London!" Ginger put her hand to her chest and looked at Ben. It would be too great a coincidence for that to be related to their London spy. Besides which, her aunt went to London all the time. . . . But why now? With everything that was going on, why would her aunt leave the country now? She shook her head. Ben's paranoia was infecting her.

"But she left instructions to make the apartment available to you." The maid beckoned Ginger in. "Please, mademoiselle. I will bring you some refreshments."

"Thank you, Bernetta." Ginger made her way to the sitting room and dropped into one of the overstuffed chairs. She leaned her head against the soft velvet and turned to stare at Ben.

He paced around the room, hopping from place to place with his agitation. The last fragments of calm had shivered free, so he had only a mesh of red and heavy grey wrapped around him. "I think you should go to the Spirit Corps billets. Better—to Potter's Field."

"I thought you wanted to get me away from there."

"At least it has walls and guards. This . . ." He gestured at the large picture window. "This is like a trap."

"Well, first I'm going to have a sandwich and send a telegram to Aunt Edie. She can make things happen from London, perhaps even more easily than here." She rubbed her eyes. God, but she was tired. "And I need to talk to the circle."

"Why?"

"To tell them about Mrs. Richardson."

Ben's brows came together. He compressed his lips and nodded, looking away. "Of course."

"Do you . . . do you remember what happened—"

"Of course I do!" The cracks in his aura widened, shattering into a whirling cloud of fury. "I'm dead, not stupid."

"No, no, of course you're not." Ginger held up her hands to try to soothe him, though she could not touch him. "I didn't mean that you—I only thought . . . never mind all that. Help me find some paper so we can draft a telegram?"

A drawer shot open, the paper within rattling in a breeze. Ginger bit the inside of her lip. "Ben . . ."

He pulled his head down to his chest, bending over until he formed an unnaturally small ball. The tight wad of soul stayed there, while a thinner, paler version of him stood, smiling bloodlessly at Ginger. "My apologies. Of course I remember what happened to Mrs. Richardson. It just slipped my mind that you would need to tell the circle. Nothing more sinister than that."

Ginger swallowed and sat down to write.

★ ★ ★

Before Ginger was finished writing, Bernetta appeared with a plate of watercress sandwiches. Ginger's stomach gave a sudden, deep growl. Good heavens. When had she last eaten? Thank heavens that Bernetta was well trained, and gave no sign of having heard the indecorous noise.

Ben, however, raised both eyebrows. "Did you bring a monster with you?"

"Thank you, Bernetta." Ginger gestured to the small table in front of her aunt's sofa. "If you could just put them there and wait for a moment. I have a telegram I'd like for you to have sent for me."

"Of course, madame."

"And while you are out, may I ask you to run to the asylum where the Spirit Corps hospitality girls are and ask Helen Jackson to come here?"

"Oh—I am sorry, but all of the Spirit Corps women have been moved inside to new dorms at the old knitting mill."

That was the warehouse they were using for Potter's Field. It had no proper barracks. There were offices on the upper floors that could be converted, but most of the women had wanted to avoid being so close to spirits when they slept. The only rooms that had been in use were for the small infirmary. "For heaven's sake, why on earth are they there?"

"It is for safety, I believe. The walls." She gave a small shake of her head. "But no one can enter without a pass, so I am not certain of all the reasons. Only what I heard Lady Penfold say."

"And I suppose you don't have a pass."

"Correct, mademoiselle."

Circling her, Ben said, "I'll go. You stay here and rest. And eat. I don't want your monster to get any bigger."

Ginger snorted and wrinkled her nose at him. "Thank you."

"Will that be all, mademoiselle?"

Ginger handed the young woman the telegram she had written to Lady Penfold. "Just this, thank you."

★ ★ ★

Ben returned in no more than a half hour. His spirit was frayed around the edges, and wisps of blue-grey drifted off of him with each movement. He hung in the air in the middle of the apartment, plucking at the collar of his shirt.

Ginger sat up on the sofa, lowering her feet to the floor. "Darling?"

His brows drew together, and he stared at her.

"Ben . . ." Ginger bit the inside of her lip. He did not entirely look as though he recognised his name. "Ben, love. Do you know me?"

"Ginger." He nodded and drew a hand over his face, shuddering. "Ginger. Yes. Sorry."

"No, no. There is no need to apologize." Her heart beat raggedly in her chest. "What is the matter? Did something happen to the circle?"

"The . . . ? Oh. The circle. No." He inhaled, as if he still had breath, and drew the folds of his soul tighter. "Give me a minute, I'm still . . . I just need a moment."

This was the point at which she would have once urged him

to sit down and pressed a cup of tea on him, or perhaps held his hand, but she could do neither of those things. Ginger twined her own fingers together and drew her legs up under her on the sofa, huddling into the corner for warmth while Ben wafted in the air. "Is there anything I can do to help?"

"Talk to me—" He waved his hand vaguely at the room. "Remind me of before."

She swallowed and nodded. "I had a letter from Dorothy Porter the other day. She's engaged to Lord Lakefield and blames it all on us. Apparently, when I brought her along to your parent's country home for that hunting party—because lord knows I was not going to go riding with the dogs—"

"Chasing the hounds."

"Chasing the hounds, then. I was not going to go do that, and certainly not sidesaddle. So Dorothy says that while she was there she met your friend Lakefield—who is a good enough chap, but a trifle shorter than her—and then met him again at a field hospital in Gallipoli. She was his nurse, I gather. Well, one thing has led to another, as they say, and they are planning to get married. I suppose they already have, given the date of the letter."

"I should have married you." Ben crossed the room and sank to sit next to her on the sofa. "That way you would at least have a widow's pension."

"Dear . . . I'm an heiress. Money is not a concern for me." Ginger slid her hand toward his and shivered at the coolness. "I wish we had married for other, more intimate reasons."

His aura blushed rosy and spread out in a soft cloud. The edges of his soul seemed better defined than when he had first returned. "Well . . . yes. There is that."

"Are you able to tell me what happened while you were away?"

He stared at her for a moment and then blinked. "Right. Yes.

There is a salt line all the way around the outer wall of the Spirit Corps. The only way in is through the nexus, and I couldn't—I tried, but . . ."

"But you are no longer primed to go through the nexus." Ginger sank back on the sofa with a groan. "Well . . . the salt line means that Helen got my message, which is good, even if it does make things a little more complicated for us."

"At least it makes the relocation of the mediums less sinister."

"True. It means Helen was taken seriously, which is all to the good." Ginger drummed her fingers on the cushion, considering her options. "Which means . . . I can just go there myself instead of skulking around sending secret messages."

"I don't think that's safe."

"Why?"

Ben opened his mouth, and then shook his head. "I just don't. You mustn't go. Do I need a reason for everything?"

"If you want to convince me, instead of simply forbidding me, then yes. I require a reason." Ginger levered herself up from the couch. As she stood, the room tipped and swayed. She pressed a palm against the arm of the sofa, steadying herself until the dizziness passed. Perhaps she should stay here and rest for a bit. "Besides which, there is Merrow to consider. If I can't reach Aunt Edie, then I have to go to Brigadier-General Davies."

"But he's—"

"Not in London, and your spy friend said 'Right about the London Traitor.'" And it seemed distinctly unlikely that the brigadier-general was the one who had strangled Ben. "We have to have help. Fact finding, I can do on my own. Rescuing Merrow? I can't."

Ben grimaced, tugging at his collar. He stood and paced around the room with his head bent. "All right. Yes. I suppose it will be safe enough."

"I'm so glad you agree." Ginger shook out her skirt. "Since I was going to go anyway."

"Obstinate, headstrong girl." He gave something like a smile. "I suppose I can't complain when it's the thing I love about you."

"The thing? That implies that I have only one lovable point."

"Well . . . perhaps more than one. Maybe two things."

"I see. And what is the other?"

"I would say your passion, but that's part of being headstrong. Or your conviction, but that's related to being obstinate. Fearless, but that is a combination of both. Perhaps, then, I shall cite your love of Brussels sprouts."

Ginger laughed outright, so that her voice bounced back from the plaster ceiling. "You are one of the least romantic men I know."

"No, no. Hear me out." He tilted his head and looked at her with that crooked grin, which brought out his dimples. "You choose the most unfortunate and ill-favoured of the vegetables, and devour it with great relish. You overlook the sulphurous taste, and its resemblance to baby lamb heads—"

"*Baby lambs* is redundant."

"—baby sheep heads, then."

"Or lamb heads, which they do not resemble, being neither wooly nor white. Although they are tiny and cute."

"Elvin lambs, then." Ben held up a finger to stop her protests, and his dimples deepened. "But you prove my point. You overlook all that is horrid about the vegetable and instead focus on the one, questionable, good feature. Though I will say that cuteness is in the eye of the beholder—"

"But they are so tiny and—"

"And, I think that if you can have a sincere love for Brussels sprouts and overlook all those flaws, then perhaps you can overlook mine as well." He took a step closer, and the shivers radiating from Ginger's centre had little to do with the chill he carried with him. "And it is not the only obscure and odd thing you can find joy in. And that—that is the other reason I love you."

Her heart would break. Had broken. Dear lord, she loved him so very much, and had so little time left. Ginger caught her breath in a little gasp. "Well. You've regained your power of flirtation, so I can assume you are feeling better."

"Always. When I am around you, I am a better man. Or ghost, as the case may be."

Ginger shook her head, smiling slowly at him. "You make me look forward to falling asleep tonight."

"Do I now?" He winked. "Well, Miss Stuyvesant, that seems terribly forward—"

Someone pounded on the door. Ginger jumped at the sudden sound, putting her hand to her chest as if she could still her heart. For pity's sake, it was only the door, not gunfire or anything else threatening. The pounding repeated. Of course. Bernetta was still out with the telegram. She was rather surprised it had taken the girl so long; the hotel had a telegraph counter at the front desk. She turned toward the door, as Ben zoomed past her in a blur of agitated colour.

When she entered the foyer of the suite, he was just re-emerging from the door. His face was ghastly white. "It's red-caps."

Redcaps? Why would military police be at her aunt's door? No one knew she was here, save Bernetta—oh. It became less surprising that the young woman was still gone. Ginger wet her lips and kept her voice at a whisper. "How many?"

"Just two. Is there another way out?"

She shook her head.

"Damn. I was hoping for a servant's entrance."

"To the hotel, yes. Not the apartment. Though I would love

to be mistaken." She flinched when the pounding repeated, followed by the knob rattling.

Ben stuck his head through the door. "They have the manager, who has keys." He spun in place. "I can't search for another entrance fast enough."

Ginger stepped to the side of the door. When it opened, she would briefly be obscured. "Can you throw a book in the parlour? Only one. I don't want you to—"

And then the knob turned. Ginger pressed herself against the wall, holding her breath as the door swung open. Ben caught the edge of the door and nudged it so that it swung fully open, hiding her behind the door. He streaked away into the parlour.

The MPs entered, boots clattering against the marble of the foyer. In the parlour, glass shattered. One of the MPs said, "What the devil?"

Ginger wondered what Ben had done as well, but as soon as she heard the MPs run for the parlour, she eased around the door, standing on her toes to keep her heels from making noise on the hard floor. With as much stealth as she possessed, she slipped into the hall.

The hotel manager was standing by the door. His eyes widened at the sight of her. Ginger raised a finger to her lips, with her brows raised in pleading.

His eyes narrowed, and he inhaled to shout.

Ginger didn't wait; she turned and sprinted for the stairs. Behind her, the hotel manager shouted, "Messieurs! She is here!"

Lifting her skirt to her knees, Ginger ran down the stairs.

"Stop, miss! Aw, bloody hell . . ." The MP's voice echoed down the stairs from above her.

Ben appeared by her side. "Get off the stairs at the second floor."

That made no sense. She couldn't jump from that far off the ground. As the MPs started down the stairs, their heavy boots clattered on the marble and echoed through the stairwell. Ginger hit the second floor and, trusting Ben, pushed the door open.

He was standing there as she came through and pointed toward the end of the hall. "Servant stairs." Then he caught the door to keep it from slamming shut. Wisps of his soul curled around the edges.

Gritting her teeth, Ginger ran for the servant stairs. At the end of the hall, she yanked open the door into the dark, narrow stairwell. The worn wood creaked under her feet as she ran down the steps.

At the bottom of the stairs, Ben waited for her by the door. He held up a hand to stop her, and then shoved his head through the door. Pulling it back, he nodded. "Out. Then left. Walk."

Ginger trembled with the urge to run, but kept her pace to a walk. Her palms were coated with sweat, and her breath came in short gasps against the hard lines of her corset. Her cheeks must have been flushed, but none of the pedestrians she passed gave her a second glance.

Ben gestured to a street. "Right."

He was back to single words. Damn. Damn. Damn. Ginger set her teeth and kept walking. First they had to get away, and that seemed anything but certain.

★ ★ ★

Ginger pushed open the door of the barn that Ben had led her to. Her feet ached from the miles of walking they—no, really, *she* had done the walking. Ben had just floated alongside her.

Although, looking at his ragged figure, the toll that the journey out of Le Havre had taken on him was all too clear. His whole form waved like a piece of limp cheesecloth, ragged and full of holes. He pointed to the ladder that led to the hayloft. "Up."

"Must I really?" Tromping through fields after the sun went down, she had tripped more than once on the way here.

"Safer."

If it hadn't been for him scouting, she would never have evaded the MPs. It seemed silly to second-guess him now. She nodded and limped across the barn to the ladder. Grimacing, Ginger tucked her skirt into her waistband and climbed. The rough wood stung her hands where she had scraped them during one of the falls. Her shoulders and arms ached.

At the top of the ladder, she crawled into the hayloft, not even bothering to stand. All she wanted was to lie down. "Anything else?"

"Sleep."

"Perchance to dream." She curled into a ball in the loose hay, squirming to form a little nest, and then was asleep.

★ ★ ★

She is in the recovery ward at Number 1 General Hospital, going from bed to bed on her rounds. There is a new ghost in the room. When she is off duty as a nurse, she will have to see about forming a circle to try to set him at rest. Lt. Plumber, in the third bed, is a sensitive, but hasn't had any training.

Helen is pushing a mop around the floor—only it isn't Helen, it's Merrow. The bucket is full of blood, and he's smearing it on the floor.

"What are you doing?"

"Washing up, dearie." Mrs. Richardson lifts her mop and sets it into the bucket of clean water. She beams at Ginger over her knitting needles from her place by the fire. "Come have a seat next to me."

Ginger sits at the fireplace in the nursing lounge—only it isn't the lounge, it's her father's house. Ben is with her, and he's knitting. He looks at her over the edge of the muffler. The red yarn pools in his lap and drips down onto the floor. "Are you all right, darling?"

"I'm fine." Ginger picks up her cocktail, which must be filled with Campari to be so red. "Is there anything we should talk about?"

"She is dead." His voice is wrong.

Ginger lowers her cocktail. Knitting needles are jabbed deep into Ben's eyes. The blood drips into the muffler and mixes with the yarn in his lap.

★   ★   ★

"No!" Ginger yanked herself awake, sitting up, and had no idea where she was. The room was dark, and her bed was lumpy. The moon shone through the window, but it wasn't as high as the window of her room at the asylum. She put her hand down, and the crisp hay reminded her of where she was. The hayloft.

Ben crouched next to her, wearing worry like a dark blanket. "Are you all right?"

"Were we—were we lucid dreaming?"

"No. I thought it would be better if you just got some rest." He reached out as if he could brush her hair back and just cooled her brow. "Nightmare?"

She wiped her face and lay back on the straw. "It was fairly dreadful, although too jumbled now to make any sense."

"Try to go back to sleep. I worry about you."

"I can see that."

Ben glanced at the steel blue shrouding him and gave a dry chuckle. "Yes . . . well. I suppose this is like wearing my heart on my sleeve. Although you could always read me like a book."

"My favourite book." The unease from the dream still clung to her. Mrs. Richardson was dead. She knew that, and yet all the horror of it had come back. She looked out the window and sighed. The moon had moved quite a bit while she dreamt. She wouldn't be able to sleep again.

Ginger sat up and picked the straw out of her hair, then crawled to the ladder.

"What are you doing?"

"If I can't sleep, I might as well walk toward Amiens while there's a moon." Mrs. Richardson might be dead, but Merrow wasn't. She remembered the blood in his mop pail and shuddered. But he was not dead—he couldn't be.

Chapter Twenty-One

★ ★ ★

Ginger waited for Ben in the alley behind Reg's building in Amiens. She pressed back into the shadows, desperately hoping that no one would notice her. Ben had approved the alley, as it had two exits. And it was empty, which was more important when one was a woman, alone in the middle of the night.

Hopefully the farmer's clothing she was wearing would at least slow down the realization that she was a woman, even if it didn't entirely hide her figure. She had another pang of guilt at stealing them, but she needed trousers. And she needed to be wearing something different from the nurse's uniform.

Ben sank from the second story to stand next to her. His entire aura was aglow with excitement, and he had more anima-tion to his features than he'd had for days. "Merrow is inside."

"Is he all right?"

"Some new bruises, but otherwise looks unharmed. He's trying to open a safe that's in the same room."

"A safe? They put him in a room with their safe?"

Ben shook his head. "It's in the cellar. No windows. I'm guessing that it was the most secure place. And—he's unguarded, thank God." Ben wet his lips and looked toward the entrance to the building. "Reg isn't there. The house is empty."

"So I can just walk in?"

"That seems too easy."

"I agree." Ginger stared toward the building. "Do we have an alternate plan?"

Ben worried at his collar, tugging on it as if he were having trouble breathing. "Damn it. No. Let me scout for you, and if I see anything out of the ordinary, just run."

She bit her lips and nodded. As much as she wanted to protest that she couldn't leave Merrow behind, neither would she be able to rescue him if she were a captive herself.

She followed Ben through the small backyard of the building. Chickens in a hut clucked lazily as she passed, but gave no cry of alarm. One of the wooden stairs creaked underfoot, and she stopped, waiting to see if anyone would respond. The windows remained dark, which made sense if the house was truly empty. Breathing out, she eased up to the small landing outside the house and tried the door.

It swung open, already unlocked and not fully latched. Shivering, Ginger glanced behind her at the tiny yard and the alley behind it. "This seems . . ."

"Suspicious, yes. God . . . this feels like a trap."

"But the house is empty."

Ben nodded. "And I checked in a three-block radius and don't see anyone watching it. No one on the rooftops. Nothing."

It was difficult to feel entirely at ease with the door unlocked.

Ginger swallowed and entered the narrow plaster hall cutting through the middle of the house. A door to the right led into a kitchen.

Ben nodded to the door on the left, which was shut. "Servant's room, but now an officer's billet. Empty."

He led her to a door in the kitchen, which opened onto a narrow flight of stairs leading down. She felt her way to the stairs and grasped the rail. She did not dare light a candle, not without risking someone outside seeing it. Feeling her way, Ginger walked down to the cellar with her heart hammering in her chest.

In the cellar, two small windows let in a little light, but only enough to show that the room was crowded with boxes and discarded furniture.

Ben beckoned her to a door on the far side. A thin line of light showed underneath it. "Here. He's in here."

This door was locked. Ginger sighed, resting her head against the wood. "Well, that streak of luck couldn't continue. I don't suppose you saw the keys during your scouting?"

"Alas, no." Ben crouched by the door. "Have you any hairpins?"

"Have I . . . ? How do you think I keep my hair up? Of course I have hairpins." When her hair wasn't pinned up, it was down to the middle of her back. Ginger pulled a pin loose. "How many do you need?"

"Just two."

"And what will you do with them, O Phantasm of My Heart?"

He glanced up and grinned, dimples shadowing in his cheeks. "Pick the lock."

Ginger paused, holding the hairpins. "Ben . . . you can't."

"If I can throw books—"

"No." She folded her fingers over the pins. "When you are distressed and burning through energy at an alarming rate? Yes.

You can throw things. And then you are—you are not right for quite some time after that."

"That is my choice to make." He rose, shoulders setting inside a grim cloak of violet determination.

"It will be easier on you if I simply channel you and give you a body to pick the lock with."

"And what about you?"

"That is my choice to make." Ginger held up her hand to stop him. "If you try poltergeisting and fail, then you'll be exhausted and incoherent, and you won't be able to lead me out. We know that channelling will work, and it leaves you more coherent."

He glared at her, aura swelling around him. It exploded outward as he turned with a growl, fissioning into multiple versions of himself. They all snapped back together, leaving only Ben, staring across the cellar away from her.

"I hate this."

"I know." Ginger closed her eyes so she could not see the weary set of his shoulders, or the heavy grey despair that dripped into a pool at his feet. "I know."

"And you are right." He had a wry tone to his voice. "Which I am sure you are going to lord over me."

"I don't know." Ginger opened her eyes and tried to match him. "Can one 'lady it over' someone?"

"My lady, I believe you do that all the time."

"Ah . . . but I'm not a lady, am I? Simply an American."

"Well, you can definitely American it over someone." Ben sighed and came back to stand at the door. "Shall we? If we're going to?"

Ginger nodded and, with the hairpins clenched tightly in her fists, reached out her soul to meet his.

She is kneeling outside the painted green door of the commandant's office. Her German uniform chafes at the neck, but then it wasn't hers originally. She is supposed to be on guard duty, but has left the perimeter to come here. No one will look for her for another half an hour, by which point she should have the battle plans she needs to steal and be away. With her eyes closed, she concentrates on the tiny vibrations of the pick and torsion wrench in the lock. It is a simple lock, but her hands are still cold from standing sentry duty.

The wrench slips. She grimaces and repositions it to try again. Frowning, she eases the picks again, and—

The door unlocked.

Ginger stared at the rough wood door in front of her. It had been green paint a moment ago. She closed her eyes and opened them again, letting out a sigh. Right. Ginger turned her head to look for Ben. He was hovering next to her, his brows drawn together in confusion.

Bracing herself on the doorjamb, Ginger rose to her feet. Her hands were so cold. "Good job."

"What? Oh . . ." Ben looked at his hands. "Thank you. What . . . what am I supposed to do?"

"You were going to watch the doors. To warn me. If someone comes."

"Warn you." He nodded slowly and rose through the ceiling. "Warn you, yes."

Shivering, Ginger turned back to the door and opened it. Lit by a single candle, Merrow stood on the right side of the room with his ear pressed against a safe set in the wall. He was no longer in hospital blues, but in a regular soldier's uniform. The cloth bandage was gone from his head, but a fresh bruise on his jaw made it clear that he'd been in some sort of altercation.

He gave no sign of hearing the door open.

Ginger came farther into the room and tried to catch his gaze, but his eyes were shut, and his entire concentration was on the knob he was turning. She bit her lip, trying to think of how to alert him without startling him. Touching his shoulder would likely give the poor man a heart attack. His aura was already dark with fear.

But unless she touched him, he couldn't access the psychic vibrations, and without those, he could hear nothing.

Vibrations . . . perhaps that was the key. Ginger stomped her foot on the floor.

Merrow's eyes shot open and he whirled, grabbing her arm. Ginger shrieked as he twisted it. She dropped to her knees.

"Oh, no—" He released her hand and backed away. "I'm so sorry. I'm so, so sorry. I didn't know—"

Ben erupted from the ceiling, anger flaming around him like the fires of hell. He flew between Ginger and Merrow and threw the young man back against the wall.

"Ben! No—he didn't know it was me." Ginger scrambled to her feet. "I frightened him."

She thanked God that Merrow could not see Ben and wished she could not either. His jaw hung slightly open to accommodate an unnatural number of teeth. The weight of it pulled his neck forward, jutting out like a bull's, and his hands . . . his arms were too long and ended in talons.

With a grunt, he pressed one of those against Merrow. Even without being able to see, Merrow began to shiver uncontrollably. His breath wheezed in his throat.

Ginger staggered forward and rested her hands on the cool air of Ben's back. "Please, Ben. Beloved. Please."

"He hurt you."

"No. He didn't. We just frightened each other." She had no book of poetry to read to Ben this time to soothe him. But Ben had always been a man who believed in duty. "Ben . . . you have tasks unfinished, and I can't do them alone. I need Merrow, and

I need you. I need you here, with me, and calm. My darling, can you please, please be calm for me?"

Ben lowered his head even further and raised those talons to wrap the overlong arms around his head, but at least he released Merrow. Backing up abruptly, Ben rushed through Ginger, leaving her gasping with the cold of his passage. She turned to find him huddled in the exact centre of the room, not on the floor, but in the air.

Her poor, sweet boy. His own instincts would shred his soul. He needed time to recover from that foolish, foolish manifestation. God. What was it about men that made them so quick to leap into a fray? Squeezing her eyes shut for a moment, Ginger held her breath, trying to regain some sense of her own equilibrium. Ben would need time. Meanwhile, there was Merrow. She breathed out slowly before facing the young man.

He still cowered against the wall, his aura stark with fear and apprehension. She reached for him, and he flinched.

Pausing, Ginger turned her hand over and held it out, palm up, entreating Merrow to take it. He glanced at Ben, before wetting his lips and lowering his sweating palm into Ginger's hand.

She squeezed it. "Are you all right?"

"Fine, miss." His aura said that was anything but true. He was a bundle of anxiety.

"How did you come to be here?"

"I'd gotten off the train in Amiens, thinking that—it was bound for Étretat, I thought and—and we needed to catch the Le Havre train. I figured we were just using the soldiers to get inside the terminal."

"Ah . . . you wouldn't have heard the announcement. It turns out that it was a Le Havre–bound train."

"Well. Damn." With his free hand, he rubbed the back of his neck ruefully. "When I couldn't find you, I assumed that

Capt. Reginald Harford had you, and I was going to try to rescue you, but . . ."

"You were caught instead."

He nodded, face turned down. "Thought I'd see what was in this safe." Shrugging, he tugged on his ear. "Not much luck."

"Have you cracked a safe before?"

He raised his brows in apparent surprise at her use of slang. "I do read, Pvt. Merrow. Novels. Sherlock Holmes has more than one fan."

With a faint smile, Merrow gave a little nod. "Yeah. I learned how. Just not that . . . well."

Ginger eyed the safe. It would be good to know what Reginald was hiding. If he had Ben's things, the notebook in particular, then the safe was one of the most likely places to put them. Unless he had it on him, of course. She would deal with that if it came to it. "Do you think you can teach me?"

His face scrunched with concentration. "I can tell you, but as to the doing—as to the doing, that's harder. You turn the knob slow to the right, until you hear or feel the tumbler drop. Then to the left. And so on. It's the learning to feel or hear that . . . I can't. I can't show you that."

"Well. I'll give it a go, and if I can't, then we'll just leave it." She glanced toward the door. "It's only a matter of time before they come back."

"They're at the front."

Ginger's brows rose with surprise at this. "And they left you here? Without food or water?"

"I don't suppose they much cared." Merrow spread his hands with a shrug. "But it gives us some time."

"Indeed." Ginger approached the safe and laid her ear against the cool metal, as she had seen Merrow do. Closing her eyes, she turned the knob slowly. There was, indeed, a faint clicking as the dial advanced. How in the world would she be able to tell when a tumbler dropped? What did that even mean, anyway? The dial made a complete circuit, and she heard no distinguishing noises. Lifting her head, Ginger sighed. "I didn't hear anything out of the ordinary."

"Sometimes, you have to go round multiple times. Like three around to twenty-five or something."

"Then I shall keep on."

Beyond Merrow, Ben had turned and was watching her. He was still wrapped in a tight ball, and only one eye was visible. It stared, unblinking, at Ginger. Shivering a little, she closed her eyes and concentrated on the task at hand.

She did, finally, on the fourth revolution, hear a faint *tink* that differed from the rest, but her surprise made the dial jump and she had to start again.

How long she endeavoured to hear the minute differences, Ginger did not know. The room grew cooler, and the metal chilled to an almost intolerable cold.

"Stop," Ben whispered in her ear.

Ginger jumped, with a cry of alarm that sent a flush of embarrassment to warm her cheeks. She opened her eyes, and the sight did nothing to calm her.

Ben hovered directly in front of her with his head stuck inside the door of the safe.

"Benjamin Harford! What the devil are you doing?"

He pulled his head out, the features elongating as if they had been stuck in the metal before snapping back into their regular arrangement. His brows were drawn together in concentration. "Helping."

"You need to rest."

Ben shook his head, brows still compressed, and pointed at the safe. "I—I, I, I . . . watch."

"You watch?" What could he possibly see inside the safe? "Can you see the papers inside?"

He shook his head, digging his fingers into his scalp. "No. No! Watch, clock, dial . . . watch, watch . . . turn. Turn! You turn. I watch."

"You can . . . you can see the tumblers?" At her question, his whole aura illuminated with disproportionate pleasure. His brows relaxed from their scowl, and he beamed like a small child. Ginger swallowed, her throat tight, and nodded. "Well done. Let's try it, then, shall we?"

She took hold of the knob, not troubling to lay her head against the door, as Ben slid his face back into the safe. With her attention fixed on him, Ginger turned the knob slowly to the right, spinning it around the four revolutions and then slowing so that it clicked forward one number at a time.

Ben raised a hand. "Now."

She stopped, then began to turn the knob slowly in the other direction. After only one revolution, Ben raised his hand again. "Now."

It took only another quarter hour of inching progress, turning the wheel back and forth at Ben's direction, and then— even to Ginger's untrained hand—the final tumbler dropped with a clunk. "Ha! Take *that*, Mr. Sherlock Holmes."

She waited until Ben had pulled free of the safe and then twisted the handle to open the door. Merrow gave a gasp behind her. "You did it!"

"Thank heavens, yes." She peered into the safe. It was filled with papers. "I wonder if that's the secret to being a good sleuth. Keeping a ghost around for nefarious purposes."

"Watson." Ben patted his chest with a grin.

"More useful than that, my dear." Ginger pulled a stack of papers from the safe, handing them to Merrow as she reached in for more. Most appeared to be reports, but there was a German passport and some currency mixed in. Quite a lot of currency, actually. Most of it British pounds, which would be close to useless in France.

"Miss! His notebook!" Merrow held up Ben's notebook.

"Oh, thank heavens." Ginger turned from the empty safe and set the papers she was holding on the floor. "May I see it, so Ben can look?"

The familiar black notebook was in better shape than it had any right to be, considering that it had been in an explosion. No blood and very little soot stained it. She flipped through the pages, with Ben leaning over her shoulder. Merrow rested one hand on her arm so he could hear them both.

Pages had been torn out of the notebook. She fingered one of the torn edges. "Did you do that?"

"No." Ben frowned. "I think."

Which was the challenge, of course. At this point, just because he didn't remember doing something didn't mean that he had not done it. Still, this stood as the best chance of jogging his memory. She turned the pages forward and found strings of letters—completely random letters.

"Do you recognise your code?" She glanced over her shoulder at him.

He smoothed his mustache, frowning at the page. "Notes."

"Can you read it?" If he had been making notes to himself in code, it would surely be worth knowing the subject.

"I wrote it."

Which was not at all the same thing as being able to read it. Ginger gnawed on her lip, trying to remember what he'd told her about codes.

Merrow asked the question before she could. "Maybe—if you remember what the code was—we could translate it for you?"

"Brutus." Ben squeezed his eyes shut and a veil of violet concentration shrouded his features. "Not Brutus—"

"Caesar? A Caesar cipher, sir?" Merrow nodded, relief and triumph blossoming in his aura, followed by confusion. "Caesar's the easiest to crack. I'm surprised you used it."

"Baker's tale."

Ginger turned to look at him, letting Merrow take the book. "Pardon?"

"Baker's tale. No—Baker's wife. The knight, the canter, the . . . Chaucer!"

He'd said it was a Caesar cipher, but perhaps he used more than one method to encrypt it. "It's a book code using *The Canterbury Tales?*"

Ben shook his head and pointed at the book. "Chaucer!"

"I'm sorry. I don't understand." Perhaps if she were not close to fainting with exhaustion, she might be able to follow him.

"Chaucer in the centre. It's. I was—in the centre. I was chaucering."

"You were chaucering?" She could make no sense of it. He'd studied the classics at university, with an eye toward historical texts—before the war, that was. She grasped at straws. "You were writing in Middle English?"

"Yes!" Ben shot to the ceiling and zoomed around the tiny room. "Yes, yes, yes!"

"Well . . . I'm not sure you needed to do anything more than that to encrypt it." Ginger put her hands on her hips and turned to Merrow. "I don't suppose you have Middle English among your tricks, do you?"

He shook his head, frowning over the text. "But there are three names . . . At least. Yes. See?" He held the book out and pointed to a short list.

NGXLUXJ

GDZKRR

YOTIRGOX

"And those are names? How in the world can you tell?" Ginger frowned over the text.

"I guessed, to be honest." He squinted at them and pointed at the first. "If this were Harford, then the next would be . . . Axtell."

Ginger shivered, but there was no real surprise there. "And the third?"

"Sinclair."

She shook her head. "I don't know him."

Merrow looked uneasy, glancing at Ben to see if he'd explain, but language still seemed far away from his grasp. Turning through the pages, Merrow said, "That's Ben's superior in London. I figure . . . I figure that's who the German spy was directing him to."

"And that would be why he didn't want to put this in plain text or in any reports." Ginger covered her face with her hands. Reginald, Ben's cousin, of whose guilt she could have no doubt. German on his mother's side, and with other reasons to wish his cousin might not return from the war.

It likely also explained why Axtell was investigating the Baker Street trench. He wasn't looking for foreign spies there; he was trying to find Ben's contact.

"So we—we should head to London, I guess."

"To London? Why? Axtell and Reg are here."

"Well . . . to warn the London branch of mediums. About the bombing. That's where the main branch is, right?"

"To—" She stopped and stared at Merrow. She had forgotten that she had lied to him. Only a small corps of people knew what happened in Potter's Field. "The bombing the German spy warned us about. Targeting the London Branch—that's a code name. The London Branch is here. It's the women working for the Spirit Corps in Le Havre."

Merrow swore, shock running through his aura. He cleared his throat. "I'm betting Captain Reginald didn't go to the front at all. Not if he thinks we're close to finding all this out." He looked from her to Ben. "I'll run word. As a soldier, I'll be able to travel faster than you. And the captain . . . he needs looking after."

Ginger hated to send Merrow alone, but he was right and she was, frankly, exhausted. "Thank you."

Merrow folded Ben's notebook and tucked it into his pocket. He started sorting through the rest of the papers. "Wish I'd thought to bring a bag."

Groaning a little, Ginger stood and walked to the door. "I'll see if I can find a pillowcase."

"There's a bedroom at the top of the . . ."

Ginger stopped. Merrow had heard her.

She hadn't been touching him, and he had heard her.

Heart pounding, Ginger stood in the doorway, praying that she was wrong. Merrow had said that he might get some hearing back. And she had seen the blood at his ears after the blast—but she knew how to fake that now. No—no. He had been locked in this room.

Or had he locked himself in? The door to the house had been unlocked.

Ginger shivered. She was simply overtired, and Ben's paranoia was creeping in.

She turned. Merrow was watching her, and any doubt dropped away at the sight of his aura. It was a mixture of spikes of alarm and the murky brown of someone regretting a mistake.

Ginger took a step back, reaching for the door. Merrow surged to his feet, scattering papers around him.

She broke into a sprint and raced for the stairs to the upper floor.

Footsteps pounded after her. With a roar, Ben spread out to

fill the cellar in a wall of red rage and wind. Loose boards and debris kicked up in a maelstrom, blinding Ginger for a moment. She stumbled.

Ginger landed hard on her knees, scraping her hands on the rough floor. Glancing over her shoulder, Ginger staggered back to her feet. Merrow was not five feet behind her, one arm raised against the onslaught of wood and paper that Ben hurled at him. The other hand held a loose coil of wire. A garrote.

He kept coming, pressing through as boards flew at him.

Ben would shred his remaining memories. His spirit was already dim and hazy amidst his tangible anger. Ginger had to stop Merrow while there was still something of Ben left. If she could lock him in the cellar again . . .

She snatched a board from the air and ran at Merrow, screaming at the top of her lungs. Sheer surprise carried her past his guard and into range to land a blow solidly on the side of his chest. He fell back a step.

Ginger swung again, but this time Merrow stepped to the side and dodged the board with ease. He reached past it to catch her wrist, twisting it hard. The board tumbled from her limp fingers.

With an inarticulate cry, Ben grabbed for Merrow, and his hands passed through him. The papers and wood dropped to the ground as he tried again and again to catch hold of the man. Disregarding him, Merrow pulled Ginger toward him, twisting her arm until it cracked.

Ginger dropped to her knees, half-blind with pain.

Leaning over her, the hard set of Merrow's jaw made his apparent youth a lie. He cuffed her with the back of his hand, knocking her head to the side. Ginger raised her free hand and tried to slap him, but came nowhere near his face.

Merrow hit her again, and the room went black.

Chapter Twenty-Two

★ ★ ★

Ginger is in the ocean, within the shelter of a canvas bathing machine. She hasn't seen one of those since she was a little girl. The waves are muted by the structure so there is only the barest tug at the pantaloons of her bathing costume. The ocean is cool, but a welcome relief from the summer heat. Thank heavens Ben suggested a trip to Brighton.

The stony shore is so refreshingly novel compared to the beach at home.

A shadow passes across the ceiling of the little box as a bird wheels overhead. Ginger closes her eyes and relaxes into the embrace of the ocean. It supports her, while the bathing costume pulls her down, encouraging her to sink into the waves.

"Oh." Ginger raised her head and turned to look around the canvas. "I'm dreaming. Ben?"

"Here." His shadow appeared on the outside of the canvas.

She sighed. It had been too much to hope that Ben would be restored *to lucidity just because it was a lucid dream. Still, she reached for the door to step out of the canvas.*

"*I wouldn't.*" *His silhouette bent its head, a bead of water dripping from his curls.* "*If I were you, I would stay put.*"

She pressed her hand against the canvas. "*Are you feeling better?*"

He shrugged, and she could hear the grin in his voice. "*Well . . . that's an interesting question, coming from a woman who has been knocked unconscious.*"

"*We are discussing you.*" *She stirred the water with one hand, anxious to be out of the canvas box.* "*Now. Your state is . . . ?*"

"*Fine.*"

"*Truly?*"

"*Another interesting question. Is my answer true, or simply what you want me to say?*" *The shadow-Ben laid a finger over his lips.* "*Sh. Don't answer, dearest. I couldn't bear to hear that you are happy to have a fiancé who parrots your thoughts.*"

"*Oh! You are such a tease.*" *She left aside the question of if he was still truly her fiancé since there was no possibility of marriage.* "*I am going to take that as proof that you are speaking your own mind.*"

"*As you wish.*"

Ginger narrowed her eyes at his shadow. "*To your original question . . . Merrow was pretending to be deaf. Why? It doesn't make any sense.*" *Certainly, his other injuries had been real enough, like the contusion on his forehead from the explosion.*

Or from being hit by someone's head while, say, strangling them.

"*I dunno. It made eavesdropping very easy, and it forced you to stay close to him.*"

"*Which brings me back wondering why. I mean, why go around with me?*"

"*Well . . .*" *Ben tilted his head, considering the question.* "*According to the message from my German contact, they were trying to figure out how the Spirit Corps worked. You'd be a logical person to go to for that.*"

"Are we certain that's what they are after? Merrow translated that message and the list of suspects, which means he could have lied about either or both."

Ben turned so his fine patrician nose showed in profile and stroked his mustache. "My guess is that he only altered parts of it. He wouldn't want to risk screwing up a confirmation passphrase."

"A what?"

"Like the salutation we used in our letters. My dear . . . *meant I was safe. Or, at least, thought I was."*

"So, we are once again in a position of needing to get our hands on your notebook."

He laid a hand against the canvas and drew a circle. The moisture from his finger glowed in a translucent trail upon the fabric. "First step: you'll need to wake up."

★ ★ ★

The transition between sleep and waking was difficult to define. Ginger still had the sensation of swaying in the ocean, but without the warmth. Turning her head, she looked for Ben's shadow, but her entire vision was filled with shadow.

The pain in her head was the only thing that gave her any certainty that she was awake. She stared up and slowly gathered her senses about her. At the moment, she was not in the ocean, but lying in the dark on a hard floor.

Ginger shifted and winced as a rope dug into her wrists. "Lovely."

Ben crouched next to her. Oddly, she could see him via the spirit plane while her own form was invisible. His brows were drawn together in concern. "Awake?"

"Barely." Ginger flexed her legs, and a hard coil of rope at her ankles told her she was bound there as well. "I wonder why he didn't just kill me. Not that I'm complaining."

"Fabergé." Ben made a low growl and tapped her forehead, his finger leaving a chill. "Fabergé—egg."

"Are you saying I'm expensive and gaudy? Hm. I shall choose instead to think you mean that I'm smart and contain a wealth within."

"Yes." The relief in his voice concealed a sob.

"I'll make a note that you think so." She pressed an elbow into the floor and struggled to sit up with her hands bound. The sense of being in the ocean returned, and she had to stop, buffeted by a tide of her own pulse in her head. "I don't suppose there's a blade of any sort in here, is there?"

"He is too great a niggard that will werne a man to light a candle at his lantern; He shall have never the less light, pardie."

She squeezed her eyes shut, thinking. "Is that a random use of Middle English, or are you suggesting that there is a candle that I might light?"

"There is a candle that you might light."

As much of a relief as it was to hear Ben reply in a full sentence, Ginger was painfully aware that he had only parroted words. It didn't matter. His soul was still Ben's, even if he had to borrow language to communicate. "I presume there are matches too, or you would not be so cruel as to mention the hope of light."

"Yes."

"Well, then. Lead on. I can see you, even if I can see nothing else in this dismal room." She inched after Ben's glowing figure, again grateful that she wore trousers. Ginger had to assume that she was still in the cellar where they had found Merrow. In hindsight, it seemed clear that Merrow had broken into the building rather than being held here against his will. It would explain why the exterior door was unlocked. Had he locked the cellar door when he heard Ginger upstairs?

Ben stood and rested his hands on . . . something. For all the glow he emitted in her second sight, he illuminated nothing in the physical world.

Gritting her teeth, Ginger sat up on her haunches and reached out. A rough wood beam met her hands. A table leg, she thought. Ginger followed it up and fumbled over the surface with her bound hands until she found a smooth, waxy cylinder embedded in the middle of Ben's icy hands. "Candle achieved. Now . . . matches?"

With a wink, Ben moved his hands only a little farther away. She put her own hands into his and felt the box between his fingers. With a sigh of relief, Ginger sank back to sit on the ground. It took a few tries before she found the best way to hold her collection.

She bit the candle, gripped the matchbox between her knees, and struck the match with her bound hands. When the match flared to life, Ginger nearly dropped the candle with relief at the light. Hands shaking and eyes crossed, she managed to bring the match to the wick.

With the light, Ben was dimmer, but still present. The room itself was in disarray, as if a windstorm had blown through it. Ginger pulled the candle from her mouth and said, "I shall have to call you Tempest from now on, I think."

"I'll show thee every fertile inch o' th' island; And I will kiss thy foot: I prithee, be my god."

"Flattery. Although . . . if you are able to quote Shakespeare at me, could you try for something more useful?" The room still spun alarmingly, and the candle seemed to have two flames. Concussion, clearly, which was not even remotely surprising considering how hard Merrow had hit her. Tears pricked unexpectedly at her eyes. God. Merrow. She had liked him. Ginger shook her head to try to clear it. "No sharp implements? Mirrors or vases to break?"

"Alas."

Tipping the candle on its side, she let wax dribble onto the floor, then secured the candle in the pool of wax. With gritted teeth, Ginger held her wrists over the flame and began to burn her way through her bonds.

★ ★ ★

Ginger slowed to a stop in the street, leaning against an unlit streetlamp. Ben kept reaching out, as if he could touch her. Each phantom brush of his hand sent chills along her arms and back.

"You're hurt."

"Not anything life threatening." She smiled at him. "I would lie to you, but you're reading my aura, aren't you?"

"Yes." He ran his hands through his hair and paced around her, the folds of his uniform wafting out from his body like shreds of silk.

"Turnabout is fair play, I suppose." Keeping her voice jaunty took almost as much effort as simply standing. She rested her forehead against the lamppost. Thank heavens the lamps were not lit at night, to make targeting the city more difficult, or she would certainly have called attention to herself by now. A woman alone at night under a streetlamp, dressed in trousers . . . she did not want to have that conversation with anyone.

She needed to get to Le Havre, and walking would take too long. Who could she trust here? "Ben? Is there anyone in Amiens who you trust?"

"Not sure." He tugged at his hair as he circled her.

"The chauffeuse at the hospital near Amiens would give us a ride, but it will take nearly as long to walk there then drive to Le Havre as just to walk." She pushed away from the lamppost and headed for the train station for want of a better direction. "Maybe there will be a night train." But that would more likely run from Le Havre to the front than the other way around.

"Truck." Ben lit up and beckoned her forward. "Truck driver."

Truck driver? She didn't know a truck driv—yes. Yes, she did. Mrs. Richardson's friend Cpl. Patel drove a truck and was stationed here. "You are brilliant, my dear."

"Stupid." He tapped his head.

"Well . . . you have been a wittier conversationalist, but the content of your ideas is not suffering. And it's easier to get a word in edgewise now."

He snorted but smiled. God. His smile, all lopsided and dimpled, would break her when it was gone. He led the way down the lane, and Ginger followed.

★ ★ ★

The Indian Army brigades did not rank proper billets, but were housed in tents not far outside of town. Ginger paused outside the one that Ben had guided her to, acutely aware that calling on a man in the middle of the night was beyond improper. Of course, the whole bloody war was beyond improper, and she was wearing trousers, so it probably couldn't get much worse.

Unless he slept in the nude. Ginger closed her eyes. Please, God, do not let him sleep in the nude.

Ginger parted the tent flap and crept inside. "Cpl. Patel?"

He woke with a jolt, sitting up in bed. "Who is there?"

"It is Mrs. Richardson's friend. Miss Stuyvesant."

"Oh my goodness! Go outside! Go outside at once. It is not proper for you to be in here. I am a married man." He scrambled at his bedside and grabbed a bundle of cloth. "I will be out in only a moment. Please."

"Of course." Ginger ducked back out into the night and rubbed the ache in her temples.

Ben paced around her, sometimes jumping several strides ahead. He straightened, looking back at the tent, and Cpl. Patel emerged. He wore his uniform and was tucking the end of his turban into place.

"I am so sorry to bother you."

He waved a hand to stop her. "No bother. No bother at all. I was only alarmed—and, good heavens, what my wife would say if she knew." He shuddered. "An excellent woman. Excellent. But I do not want to give her any cause to doubt me while I am away."

"But she—"

"Wouldn't know? But of course she would, because I will have to tell her what happens tonight. I would not lie to her. Not for all the world. And there is an emergency, yes? That is why you have come?"

"I—yes." Ginger wet her lips and faced the first person she would have to tell about Mrs. Richardson. "I am afraid that Mrs. Richardson is dead."

"Oh . . . oh, I am very sorry to hear that." He touched the muffler that was wrapped around his neck. "You have my sincere condolences."

"Thank you. But that is not the emergency. I believe that someone is going to try to bomb a facility in Le Havre, and I need to get there quickly. Can you drive me?"

Cpl. Patel grew very still and studied her for a moment. He tilted his head to the side, eyes narrowing. "That man. The one on the road? Johnson. That is why you cannot go to an official?"

She nodded, grateful for his perception. "Exactly."

Dusting his hands together, Patel nodded. "Then. We drive."

"Thank you."

"It is no trouble." He beckoned her to follow him along the path between the neat lines of tents toward a row of vehicles that stood silhouetted against the predawn light. "It is no trouble at all."

"I am afraid that it is." Ginger pressed her fingers against the headache behind her right eye. "Dragging you out of bed to drive to Le Havre . . . you have my sincerest thanks."

He smiled, his lips compressed under his heavy black mustache. Tapping his forefinger alongside his nose, Cpl. Patel glanced briefly toward his truck. His finger tapped again, and he squinted. His aura spoke of an internal struggle between the yellow-green of caution and the bright yellow of need. With a nod, as if to himself, Cpl. Patel inhaled and spoke. "About the trip to Le Havre . . . I would like to set you down outside the city. With apologies—deepest apologies—for not taking you all the way in."

"Oh. Of course." She had no right to ask him for anything, and was grateful for what he could offer.

Ben murmured, "Safer . . ."

Cpl. Patel nodded. "Exactly so. It is safer."

Ginger jumped in her tracks, coming to a stop on the wooden duckboards. "Pardon me?"

"The ghost you are travelling with . . ." He gave a little shrug. "I did not see him—I assume he was with you the other day on the road—but I did not see him. Tonight? Still half in sleep? I was between worlds, and he is . . . he is very present. Very present indeed."

"You are . . . you are a medium?"

"I would use a different word, but as the English describe it—yes." He gave another shrug, still not meeting her gaze. "My wife and I, we . . . I miss her very much. It is why my mind was in a position to notice your ghost."

Lucid dreaming. He could mean nothing else. Ginger tried to meet Ben's gaze, but he was staring at Cpl. Patel with a hungry green mantle of envy cloaking him. As so often happened with auras, Ginger could see the emotion, but not understand the reason behind it. Knowing that Cpl. Patel could see and hear Ben kept her from asking him what was troubling him.

"Well . . . to return to the original topic, setting me down outside town is perfectly fine."

"Thank you." He inhaled, straightening his shoulders and tucking his chin down, as if preparing for a fight. "And now, I need to ask you for a favour—understanding that it may not be within your power."

"If I can grant it—"

"Wait—" Patel held up a single finger. "Make no promises until you know the request."

"All right."

He fumbled at the collar of his uniform and pulled out the identity tags that every soldier wore. "I want the third tag for the Indian Army."

Ginger froze, utterly unprepared for this request. "I beg your pardon?"

He rattled the discs, looking directly at her, and she had no doubt that he was looking at her aura. "We have only two. British men have three. We are not trained to 'report in.' British men—*white* British men are. It is not so difficult to imagine the connection."

She prayed to God that it was far more difficult than that to imagine the connection. The number of people who understood what the third disc on British ID tags did was numbered no more than twelve. Every soldier had the black disc, which stayed with their body after death. The red disc—that was pulled from the bodies of corpses on the battlefield for the death records.

The blue disc . . . it was pulled from the necks of soldiers who were injured and would not return to the battlefield. Ostensibly, it was part of tracking the medical records. In fact, it was the key that bound British soldiers to the nexus at Potter's Field. The real reason for removing it from wounded soldiers was so that they did not report in if they died in the hospital with nothing useful to say.

"I think it was a mistake to not issue them to the Indian Army."

He snorted. "Because it gives the game away. Not because you think we have anything of value to add to the reports."

"Both." Ginger wiped her hands across her face, shivering. "I will make the recommendation to my superior, but I can offer no assurances beyond that."

He broke into a sudden grin. "Considering that I thought you would lie to me—I will take it. And thank you for trusting me."

"I am not certain I have much choice, since you could expose me with a single shout."

Cpl. Patel blanched. "Oh my goodness. I did not think of that. I beg your pardon. Most sincerely, I beg your pardon. I should have waited until we were not—"

"Please—" Ginger reached across the gap between them and rested her hand on his arm for a moment. "You are correct, and have nothing to apologize for."

"Thank you."

Ginger nodded and stared out at the path in front of them, looking through Ben to the truck that would carry her to Le Havre. "Tell me about your wife as we go?"

Cpl. Patel glowed with a rosy mist of adoration and pulled a set of keys from his pocket. "Her name is Arundhathi, and she is a most excellent woman."

Chapter Twenty-Three

★ ★ ★

Ginger leaned against the wall behind a rosebush overlooking the street that led to the Spirit Corps warehouse, waiting for Ben. It seemed that she had spent most of her time over the past days waiting for Ben, but without his ability to scout ahead, she would probably be in the clutches of Merrow or Reg or Axtell or . . . She clenched her teeth. She was no longer certain who the enemy was, only that there was one. More than one.

Rubbing the bridge of her nose did little to relieve the headache that had taken up residence there. She hoped, very much, that Cpl. Patel had made it safely back to his camp after dropping her off. Just as fervently, she hoped that his unique position as a driver who was a medium also made his guess about the blue ID discs unique.

Morning sun slanted down the street, cutting black shadows

with golden light. Ben wafted down the street and passed directly through the rosebush to stand by her with the branches sticking through his body. A bloodred blossom emerged from his neck like a boil. His jaw was set and firm.

Ben pointed down the street toward the train station. Images of him stuttered around the bush, moving toward the wall surrounding the warehouse that housed Potter's Field, before evaporating back into himself. "Merrow."

"Damn it." Ginger squinted down the street, but didn't see the man. She gnawed on her lower lip, thinking. "Is he alone?"

"Yes." Ben grabbed at a rose branch as if he could snap it off. Great red wings of anger snapped behind him and then curled tightly around him.

Closing her eyes, Ginger tried to run through all the possible choices in front of her, but she was so fatigued that only one seemed viable. "Change of plans. Since we know he's here, I'm going to go to Brigadier-General Davies."

"No!"

"Yes." Ginger pushed herself away from the wall. "Davies can't be the traitor, because if he were, they would already know where the Spirit Corps is. He might arrest me before he lets me talk, but at least that will put him on alert."

"Ginger . . ."

"I know, I know. You think it is not safe." She straightened her jacket, wishing she were in her Spirit Corps uniform for this purpose. "But *nothing* is safe, so that provides little reason not to proceed."

The space between Ginger's shoulder blades itched as she stepped out from behind the rosebush. She shoved her hands deep in the pockets of her jacket as she walked toward the main street. Every part of her soul screamed at her to run, but running would draw attention.

"Hide." Ben zoomed past her, grabbing for her arm as if he could hurry her along.

Behind Ginger, a bottle rattled on the pavement. She murmured, "Is he . . . ?"

"Yes."

The itch between her shoulders grew until she shuddered. Merrow wouldn't shoot her, because that would draw attention.

Attention—Ginger had planned to head away from the gates to Potter's Field, because Merrow was there. But so were the guards. Merrow had been hiding from them, so that meant they weren't on his side. She hoped. Abruptly, Ginger turned around and ran screaming toward the main gate of Potter's Field.

Toward a distinguished British officer.

He had white hair, a hoary mustache, and a brace of medals on his uniform. This was who had been behind her?

The man's eyes widened, and his stance settled, in a movement at once strange and familiar. She had seen Merrow do that on a train.

God—this *was* Merrow, but he somehow appeared two inches taller and broader through the shoulders. And with pale hair.

Ginger screamed louder. Her throat and soul tore with her screams.

The MPs came running out of the gatehouse and aimed their weapons at her. Too late, Ginger realized what this looked like. She was dressed like a French farmer. Merrow was dressed like a British officer, and she was charging him.

Ginger pulled to a halt and yanked her hat off, tossing it aside. Please, God, let Lt. Plumber have been right that she was unmistakably a woman, even in men's clothing. "Please! Help me. This man is—"

"Oh, for God's sake." Merrow grabbed her, and Ginger gasped

as his hand closed around her injured wrist, pressing into the blisters there. He twisted her arm behind her. When he spoke, his voice was hauntingly familiar, but not as Merrow's. He sounded like the officer who had drowned Capt. Norris in the baths. He sounded like an aristocrat, bored and utterly in charge. "A word of caution, gentlemen. Do not flirt with Americans: they'll try their best to entrap you."

"Bloody Americans." One of the gate guards spat on the ground.

"It's my own damn fault. The henna should have been a clue to her desperation."

"Henna?!" Ginger tried to stomp on his foot, but he dodged nimbly. "This man is a traitor and—"

He twisted her wrist again, and her vision went white with pain. "Really . . . that fiction did not work any of the other times you tried it. Do you think these gentlemen are more foolish?"

"She been giving you trouble? Want us to take her along to the MPs?"

"No . . . no, thank you. You have a gate to guard." Merrow sighed with upper-class resignation. "And I do not want my own indiscretion to inconvenience anyone but me."

"What're you going to do with her?"

"I'll walk her down to the hospitality hut where I met her and turn her over to the matron there." Merrow turned Ginger as easily as if she were a puppet, so she faced away from the gate to Potter's Field. "Wish me luck that they actually send her back to America this time."

Ginger tried to struggle free, but his grip on her gave no room for leverage. With her hand twisted up behind her back, she had to move forward to keep from falling. Though perhaps falling in the street would be preferable to wherever he was taking her.

Ben reached for Merrow and jerked his hands back with a

hiss of pain. He issued a string of curses, which demonstrated that his language had not been impaired on that front.

Behind her, Merrow made a grunt of satisfaction.

"What did you do to him?"

Merrow didn't answer her, just continued marching her down the street. Ben circled them, balling his hands with rage. Red swirled around him as if the very air were boiling. "Salt. Clothes—"

"Salt? How did you introduce it to clothing?" She waited for Merrow to answer. When he didn't, she continued on, hoping she could provoke some sort of response. "Bathing it in a solution of salt water would work, I suppose. I wonder at the ratio. Is it scratchy and uncomfortable? I do so hope it is."

He turned Ginger abruptly, and she stumbled. His grip on her arm kept her from falling, but it left her nearly blind with pain, as something in her wrist snapped. When her vision cleared, they were back in the alley that ran down one side of Potter's Field. It had been used, at one point, to load materials into the warehouse and still had the remnants of boxes littering the cobbled surface.

He stopped and sighed. "Did the captain untie you?"

Even if she *had* possessed the breath to speak, she was not going to answer his questions, by God.

Merrow sighed again. "That isn't a state secret. Did he untie you?" When Ginger remained silent, he put a hand on her shoulder and forced her to her knees. "Captain, please tell Miss Stuyvesant the rules when facing interrogation. She won't believe it from me."

Ginger swallowed and cursed internally when her voice shook. "So you are going to interrogate me now, instead of spending days pretending to be a friend? Why? Why are you betraying your country?"

"Betraying my—" He gave an ugly laugh. "I have to ask, what did you think Capt. Harford was doing, when he was behind German lines? Making friends? Being loyal to Germany?"

She had no answer for that. Darkness swam in front of Ginger's vision. For a moment she thought she was going to faint, and then she realized it was the leading edge of Ben's aura. He drifted in front of her, radiating fear. "Answer anything not critical."

"Well, won't he just know what's critical then?" She turned her head as far as she could toward Merrow. "Fine. No. He did not untie me."

"Damn."

"Why damn?"

"Because I was looking for a reason not to kill you. And if you had that much control over the ghost, that would be useful technique to extract." He sighed again. "Please believe that I have been trying very hard not to place us both in a position where that was necessary."

"That is hardly a comfort."

"No. I suppose it isn't."

"Why now?" She searched the ground, looking for something to use as a weapon. There was a board just in front of her, but not quite in reach. When Merrow was silent, she looked over her shoulder. "You don't want me to go to my grave wondering. Unless you want me to haunt you."

Ben reached over her, passing his fist into Merrow's head. "Two ghosts."

The man shivered and then gave a shrug. "Because at the moment, you are the only person who knows I'm a spy."

"Ah, but I'm not." Ginger wet her lips and looked forward again.

"You are. If you had told anyone, then you wouldn't be alone."

Cloth rustled behind her. "At least you'll get to be with the captain again."

Merrow let go of her wrist. Ginger lunged for the wood and was yanked to a halt. A tight line ran around her throat.

Ginger could not breathe. She clawed at the wire. Struggling to rise, she could not draw a breath to scream. Ben screamed for her, and the spirit plane shuddered with the waves of blue-black anguish that rolled out from him.

Ginger gripped Merrow's wrists and the rough braid of a British officer. She dug her nails into his flesh, trying to peel his hands away. She could not breathe. Could not breathe—

Metal clanged against brick.

Above her, a meaty thud, and then Merrow grunted. The pressure at her throat slackened. Ginger dropped forward, rolling onto her back.

Lt. Plumber balanced over her and brought his crutch around for another blow. Merrow caught it, blocking the blow as he kicked the lieutenant's remaining leg out from under him.

Mr. Haden appeared from somewhere and stabbed a knitting needle deep into Merrow's back. Face blanching, Merrow dropped to his knees. Lt. Plumber swung his other crutch up from the ground and caught Merrow in the jaw. He fell forward, still somehow catching himself on his hands. As he struggled to get his legs back under him, Mr. Haden jabbed another needle into his thigh.

Edna ran forward, her skirt flapping, and kicked Merrow onto the ground. In moments, she had his hands and feet trussed together as if he were a sheep.

Ginger pushed herself up as Joanne and Helen caught her. She looked up at her circle in bewilderment. "How—"

Mr. Haden leaned down to help Lt. Plumber up. "I had a visitor from beyond the grave. . . ." He pulled another pair of knitting needles from his pocket, his aura dark with grief. "This bastard thought he could get away with strangling Mrs. Richardson. Set off a shell in the bunker to cover his tracks, but she reported in. To me."

"So we've been watching for you." Helen stood with her hands on her hips. "That scream of yours made quite the ripple in the spirit realm. Good thing too."

Ginger stared at Merrow, her stomach turning. Mrs. Richardson. Strangled? She had wanted to be wrong. Ginger turned to Ben for reassurance. Where was he?

The air in the alley was warm and still.

The auras of the mortals glowed in a mix of angry reds, triumphant golds, and the deep violet of grief. But Ben . . . God. She pressed her hand to her mouth. His unfinished business had been finding the traitor.

He couldn't be gone already.

Ginger's gaze dropped to Merrow again, bound in the middle of the alley. She had so very much wanted to be wrong. She had wanted to be simply tired and confused and paranoid. Ben and Mrs. Richardson and . . .

"Why Mrs. Richardson?" Her voice cracked. "Why not me?"

Merrow closed his eyes, face blank. His aura crept with grey-brown resignation, but the ever-present fear had vanished.

Lt. Plumber prodded him with his crutch. "The lady asked you a question."

With his eyes closed, lying down, Merrow looked even younger than before, like a teenager taking a nap. If that teenager were bound and bloody. The knitting needle in his back shifted with each breath. Red rimmed the cloth around it in a widening circle.

Ginger wet her lips and turned to Mr. Haden. "Did Mrs. Richardson say anything else?"

"Aye. That she did. She—"

"Wait." Helen held up her hand. "Best not to let this one know what we know."

Lt. Plumber nodded. "I can help with interrogating him." He ground the tip of his crutch into the earth. "Be a pleasure, in fact."

"I think we'd all be glad to help with that," Joanne said, cracking her knuckles.

Edna simply stooped and lifted Merrow off the ground. She grunted as she heaved him over her shoulder like a sack of grain. "Where do I take him?"

Helen eyed the warehouse that housed Potter's Field. "Well . . . it seems to me that since he wanted to see the inside so much, maybe we ought to let him. It's not as if he'll be able to tell the Huns about it now." Tapping her finger on her lower lip, Helen turned back to Ginger. "How stable are you?"

"Fine." It had been so long since she had truly been well that it did not even feel like a lie.

Snorting, Helen shook her head. "I don't know why I expected you to tell me the truth."

"I mean, tired, obviously, but well enough. All things considered . . ."

"And Capt. Harford?"

Ginger looked around them again at the quiet, warm alley. She tried and failed to smile. "I—we know who killed him, now." That question had been all that had kept him there.

"Ah . . ." Helen's aura dripped grief across the space between them. "I am sorry—and not, all at the same time."

"Me too." Ginger wiped her eyes with the back of her hand. She had thought she would be able to say good-bye. "It had become . . . difficult, at the end. Why did you ask me about my stability?"

Helen gestured toward Potter's Field. "We've made some changes."

"Thank heavens. I wasn't sure if you got my message."

"We did." Helen cocked her head. "Did you get ours?"

"Yours . . . ?"

"We didn't know where you were, so we tried lucid dreaming at you." She jerked a thumb toward Merrow. "About that one."

"Oh." She had thought that was just a nightmare. "Almost. What sort of changes?"

Helen eyed Merrow and grimaced. Crossing to Ginger, she crouched down and whispered to her. "The Germans have been attacking hospitals and men at rest. We've been flooded with useless reports, so . . . we made a holding area. On the grounds."

Now her question about Ginger's stability made sense. Walking through a ghost was difficult for a medium under the best of circumstances. Walking through a courtyard thick with them? It would be hellish. "Ah . . . well. I'm fine. Really."

Snapping her fingers, Helen scowled at her. "You are lying."

"And you've done your best to warn me, so consider any consequences on my head." She tried to stand, wincing as she put weight on her wrist. "We can't wait around coddling my delicate sensibilities."

"Now you sound like a Jane Austen novel." Helen straightened, offering a hand.

Clasping it with her good hand, Ginger felt a wave of warm comfort flow between them. The tangible sympathy made her eyes burn with tears. She tightened her lips and let Helen help her off the ground. Mr. Haden joined them, offering Ginger his arm. She followed their small procession to the iron gate set in the wall that surrounded the warehouse grounds.

Joanne pointed down as she entered the gate. "Careful there."

A line of salt sparkled in the morning sun and followed the path of the wall all the way around the grounds.

Ginger leaned on Mr. Haden as she stepped across, careful not to disturb the grains. The temperature plummeted from July to November. Souls pressed against her from every side.

She is lying in bed, smiling at the nurse who brought the evening meal. If she had both her legs, she would flirt, but that is utterly pointless. Something crackles. A light flares—

She is shaking the dice in her hands, laughing at Branson. He has had terrible luck with the dice all night, and wonders if someone might want the ratty kidney belt his aunt made him. Something crackles. A light flares—

She is cold. It seems that she can never get warm in these damn tents. And stupid Cody won't stop snoring. She reaches for her shoe to pitch at him. Outside the tent, something crackles. A light—

"Ginger!"

Of all the voices in the world, that one could cut through a crowd and find her. Ginger raised her head, shaking. Mr. Haden had his arm around her waist, supporting most of her weight. Turning back to the gate, she saw a bare shimmer of grey beyond the iron.

It was only a shadow, even in the spirit realm, but the shape of Ben's soul was still unmistakable. He pressed against the barrier. And he was trapped on the other side of the salt.

"Ben?"

Ginger stretched her soul out of her body, reaching for the shadow of Ben's voice. The souls around her buffeted Ginger in a maelstrom of death and pain. The weight of her mortal form dropped away.

Wordless, Ben shrieked, and Ginger left her body lying on the ground.

Chapter Twenty-four

★ ★ ★

From the spirit plane, most of the mortal world seemed grey and uninteresting. The line of salt, however, made a shimmering translucent dome over the entire grounds of the Spirit Corps. Ginger slipped through the souls of soldiers to the barrier. She could just make out Ben on the other side.

If Ben was still here, did that mean that Merrow wasn't the traitor? Or . . . he'd said that the traitor wasn't working alone.

Crouching, she tried to move the salt so he could come in. Her fingers burned and slid off the surface as if it were hot glass. Well . . . if that was what it felt like, no wonder Merrow's modification to his uniform had been effective. Damn him.

"What are you doing?" A soldier stood next to her in the spirit realm. More than one, actually. She seemed to have attracted a bit of notice, as the sole woman among these spirits.

Standing, Ginger shook her head. "Nothing effective. My fiancé is on the other side of this. . . ."

The man squinted at the wall. "He's dead."

"Yes."

"But you aren't."

"Not . . . no. I suppose I'm not." She glanced back at where her body lay sprawled on the ground. Lt. Plumber was compressing her chest. Ginger had probably stopped breathing again. The rest of the circle had linked to each other and were concentrating on her.

They had left Merrow tied on the ground. Without the weight of her physical form blocking the view, his aura stood out with a stark clarity. The fear that had been so present the entire time she had known him was gone. In hindsight, it was easy to see that he had been scared he would be caught. A dull resignation and resistance had replaced it.

Now that he *was* caught . . . well. She would have to see if she could give him something new to be afraid of. Ginger turned to the ghosts surrounding her. "Do you see that man on the ground? He's a traitor."

"Is that so?" The edges of the soldier's spirit hardened into knives.

"He killed my fiancé and tried to kill me." She turned back to the wall of salt. A hazy shadow of Ben paced outside it.

"Bastard. Oh—sorry, miss."

Ginger held up her hand—or rather, the memory of her hand. "Please. I have heard far worse." He looked unconvinced. "Damn far worse."

The soldier broke out into a grin, and the apricot haze of amusement spread among his fellows. Ginger eyed the salt wall again and turned back to Merrow.

She slid through the soldiers to crouch next to Merrow and ran her finger across his throat. "You can hear me, can't you?"

He shuddered.

Lt. Plumber was sitting up, his head hanging. Edna patted him on his back, saying something to him. Helen was standing, her aura spread out in great steel blue wings laced with bloodred fury. Ginger's body seemed to be breathing again, which was something.

"All that time, pretending not to be a sensitive." Ginger laid her hands upon his neck, and her fingers sank into his flesh. "Was that something you had to learn to do in Germany? They burn witches there, right?"

His breathing got faster, and he closed his eyes.

"So, I'm betting you've had no training. No one to teach you how to guard your mind from unwanted brushes with other souls. Have you ever felt another man's death?" Ginger looked up at the soldiers surrounding her. "Gentlemen . . . may I show you how to haunt a man?"

One of the soldiers chuckled. "I bet you've haunted plenty of—ow."

"Shut it," another replied.

"Thought I couldn't feel pain once I was dead."

The memory of Ben jerking his hands away from Merrow bled into the group. "Oh, you can still feel pain. And you can inflict it too."

"Crikey."

Ginger bent her head and whispered into Merrow's ear. "Just wait until you go to sleep. There are thousands of soldiers here, and we will haunt you. The ghosts of all those whose deaths you are responsible for will visit you every time you shut your eyes. Every time you open your eyes. For every moment that you live. I have no reason to wish for mercy for you, and very, very unfinished business."

★ ★ ★

Ginger lost time waiting for Merrow to fall asleep. They put him in a closet with a guard outside, and the sun was shining. Then it was dark. Intellectually, Ginger was aware that it was a very bad sign that she had lost the sense of time passing. If she wanted to return to her body, that is, which was becoming increasingly unimportant.

She drifted through the door and settled down next to Merrow.

Ben had said that he'd entered her dreams. It hadn't occurred to her to ask him how he did that. With regular lucid dreaming, you fell asleep, reaching for the other person. She supposed . . .

Ginger reached out a tendril of her soul and pressed it into Merrow's head, reaching for him.

She is in a small hut, but not quite there, not really. She is watching Merrow, who is sitting at the table, picking his name into the wood with a knife. A woman stands at the sink, washing dishes. The sound makes her turn.

"What are you doing?!"

Merrow jumps, and the knife slices through his finger.

Ginger snorted in satisfaction. He turned and stared at her, eyes widening. "What are you doing here?"

"I told you I would come to haunt you." Ginger walked closer to him, past the rows of beds in the field hospital. Outside, the crack of guns was constant. The men in the beds watched them, all with identical knitting needles jutting from their eyes.

Merrow backed away. His finger was still bleeding, and the blood ran up his arm to soak his sleeve. "This is a dream."

"Yes. How does that make it better?"

He turned, looking for the exit, but the canvas walls stretched away from Ginger in all directions. Row after row of beds surrounded them. "You can't hurt me in a dream."

"I can make you remember." Ginger put her hand on the back of his neck and gave him the memory of Capt. Norris's death.

A man in British Army uniform is on him. Has him by the shoulders and pushes him down under the water. He thrashes, trying to get free, but in the big tub, there is no leverage, and he is still too drunk to be coordinated. Dammit. He didn't survive the shelling to die like this. His lungs burn, and he coughs, sucking in water.

Merrow twisted in her grasp, but Ginger held on and leaned closer. "Every night. I have thousands of memories of death." She pressed him into the memory of Ben's death.

His throat burns. He can't breathe. Why can't he breathe? The burning darkens into pain, and he claws at his throat. A garrote.

He tugs at the hands holding the piece of wire around his neck and staggers, trying to throw the man off. They stumble together, and, for a moment, in the window of the cabin, there's a distorted reflection.

A man with light hair and a British uniform. It is himself.

He can't breathe. He can't breathe. He is on his knees. He can't stop strangling himself. Breathe. He can't. He—

Merrow screamed. Ginger flew out of his body. He was still screaming, awake and screaming, and his aura was dark with fear.

"Stop! Stop—for the love of God! Stop. I'll talk." He pushed back into the corner, staring at where Ginger floated in the closet. "I was assigned to find out how the ghosts worked, because we've been trying to re-create it with no success. It seemed easy at first, getting placed as Capt. Harford's batman, but he was so careful, and all I knew was that there was conditioning, but not how it worked, even though I was put through it. I remember being given tea—we even managed to steal some tea, but it was just chamomile and lavender—and I remember the lessons about how to report in and what to notice, but I couldn't get any more than that, and I kept getting shut out of the meetings, and he always wrote his notes in code—God. Middle English. No wonder I couldn't crack it."

He was trying to deflect the conversation. Ginger drifted closer. "So why did you kill him? You did kill him, didn't you?"

"Yes." Merrow clutched both sides of his head. "I had to."

"You had to." If she could render him unconscious and make him live that death again and again, she would. "Why?"

"We needed him."

"Come now. If you want to sleep peacefully ever again, I need specifics. Who is *we*, and why did you need Ben?"

"We is—we are Thackeray, Johnson, Vale, Williams, and Schmitt."

Interesting that Reginald and Axtell were not on the list. Thackeray . . . that had been the head of the prison camp. Johnson and Vale were two of Reg's flunkies. Williams she didn't know. Schmitt—the German medium. "So I take it Schmitt's defection was a sham."

He nodded. "He doesn't speak English, but he needed to be on this side of the line. He thought we could bomb the camp so that the massive amount of concentrated and simultaneous deaths would clog the mediums and act like a banner to try to locate the Spirit Corps."

"And Ben?"

Merrow sighed, and his soul was grey-brown with resignation. "Schmitt needed a soldier who consciously knew where the Spirit Corps was located as a . . . a sort of homing pigeon. So I—I strangled Captain Harford. Schmitt isolated his soul and tried to follow it, but . . . it didn't work."

That explained why Ben had been killed before the explosion, but didn't show up until after the wave of other soldiers came in. It also explained why Ben had deteriorated so quickly. Maybe . . . maybe it was possible to put him back together again. "In what way didn't it work?"

"When they released his soul from isolation, it—it vanished, just like all the other souls. The beacon didn't work, and we don't know why. We . . . we need to know how the souls are conditioned, which Capt. Harford didn't know."

Ginger straightened in understanding. There were, perhaps, a dozen people who knew how the binding worked. Ben was not one of them, not fully, but he knew who had invented the technique. He would have made notes in his book, perhaps in Middle English and under a cipher, but Merrow knew how to read that now. "That's why you needed his notebook."

Merrow spread his hands with a desperate laugh. "A black woman. Why would we have thought she was important?"

They knew about Helen.

Ginger blew out of the tiny room and headed for the stairs to the first floor, passing ghosts who crowded the halls. One slid through the wall, and Ginger pulled to a halt. Why did she need the stairs? She sank through the floor and emerged in the hall outside Potter's Field. Here, mediums and mundanes walked in the hall as they came off shift. They had their heads down and their arms tucked around their bodies. Every single one of them had their soul curled into a tight ball in the centre of their selves, trying to avoid contact with the ghosts that crowded the building.

Ginger slipped through them, catching brushes of thought. What is happening? When can I leave? Why am I here? How did I die? She passed through the door and stopped. A translucent wall surrounded the room.

"Bloody hell." She at first thought that they had moved the salt line to surround the warehouse grounds, but there were evidently two lines. In this form, Ginger couldn't cross it. She turned to the nearest medium. "Excuse me."

The woman kept her head down and continued walking. In this crowd, Ginger's plea blended with the other soldiers.

Ginger needed to find her body.

Chapter Twenty-five

★ ★ ★

Ginger's body was not difficult to find. It lay in the infirmary on the third floor of the warehouse. Three other mediums were in the room. Or rather, their bodies were, but no animating aura surrounded them. She hadn't realized that they'd lost more souls. Each lay still and breathing, but with the lax face of the inanimate.

Her own body had been cleaned of the dirt that had accumulated during her days at the Front, which only made the dark circles under her eyes more apparent. When had she become so alarmingly gaunt? Though, when she thought about it, Ginger could not remember the last time she had eaten. It simply had not seemed important.

There would be time to worry about that later. She eased into her body and the flesh slid around her like scum on a pond.

Ginger gritted her teeth against the stink of decay until her jaw ached. The ache distracted her from the churning nausea in her gut.

Sandbags rested upon her lids and she strained to open them. Everything weighed on her, pressing against her soul and pinning it to the world. She blinked against the harsh light of the ward and groaned.

Someone gasped. "Ginger?"

Ginger turned her head, which throbbed with the movement. She knew the voice. "Aunt Edie?"

"Oh my heavenly stars! You have no idea how worried I have been."

"I thought—" Her voice scratched her throat like broken glass. Ginger stopped and coughed. "I thought you were in London."

"London? Whatever gave you that idea?" She sniffled and wiped a finger roughly under her eyes. Her aura had relief breaking through the patches of grey.

"Your maid said you had gone there."

"London branch. Oh, that stupid thing. I told her to tell you I was going to stay with the London *branch*. I knew I should have left a note, but then I was afraid it would fall into the wrong hands. Going gallivanting off to London after seeing you leave on a train with a gun and a ghost? I've never heard of such silliness. Oh—my dear, I'm so glad you're awake. But you are absolutely forbidden from ever frightening me like that again."

Ginger winced. It had not occurred to her what it would do to her aunt—or to her circle, for that matter—if she didn't come back. Foolishness. She had seen the effects of death so often that she had become inured to it. "I am sorry I frightened you."

She tried to push herself up on the bed, and the room spun

around her. Ginger dropped back, nauseated as the pitching sensation continued.

Worry clouded her aunt's aura. "You should rest."

"Can't." Squeezing her eyes shut, Ginger covered her face with her hands. "Helen is in danger."

"Why Helen?"

Of course . . . her aunt didn't know, because she'd specifically asked not to be told any of the details. "Do you know where she is?"

"Oh! That's something nice. Brigadier-General Davies is apparently going to reconsider your suggestion to have her be the liaison. He just sent a man to fetch her, so she is at his house."

"His house. Really? He's having a meeting with her in his home?"

"Do you think that put her in danger? He only agreed to it today, so I hardly see how the Germans could know yet."

Opening her eyes, Ginger stared at her aunt. "Do you really see the brigadier-general receiving a woman of colour in his home?"

"I—well . . . no. I wish I could, but no."

"Do you know who came for her?"

"Oh . . . no, but his name was literary."

"Lt. Thackeray?"

"Yes!" Her aunt tilted her head. "Which I can see by your aura is terribly bad news. My dear . . . I know I have told you not to keep me informed, but I think I will be more helpful if I know what is going on. Why Helen?"

"Because Helen created the process that imprints the soldiers. And Merrow had Ben's notebook, which mentions that, and he's told the Germans everything he knows." Ginger reached for Aunt Edie's hand. "Will you help me up, please?"

"Oh, my dear . . ." Her aunt looked stricken, then furious.

"I know. Honestly, I'm not sure if Davies is involved, or if the message from him was faked. We *thought* they were looking for the Spirit Corps, which would mean that the traitor couldn't be Davies, because he knew where we were. But they were looking for the *process* to imprint the soldiers." Ginger forced her elbow into the cot and levered herself up. She sat, clutching the edge of the bed with both hands. The swimming sensation continued. She had no idea if it was from the concussion Merrow had given her or because . . . because she had died. If she was being clear and honest with herself, Ginger had died for a few moments, until Lt. Plumber got her breathing again. "Now, will you please help me stop them?"

"But you should—"

"Rest. I know. But I have a duty, and I mean to perform it." She looked at the other women, lying prone and nearly lifeless in the other beds. "But we need the rest of my circle. I am, as Helen puts it, rather loose in my skin."

★ ★ ★

Lady Penfold's comportment would have made many officers ashamed of their own posture. She marched down the hall, leading Ginger's circle out of Potter's Field. Ginger leaned on Edna as they left the warehouse.

Her joints ached with every movement, although *ached* was perhaps the wrong word. Ginger was acutely *aware* of her physical form and the bunching of muscles, the grinding of cartilage, and the rumble of digestion. Her tongue filled her mouth with the taste of decay.

This constant reminder of the mortality of the body was probably why those other women's souls had not returned. The sense of rot filled her, and just there, just beyond the boundary of her skin, floated the soft currents of the spirit world.

Ginger ground her teeth together, focusing on the deliberate tension in her jaw. She had work to do, and she knew full well that the spirit plane was not all beauty and light. Around them, the souls of soldiers who had died meaningless deaths swirled in unrest. Even with her soul pulled tightly into her body, she could feel their unease prickling her skin.

They wanted to do something useful.

"Stop here a moment, would you?" Ginger squeezed Edna's arm. "I need a circle. Aunt Edie, would you anchor me?"

Lifting her head with a sniff, Lady Penfold pivoted on her heel. "You are not seriously contemplating leaving your body, are you?"

"I am just going to push out a little."

"Absolutely not."

"Then I will do it anyway, and I am too tired to stay anchored." Ginger tightened her grip on Edna and reached for Mr. Haden. He stepped forward and placed his hand in her left with a nod.

His warm, familiar calluses and the slight scratch of his fingerless gloves were the first things that had felt comfortable since Ginger had awoken. She squeezed his hand, and the wool seemed to carry a whiff of Mrs. Richardson. Edna stayed in Mrs. Richardson's spot on Ginger's right, and Joanne stepped up to take her hand. Lt. Plumber balanced on his crutches, joining hands with Mr. Haden.

There was a gap where Helen should be. With a glare, Lady Penfold stepped into place. "You are as stubborn as your mother was."

"I take that as a compliment."

"I meant it as one." Deftly, her aunt stitched the circle together, and all of them put their weight on Ginger, even before she reached out.

True to her word, Ginger tried to stay just past the surface of her skin, even though the currents tugged at her. It would be so much easier to let go and drift in the lemon gold warmth. Ginger looked about them.

Lost men. The yard was full of lost men, wanting an opportunity to fulfill their duty. Ginger drew strength from the circle and projected her words into the yard, filling the space between the salt barriers. "Gentlemen!"

The swirling slowed, and they turned, the silvery blue-green of curiosity leaping like a spark from soul to soul.

"I need some volunteers to help me stop a traitor. I want to be clear and honest that, even as ghosts, this has the potential to cause you harm."

"Getting shot at is what we signed up for, innit." A private solidified in front of her, hat cocked on the back of his head, well out of regulation alignment. "Don't see as how it matters if we're living or dead. Got a duty to do."

"Right you are." A captain—the one she had spoken to before, she thought—appeared out of the mass of ghosts. "All right, men. Any who want to come, form up."

The swirling mass changed, becoming regular squares of souls as orders sparked bright orange across the yard. They had died in their sleep, en masse, and entire battalions haunted the courtyard. The majority of them moved into formation.

"Thank you." In the distant mortal plane, Ginger had an awareness of someone weeping.

"What are our orders?"

"Do you know what a poltergeist is?"

Ginger is leaning back against Ben's chest, the remnants of a picnic spread at their feet. An ant is crawling at the edge of a puddle of honey that had spilled on one of the porcelain plates. Ben is playing with a strand of hair at the base of her neck.

Ginger wrinkles her nose and stretches against him. "If the servants weren't pretending not to watch, I might just fall asleep here."

"Would you prefer for them to watch boldly?"

"I'd prefer for them not to be here at all." She reaches up and lays a hand on his cheek. It is coarse with stubble, which is odd, since she has never seen him less than perfectly groomed. "But that would be wicked indeed."

"I should not object to a little wickedness." He nuzzles her neck. "But I am afraid that you need to wake up."

Ginger sat up. "Oh! Am I lucid dreaming? Are you really here?"

"Dear—I am so very sorry, but I need you to wake up now."

Her aunt was shaking her. Ginger blinked at her and shook her head. The field spun, tipping with the motion. Ginger closed her eyes and rested her head back against Ben's chest with a *thunk*. "Ow."

She sat up again, her hair catching on the bark of the tree she had been leaning against. Her aunt knelt at her side, with Brigadier-General Davies standing behind her. Ginger squinted up at them. "Sorry. Are we ready?"

The brigadier-general's aura was green-brown with doubt. He leaned over to Lady Penfold and murmured something. Ginger could not hear him, but the question was clear enough.

"I am perfectly fit—" She stopped at her aunt's glower. "At any rate, I am fit enough for this."

She drew her feet up so they would not knock over the picnic things, then stopped. That had been a dream. Ben was little more than her own memory of him, embodied in a spot of cold at her shoulder.

She swallowed and looked to her left, where a hand in finger-less gloves rested on her arm. Mr. Haden gave her a little smile. "We've got you. Don't you worry about that."

"Thank you." She glanced over to Edna, who sat on her right, also maintaining contact with her. At least two people had kept contact with Ginger since she had returned to her body, keeping her anchored. "Thank you both."

The young woman merely ducked her head, but her aura was ruddy amber with pride.

The brigadier-general tugged on his mustache. "Well . . . the men you requested are here. I must say, I did not know when I agreed to this that you were requesting an Indian company. This is highly irregular."

"Oh for pity's sake, George. I can overlook this in London, but not at the front. We need men who we are certain aren't compromised." Lady Penfold sniffed at him. "I suspect that the Germans will have overlooked them for the same reasons that you find their deployment 'irregular.'"

"It's not that they are Indians—it's just that it's a group of drivers. We need combat veterans for this."

"And I am that, sir. I am very much a veteran." Beyond the brigadier-general, Corporal Patel ground his rifle on the earth. "I fought at Gallipoli. I am only driving a truck because no one will send me to the front here."

"Well, it's not the front, but I need a medium among the men we are sending forward." Ginger shifted, but her legs were still strange and unfamiliar. "Forgive me for not rising. Aunt Edie, did you get the discs I asked for?"

"Yes . . . but I don't see why it matters; don't they have ID tags already?" She fished a bundle of blue tags from her hand-bag. "And none of these have the names on them."

"We'll take care of that." Ginger waited until Patel had them in hand. "Have each of your men write their full names on a tag, spit on it, and then put the disc on the chain with their others."

"Spit?"

"Technically, any bodily fluid will work, but there has been enough blood shed in the world already." Ginger let her spirit drift a little out of her body. "Now, allow me to introduce you to Capt. Wentworth. He's in charge of our ghost army. They will serve as your scouts."

Chapter Twenty-Six

★ ★ ★

Ginger sat with the full circle anchoring her. They had changed their usual positions so that Edna sat next to Lt. Plumber now, and Aunt Edie sat in Helen's spot. The ghosts had found Helen just outside of Le Havre, in a home in the middle of a field pockmarked by artillery fire. The German mediums held her in the middle of a full circle.

Ginger waited as Patel's men crept through the field surrounding a simple farmhouse. Germans dressed in French and British uniforms mustered in a wobbly circle around the perimeter. Four machine guns punctuated the line, each covering a quadrant of the surrounding field. They had not had time to dig proper trenches, or bring up significant supplies. But the Germans did not need to hold their ground forever: just long enough for Schmitt to get answers out of Helen.

A streak of burnt-orange haste zipped across the field and stopped in the centre of the circle. A young private, with a spatter of freckles across his nose, formed from the haste. He saluted Ginger. "Pvt. Tucker reporting, ma'am. Everyone is in position."

"Thank you, Private." Ginger briefly turned her attention to the corporeal world. The Indian company had spread thin all around the farmhouse, just out of range of the German guns. The ghosts were distributed likewise, but more heavily on the far side. "Brigadier-General? They are ready, at your command."

His aura was a seething ball of tension that roiled around the outside of the circle. "Tell them to proceed."

Private Tucker saluted. "I heard, ma'am. I'm learning to push into the mortal world."

"Save your energy. And remember—only one act of poltergeisting per ghost. It's too dangerous for your souls to do more."

"We'll do our duty, ma'am." And then he whizzed away, staying low to the ground as he sped off to find Patel, who would relay the order to attack to the living and the dead.

She had no doubt that they would do their duty. It was the concern that they might do too much that worried her.

Machine gun fire chattered from the far side of the farmhouse as the attack began. If the men of the Indian company returned fire, Ginger could not hear it from her position. She felt much of the stress of command in that moment just after the orders had been given. They could not be called back or halted now without endangering not only the rescue effort, but the men already committed to the attack. And yet the attack crawled along, drawing fire from the Germans but otherwise seeming to have little effect.

"My God." The brigadier-general paused in his tense pacing,

facing the farmhouse and looking off toward the attack on the far side. Whole companies had sprung out of the crater-pocked field, visible from this distance only as a seething mass of troops. They advanced on the farmhouse, closing ranks, moving no faster than a steady marching pace.

German fire intensified from the direction of the farmhouse, and shouts of alarm punctuated the rapid-fire shooting. Despite the intensifying firing, the line did not waver. Hardly a surprise, given that it was composed entirely of uniforms stuffed with straw, propelled by ghost soldiers.

"They can't have much ammunition, can they?" Lt. Plumber's aura trembled with a growing doubt. "They weren't really planning to hole up there, after all."

"We don't know what they were planning, or what uses they might have had for this place." The brigadier-general resumed stomping around the circle, the spectacle of the poltergeisting battalion palling. "If they shoot through this ruse of ours, we might have to wait them out."

"But, Helen. They have a full circle working on her." Ginger paused, seeing the brown of his incomprehension. "They can pry into her mind and get the information without her willing participation."

He tugged his mustache and stared toward the trees, over which the plumes of dust and smoke still rose. "In that case, we'll drop a bomb on them if we have to."

The circle flared with rage around him. Joanne rose to her knees. "Over my dead body! You don't just bomb someone because it's easier—"

"It's in the interests of national security. The knowledge that she has is too valuable to fall into enemy hands. If we have to sacrifice her to prevent it from getting out, that's what we'll do."

Lady Penfold sniffed. "My dear brigadier-general, I have a great deal of affection for you, but you are an idiot. They are mediums. Killing them won't keep them from reporting what they've learned."

More shouts went up around the farmhouse, alarm growing. The Germans might be wearing uniforms impregnated with salt, but that seemed to be the extent of their preparation for dealing with the dead. The machine-gun fire ramped up, then suddenly stopped. More frantic shouts, and guards began running from the far side of the farmhouse to the near side, then back again.

The machine-gun fire picked up again, yet steadily the straw soldiers advanced. The Germans shot wildly, discipline gone from their defense. A blanket of dark terror covered them.

The orange streak of Pvt. Tucker zipped toward her. He was shouting as he came, "They're breaking, they're breaking!" When he fetched up in the circle, the light of exhilaration was in his aura. The ghosts had joined the battle. "Captain says now's the time to make your move."

Ginger fell into her old role with ease. "Casualty report?"

"Two men injured, but none killed. Five spirits were shredded when they poltergeisted to lift the the living fellows clear."

Unease rippled through the cold spot at her shoulder. A whisper of Ben hissed "Shit!" in her ear.

"Did they go beyond the veil?" They had told the ghost soldiers that their business was completed if they had to poltergeist in the line of duty. Some men, like Ben, had a different sense of duty.

"Yes, ma'am."

She sighed with relief. "Is there a clear path to the house?"

"It's getting that way. There's only two guards left watching this side, and they've pulled all the machine-gun ammunition to the far side."

Ginger relayed the information to the brigadier-general.

"Very well. Launch the real attack." He grunted and bounced on his toes, still surveying the scene.

"Run to tell Cpl. Pa—" But Pvt. Tucker had already gone, the orange streak not heading to the far side now, but much closer.

Fewer than a hundred yards ahead of them, between the circle and the farmhouse, more straw soldiers rose up from the ground. The balance of the Indian company rose with them, trotting across the cratered field. Frantic shouts came from the guards on the near side of the farmhouse, but the wild firing on the far side all but drowned them out. Close by, the pop and crash of trusty Enfield rifles filled the air. One German stood as though to run, then flopped over as soon as he was upright. He did not stir, but his soul drifted free and vanished beyond the veil.

Gunfire rippled up and down the advancing line, and Ginger recognised a catastrophic flaw in the plan. Pvt. Tucker would not return to relay new orders unless the situation changed. The men advancing were instructed to kill the guards—all of the guards—with orders to try to avoid hitting the house if at all possible. But if one of the German mediums had broken Helen, he could simply run out into the teeth of the fire and be cut down, his spirit free to return across the German lines and report to a medium there.

"We need to follow the line of assault and get closer." Ginger stood, still gripping the hands to either side of her. The others struggled to stand without toppling over, and Lt. Plumber—his aura spoke of eagerness, agreement, but he could not cross the field with his crutches and maintain contact with the circle at the same time. And then there was the brigadier-general.

"Absolutely not. I will not hear of it!" He stomped up behind her, and she sensed that only a lifetime of training kept him from putting his hands on her shoulders and forcing her to sit once more. "It's dangerous enough for you to be this close to the fighting."

"We must, if we are to capture Schmitt alive. We cannot let him be killed and escape back to Germany with what he knows." Ginger broke away from the circle, and from the brigadier-general, who screamed his disapproval. She set out from the little hilltop they had occupied, hurrying down the gentle slope to the depression where the main force of the Indian company had lain hidden.

A hand grabbed at Ginger's. She pulled it away, but then Edna snatched Ginger's hand back and held tight. Another hand, Mr. Haden's, grabbed her from the other side. Rather than hauling her back—something she doubted she could physically resist at this point—they hurried along with her in the wake of the attack.

"We cannot let you go alone, ma'am." Edna twined her fingers in Ginger's. "You must stay anchored."

"Thank you." Ginger forced them into a trot across the broken field, her legs burning immediately with the exertion. The tang of cordite hung in the air, along with the scents of freshly churned earth and dry straw. An Indian soldier slipped down into a crater, and she feared he had been shot. But then she saw him taking aim and squeezing off a single shot. There was a cry from an upper window of the farmhouse, and a man and his rifle tumbled out the window.

A sniper. Had he been aiming at her? Feeling very exposed, she swallowed against the dryness in her throat.

They caught up to the advancing line just as they reached the farmhouse. Most of the ghosts had gone, rising through the veil, their energy expended by moving the straw dummies. But the Indian company, drawing together, was big enough to surround the farmhouse all on their own now. The Germans who had been on guard now all lay on the ground, dead or dying.

"I must get through," she shouted, but it came out as more of a croak. A simple trot of a few hundred yards had nearly done her in.

"Here now! You lot." Mr. Haden bellowed like a carnival barker. "The lady needs through."

The men in front of them parted, letting her and her anchors by.

She almost felt as though she could just float away at this point, anchors or no, and leave this weary body behind. But she needed her body to be able to do anything for Helen, so she pressed on.

A guard lay slumped on the ground near the rear door of the farmhouse, his back a scarlet ruin. He had been hit in the chest several times, and his back had been opened by the exiting bullets. As much as she had seen of the dead, the freshly empty bodies were new to her, and Edna and Mr. Haden besides. In their shock, she was able to pull away from them and reached down to grab the pistol the man had in a leather holster on his belt.

Cpl. Patel stood at the door, looking dusty and sweaty, but otherwise unharmed. She indulged in a flash of relief, then nodded to him. He pulled the door open and she entered, the big Colt handgun held in front of her. It was at once strange, yet familiar from other people's memories. Edna and Mr. Haden protested behind her, but she had to get to Helen, had to stop this before it was too late. Schmitt need not run into the battle to die and carry his secrets off; he could just as easily die by his own hand, here in the farmhouse.

They passed into the kitchen and heard the murmur of voices from a room to the side. Cpl. Patel stepped through the door first and she followed, then staggered back. Six people sat in chairs arranged in a familiar circle, with Helen in the middle. Auras pulsed with the frantic effort being put forth to break Helen.

What would breaking the circle do at this point? She had no idea, but she could not let them continue. "We must take them alive. All of them."

Cpl. Patel raised the butt of his rifle and brought it down hard on the shoulder of the nearest, a medium. He crumpled off his chair, and the efforts of the circle wavered and broke. One of the mundanes stood and launched himself at Cpl. Patel.

Ginger took another step toward Helen, feet leaden with exhaustion. Helen had been bound to the chair in the centre of the circle, and she looked on the edge of collapse. Shouts came from behind her. More Indian soldiers poured into the farmhouse. Familiar voices behind her as well. Edna?

She couldn't worry about that. In front of her, Schmitt, the false prisoner of war, sat on the far side of the circle. He was still working, holding tight to the anchors on either side of him. His eyes fluttered with effort. Helen fought him still.

Ginger's arm rose without much conscious thought. The pistol was primed, the hammer cocked back. Her finger caressed the trigger and the gun went off, the booming crash of the shot filling the farmhouse dining room. Schmitt jerked back, his shoulder appearing to explode in crimson, pulling away from the others as he fell.

Ginger slumped to her knees beside Helen, and then across her lap. Indian soldiers swarmed in, grabbing the others in the circle. Someone with warm, brown hands pried the pistol from her grip, and conscious thought left her.

Chapter Twenty-Seven

★ ★ ★

Everything was heavy. Gravity pulled her down into the embrace of sleep. Only a gentle murmuring slipped past the pressure of darkness to tug at her consciousness. She knew the voice. A man's. It wasn't Ben's, but it had a similar timbre.

Reginald Harford.

Ginger dragged her lids open. Sensation seemed to rush back in as she woke. Her throat scratched as she swallowed, and she coughed. The voices stopped.

Another cough tickled, and she tried to lift her hand to cover her mouth. It would not move. Someone held it. Someone held both hands, in fact. She rolled her head to the side.

Mr. Haden gave her a little smile. "Well. Look who's decided to rejoin the living."

"Sorry to trouble you." Her voice was hoarse with disuse. Ginger cleared her throat again. "Might I have some water?"

"Of course! Oh, my poor dear, you must be parched. We've been using ice cubes, of course, but that isn't the same as a nice drink of water." Lady Penfold bustled up on her other side, leaning in past Edna to hold a glass of water for Ginger. Some of the water slopped out of the glass, leaving a cold spot on the fabric of her gown, but Edna did not let go of Ginger's hand.

She lifted her head, and it throbbed with the motion. She was in the guest bedroom in her aunt's apartment. The damask wallpaper stood in stark contrast to the dull blue uniforms of her circle. They sat around the bed, hands linked together. Joanne, Mr. Haden, Edna, Lt. Plumber, and . . . Ginger let out a sigh of relief when she saw Helen in her familiar spot. "Oh, thank God."

"Eh. I think the thanks belongs closer to home." Helen pursed her lips, but could not hide the twinkle in her eyes.

Ginger gave Mr. Haden's and Edna's hands a squeeze. "You can let go. I promise I won't venture out of my body."

Helen snorted and exchanged a look with Lady Penfold. "Let's not test that just yet."

"Truly—"

"The fact is, dear . . ." Lady Penfold ducked under the joined hands of Lt. Plumber and Edna, holding her skirt off the floor. She settled on Ginger's bed. "I'm afraid we have some business to attend to, and . . . well. I think it's best if you stay linked for it."

"That . . . that sounds ominous."

From the door, a man cleared his throat. Reginald Harford stepped fully into the room. "More ominous for me than you, I think."

"What are you doing here?"

"My one good deed." He set his hat on the dresser by the door.

She was too tired to be polite. "Are you certain you can manage even one?"

He winced. "I was trying to keep you safe."

"By setting your men on me?"

"I don't expect you to believe me, but I didn't know what Johnson was up to. If it makes you feel any better, he's been . . . dealt with."

"I am not disposed to be pleased by vagueness."

Reginald sighed. "He's been arrested and will likely be shot for treason. Does that satisfy you?"

"I—" Did the death of another man matter at all in this endless bloody war? It did nothing to bring Ben back, and gave her no satisfaction.

Reginald turned to her aunt and swept a hand over his brilliantined hair. "Can we get this over with? I'm not who she wants to talk to."

Aunt Edie compressed her lips and gave a little sniff. "I'm sorry to keep you waiting, Captain." She rested a hand on Ginger's arm. "My dear . . . Ben has not yet crossed over."

"What?" Ginger struggled to sit up. This time, though neither Mr. Haden nor Edna let go, her aunt helped her. "But we know who killed him." She glanced across the circle to Helen, to reassure herself that the other medium was really safe. "And we've stopped the immediate threat from the Germans. Haven't we?"

"So it appears. We have Schmitt and the others." Lady Penfold beckoned Reginald forward. "But he is still here, and he wants to talk to you."

Ben wanted to talk to her. What did that have to do with Reginald Harford? Too slowly, Ginger's mind put the pieces together. His one good deed. "You're going to channel Ben?"

He took in a single breath and gave a nod. "I am."

"That seems . . . why?"

"I told you. It's my one good deed."

"But why you? Why not a medium?"

Reginald frowned, and the line between his brows seemed at odds with his usually careless ease. Lady Penfold cut in. "Ben is quite unstable. Helen and I believe that using the body of someone with whom he has shared experiences will help him."

"And we did grow up together."

A scrap of memory from when she had channelled Ben turned her stomach. He had loathed this man. No common memory was going to override that, surely. "But—surely there is someone else who—"

"Whom he liked?" The corner of Reginald's mouth turned up in a sardonic smile. "Yes. As the younger, poorer child, I had to take what attention was offered. Ben wanted little to do with me, but we had to maintain good relations, didn't we? Under those circumstances, I found it better to pretend that I didn't know how he felt."

Ginger stared at Reginald, mouth slightly agape. He could not mean . . . Ben had said he didn't have a sensitive bone in his body. She tried to stretch out of her body to see his aura, but her circle flexed their collective will, holding her firmly inside her skin.

Reginald's eyes unfocused a little, and he sighed. "Our maternal grandmother fled Germany with her family when her father was almost burned at the stake for being a medium. Acknowledgment of the Sight was not encouraged. So.

"I will not pretend I am anyone that you should like to associate with, but I was fond of Ben, despite everything, and if this helps him to rest . . ." He spread his hands and turned his head to look at Ginger's right shoulder, where a cool breeze lingered. "Shall we get to it, old man?"

The breeze stirred Ginger's hair, rushing past her with a sigh. She stiffened on the bed, and tightened her grip on Mr. Haden and Edna. The fabric of Reginald's lapel lifted for a moment. A strand of his blond hair blew free of its pomade. With a grunt, he staggered and dropped to his knees.

Lady Penfold sprang from the bed. "Oh, dear—"

"Sorry. That was a little more melodramatic that I would have liked." Ben raised Reginald's head. He smiled, lopsided and full of dimples. "You keep telling me that I don't need to worry about you, and then winding up in hospital."

"Only once."

"Twice. But who's counting?" He winked, and pushed up to stand. It was Reginald's body, but the posture was Ben's. His shoulders sat at a slight angle, as though he would lean against a wall if it were offered.

"Apparently *you're* counting." Ginger fought to breathe. "Is it really gentlemanly to keep score?"

Ben cocked his head and looked at her sideways, through lashes that were too light to be his. "Only when you owe a debt."

"And do you? I didn't think you were the type to let a debt go unpaid."

He took three familiar steps, then sat on the bed at her side. "I owe *you* a debt."

"Ben . . . darling. Please. You owe me nothing." She tried to reach for him, but Edna held her hand. Ginger closed her eyes, clenching her jaw against tears. "Please, please believe that you have more than fulfilled your duty. You have no unfinished business."

His hand brushed a tear from her cheek. With her eyes shut,

she could imagine that the weight shifting on the bed really did belong to Ben. "But I do."

She gave a desperate laugh. "Finding your murderer, stopping a traitor, and uncovering a plot by the Germans isn't enough? And don't you dare say that your duty is to keep me safe. Because I refuse to accept being haunted just so we can keep having the same argument."

He chuckled. "No. It has become abundantly clear to me over the past several . . . however long it's been . . . not only that you are resourceful, but that your circle is a force to be reckoned with. I mean, Lady—your aunt alone is more protection than I could ever have been."

"Ben—" She opened her eyes to look at Reginald's form and reminded herself that her love was not here. But his eyes—she had not noticed that they had the same eyes. Or perhaps it was merely the steadiness of his gaze and the way he watched her with his head canted a little to the side.

"I am sorry that I doubted your abilities."

Her breath caught in her throat, and she thought she might tear in two. "I shall miss you. So very much."

"Just remember that you've promised to grow old."

"People will quake before me as I brandish my cane at them."

"They will quake even before that." His dimples flashed again. "And then you will charm them. Or maybe you'll charm them first. Probably you'll do both, just to keep people on their toes."

Ginger could not raise her hands to wipe her eyes, but the tears streaming down her cheeks seemed almost a relief. She did not want Ben to go, but she could not keep him. Ginger swallowed and leaned on her training with the Spirit Corps in order to be able to speak at all. "Have you any final messages?"

"Thank Reg for me. Tell him I'm sorry I was a blighter to him."

"I will."

"Thank you."

She tried to smile for him. "Is there anything else?"

"Apparently I owe you a kiss." Ben took a breath and looked as nervous as he had when he proposed. "May I?"

She nodded, words completely beyond her power. Ben leaned forward, and Ginger closed her eyes to meet him. Unfamiliar cologne clung to him. The contours of his lips were new, but the warmth and passion that came through them broke her heart with familiarity.

His breath was rough, and tears dampened his cheek where it pressed against hers. "I love you very much, Ginger Stuyvesant."

"I love you too."

He pulled back, and she opened her eyes as his hands cradled her face. Ben gave a tentative smile, dimple flashing for a brief moment, and then he tilted his head to the side. "Oh. *That's* the light. It's—"

Reginald slumped on the bed, sliding off of it and landing on the floor with a thump.

Lady Penfold dropped the handkerchief that she had been blotting her eyes with and knelt by him. "Are you all right, Captain?"

His eyes blinked open, still red from Ben's tears. Ginger expected him to complain about being on the floor, but he brought his hands up over his eyes, and his breath shuddered in his chest.

"I'm fine." His voice was hoarse, and he wiped fiercely at his eyes before shoving himself to his feet. Reginald tugged at his uniform, all familiar traces of physicality gone. "Good deed is done."

The tears continued to stream down his cheeks, and his hands shook as he ducked out of the circle. He would not remember what they had talked about while Ben had had control of his body.

Ginger cleared her throat, but her own voice shook. "Ben wanted me to thank you. He said he was sorry he was such a blighter to you."

Reginald stopped at the door, his back still to them. He grabbed his hat from the dresser. "If he'd really meant it, he wouldn't have given me a glimpse of—" Glancing over his shoulder at Ginger, his face was stricken. "He loved you very much. You have my sincere condolences for your loss."

And then he was gone.

And Ben was gone.

But Ginger was not alone. Her circle rose from their chairs, still linked, and wrapped her in their embrace as she wept.

SEPTEMBER 1916

Ginger waited at the checkpoint as the guard considered her papers. The loose end of the turban wrapped around his helmet flapped in the early autumn breeze. Another guard watched, his rifle held in a casually ready position. Her aunt's car idled behind her, in case she needed to be taken back to Le Havre. She kept her soul in her skin and tried to rely on watching the guard's face to guess his response.

He grunted and folded the papers to hand back to her. "All in order, Cpl. Stuyvesant. First time to Graveside?"

"Yes. Thank you." She took her documents and stared past the checkpoint to the bunker built into a French hillside. "But I was at Potter's Field in Le Havre."

"Well, then you know what you're getting into more than I do, I suspect." He turned and gestured to the bunker. "Just down the steps and turn right to go to the command centre. The left will take you to Potter's Field."

She nodded and walked to the bunker door. It opened onto a steep stair lined with hastily poured concrete. As she went down, the air chilled quickly. Now that they were no longer trying to hide the fact that the Spirit Corps existed, the intelligence department had opted for safety as the first consideration. They had buried the mediums deep in the earth, far from the front lines. They hadn't been able to move the nexus, but with Ginger's ghost army, Helen had devised a system whereby volunteer ghosts redirected the incoming souls.

At the bottom of the stairs, Ginger glanced to the left, but the long hallway to Potter's Field curved away under the earth. She wasn't back on duty yet. Taking a breath of the cold, earthy air, Ginger turned to her right. She passed other young women moving with purpose through the narrow halls.

Rough timbers supported the ceiling, with bare bulbs suspended from them. Green doors stood at intervals along the corridors, and everywhere she walked, pockets of uncanny cold air brushed against her, whispering. At an intersection, Ginger paused and got directions from a young West Indian soldier who pointed her to the brigadier-general's office.

She swallowed and stared at the door, then raised her hand to knock.

"Enter!"

Ginger opened the door on a meeting in progress. Brigadier-General Davies looked over his glasses and nodded a greeting. "Miss Stu—Cpl. Stuyvesant, your timing is excellent. We were just discussing poltergeist training." He gestured to his right. "There's a seat by Sgt. Patel."

Sgt. Patel sat next to Capt. Lethbridge-Stewart. Across the table from them, Capt. Keatley had his usual sheaf of papers. Capt. Axtell leaned back in his chair, twirling a cigarette between his fingers. His hair had returned to its usual blond. It turned out that the brigadier-general had sent him to investigate the Baker Street trench because a leak was stemming from there. He thought it might have been Ben.

And beside him, Helen—Capt. Jackson—slid a paper across the table to Ginger's seat.

Before sitting, Ginger hesitated for a moment. "I—I haven't officially been returned to duty."

"Eh? What?" The brigadier-general pushed his chair back and stood. "My dear gir—my dear woman, if you are still recovering, you should have sent word you could not attend. We would have understood, of course."

She shook her head, aware that her uniform was too loose, despite the efforts of her aunt's chef. "No—it's not that. It's just that I need to be formally reinstated. Do I have permission to return to active duty?"

"Of course—that's why I asked you to come today. We need your expertise."

"I meant as a medium."

"Ah. That's up to your superior officer." The brigadier-general turned to Helen. "Well, Capt. Jackson?"

Helen tilted her head, and her gaze went distant. Ginger swallowed as the other woman read her soul. "I really am much better."

"You have lied to me before about your health."

Ginger blushed and ducked her head. "Yes."

"Will you again?"

"Probably." She looked back up and unexpectedly met Axtell's gaze. His genial mask had slipped, and his fatigue was clear from his features. "I think we all do, just to keep going."

Axtell nodded, then gave a huge laugh, slapping his knee as the mask slipped back into place. "That's true enough. If you wanted every soldier to be honest about their health, we'd all be home."

Capt. Jackson nodded at the chair. "Well then, sit down. We have work to do."

Ginger let out a sigh of relief and sank into the chair next to Sgt. Patel. He leaned over and whispered, "I am very glad you are better. Indeed, I am."

"Likewise." Ginger pulled Capt. Jackson's report closer and listened to the conversation about how to work with their volunteer ghost army. The Great War was far from over, and duty called.

She had unfinished business. They all did.

Acknowledgments

You know you're in good shape when John Scalzi writes your opening line for you. I was telling him about *Ghost Talkers,* which originally opened with a dinner party in London, and he explained that I was stupid—although he said it more kindly than that—and told me what my actual opening line was. So please offer him thanks that you didn't waste time reading about a dinner party.

Thank you to all the people who helped me with historical facts when I was in the early throes of this book: Scott Lynch, David Hogg, Sally Smith, Greg Vose, Norin, John Pitzel, CD Covington, Fric, Chuck Rothman, Val French, Tom Evans, and Robert Killheffer. They know terrifying amounts about WWI and helped me settle on the Battle of the Somme and Delville Wood. The mistakes are mine, but there are fewer of them than there would have been without these folks.

Thanks to Michael Livingston for pointing out that J. R. R. Tolkien was actually at the Battle of the Somme. Yes, really. And also for being willing to teach me how to speak in Middle English for the audiobook. (For the record, I'll note that Narrator Mary haaaaaaates Writer Mary. Middle English? Really? Who thought that was a good idea?)

Thanks to Tobias Buckell, who made an incredibly good suggestion while visiting for a mini writers' retreat. If you're a writer, you know that moment when you're beating your head against a wall and you say, "I wish someone else would just write this for me."

Toby said, "Why don't you ask Dave?"

He had collaborated with David Klecha before, and, man . . . was he right. My first efforts at planning the assault on the Germans were pretty shabby. I needed to learn so much about military tactics in order to stage that correctly. So I just e-mailed

Dave, since he's a combat vet, and asked him if he would write the scene for me. We chatted through my rough outline and he handled all the battle stuff. Then I went back through and adjusted the language to match my own style. Although he's really, really good, so I didn't have to adjust much.

Many thanks to Leanna Renee Hieber, with whom I spent a delightful afternoon brainstorming how the conditioning worked. Dan Wells looked at my outline and pointed out where I was being stupid about the structure.

And then there are the folks who let me blather at them while I was developing the novel and generally made me feel safe and supported: Howard Tayler; Brandon Sanderson; Lynne Thomas; Wes Chu; my husband, Robert Kowal; Sandra Tayler; Donovan Beeson; and pretty much everyone else I know. Never underestimate how important this is for a writer.

Of course, my agent, Jennifer Jackson. First reader, Michael Curry. And my truly amazing editor, Liz Gorinsky.

Historical Note

My grandmother, Mary Elois Stephens Jackson, was born in 1905 and remembers WWI ending. She said that everyone ran out into the streets, crying and cheering. Later, she married Grandaddy, Luther H. Jackson, who was a veteran of the war. When she passed away in 2014, she was one of the last remaining widows of a WWI veteran.

With war, we tend to focus on the men, and a lot of people, including me, don't realize how integral women were to the war effort. Allow me to recommend that you go out and get a copy of Kate Adie's *Fighting on the Home Front,* which is about the role of women in the First World War.

Here in the United States, the Great War had less of an impact than it did in England and Europe, simply because we entered the war later. But in England, from the moment the war began, women were "doing their part" both at home and in the theater of war. They were nurses, ambulance drivers, doctors, motorcycle dispatch riders, and often right in the thick of it.

Much of what the mediums go through in terms of "shell shock" was based on the ambulance drivers, who saw death and horrific injuries every day. They were right there, in the battlefields amidst the same unrelenting shelling that the men experienced. They suffered from PTSD in ways that are largely ignored.

There are so many women that I wanted to work into the novel and just couldn't, so I hope you'll indulge me as I tell you about some of them. An amazing pair of women, Mairi Chisholm and Elsie Knocker, were motorcycle nurses. They set up a dressing station a hundred yards from the front lines so they could retrieve soldiers and patch them up enough to get them to the official hospitals. They saved thousands of lives.

Edith Cavell was a British nurse who kept treating people in Belgium and didn't evacuate when the Germans invaded. She helped sneak wounded Allied soldiers out of the country by obtaining false documents for them, or disguising them. She was executed by the Germans in 1915.

In many ways, Edith Appleton does appear in *Ghost Talkers.* She was a nurse at the front and kept extensive diaries which detail her life during the war. I read *A Nurse at the Front: The First World War Diaries of Sister Edith Appleton,* edited by Ruth Cowen, and it completely shaped how I wrote this book. In many ways, Edith was not extraordinary, in that she could have been any one of the thousands of women who served. In other ways, she truly is. In the same entry, she can write about receiving a train of wounded and then the beauty of a sunset. Her writing makes you feel the war in ways that pictures of the trenches cannot. (Also, I used their names for Ginger and Mrs. Richardson's aliases.)

The hospitality rooms were real things. Women recognized that tending to the soldiers' emotional health was as important as their physical health, so they set up rooms, huts, and tents in which soldiers could go for a cup of tea, a biscuit, or just music and conversation. There were many, many letters written about how grateful the men were for a reminder of normalcy.

"Now go, sit down and be quiet, and leave the war to the men." This is paraphrased from the response that Dr. Elsie Inglis received when she offered a fully trained and staffed medical unit to the Royal Army Medical Offices. Their problem? It was all women. The French had no such qualms, and stationed her in Serbia. She came to be greatly admired, and the Scottish Women's Hospital units had higher survival rates than their male counterparts. They also were among the first to recognize and treat shell shock as a serious problem.

Life in the trenches was brutal, and J. R. R. Tolkien referred to it as an "animal horror." He based the Battle of Helm's Deep on the Battle of the Somme, which he fought in as part of the 11th Lancashire Fusiliers. Fortunately, he was not in the first wave, which was nearly wiped out.

This was the first time that machine guns were in common use in war. The strategy of marching forward in a line was completely ill-suited to that offensive tactic. In *Forgotten Voices of the Somme*, which is a collection, edited by Joshua Levine, of first-person accounts of the war, soldier after soldier talk about how they were the only one in their platoon to live. One man said that he thought the soldiers in front of him had just lay down, and couldn't understand why, until he realized they were all dead. Other soldiers said they could not understand how they lived. One battalion went out, and less than twenty men returned.

It was during this time that a lot of people turned to Spiritualism. I have played fast and loose with the practice of Spiritualism, and mediums, for the purposes of the book. My rationale is that the way I describe it is how it "really" works, while the public awareness of Spiritualism is camouflage to protect sensitive information. Spiritualism is still an active religion, and if you're interested in more information, I would encourage reading about its actual beliefs. My primary source was Hereward Carrington's 1920 book, *Your Psychic Powers and How to Develop Them*.

One last note, on spycraft. The British War Museum's WWI exhibit was invaluable in coming up with some of the details of how spies passed information in the First World War. Book codes were one of the most unbreakable ones, and the pages of numbers in this book really do work. I picked Rupert Burke's poems and *The Story of an African Farm* because they were both referenced in *Letters from a Lost Generation: First World War Letters of Vera Brittain and Four Friends*, edited by Alan Bishop and Mark Bostridge. Again, this was an invaluable resource. Vera and her fiancé often discussed fiction in their letters, and these were their two favorite books. I wanted to honor their memory by incorporating them. They're also worth reading. Actually, all of the books I mentioned are.

There's more. So much more about the war and the men and women who were there. Reading their firsthand accounts made me realize that I had no understanding of what bravery really meant. Tolkien based Samwise Gamgee on the common men in the trench, and he believed that men like him were the bravest of them all.